VG 11/14

He stepped closer, scanning her critically, his gaze, soft as a caress, took in her face, her neck, then moved down her dress to the tips of her shoes. There was no way she could stop her heart from jolting. It alarmed her so much she backed a step away.

"Have no fear, Meg," he told her, appearing to read her thoughts. "No more stolen kisses."

Despite his attempt at nonchalance, she sensed it was a sham, that he was watching her closely. There was an intensity about him, as if he were a stealthy lion, motionless at the moment, yet poised to spring. She discerned that if she gave him the slightest encouragement, he would seize her and wrap her in a passionate embrace. And, she suddenly realized, she wanted him to!

Books published by The Ballantine Publishing Group
are available at quantity discounts on bulk purchases for
premium, educational, fund-raising, and special sales
use. For details, please call 1-800-733-3000.

LADY SEMPLE'S SECRET

Shirley Kennedy

FAWCETT CREST • NEW YORK

A Fawcett Crest Book
Published by Ballantine Books
Copyright © 1997 by Shirley Kennedy

All rights reserved under International and Pan-American Copyright Conventions. Published in the United States by Ballantine Books, a division of Random House, Inc., New York, and simultaneously in Canada by Random House of Canada Limited, Toronto.

http://www.randomhouse.com

Library of Congress Catalog Card Number: 96-91028

ISBN 0-449-22830-4

Manufactured in the United States of America

First Edition: July 1997

10 9 8 7 6 5 4 3 2 1

For Dianne and Lindy,
with special thanks to
Elnora King, who teaches writing.

Chapter 1

"Confound it, Edward!"

In his spacious London lodgings, by dawn's first light, Richard, Lord Beaumont, heir apparent of the Earl of Montclaire, yanked off his muddied Hessian boots and dropped them with resounding thuds onto his plum-colored carpet. "I am dreading Wallingford's dinner tomorrow night," he said in his deep, baritone voice. " 'Twill be nothing but a giant bore. I forget what madness made me accept." He bent to light a fire in the iron-and-steel-grated fireplace. "Cummings's job," he commented tersely, referring to his valet. "I regret I told the lazy beggar he could go to bed."

Lord Edward, the affable fourth son of the Marquess of Semple, slung his slender frame into Richard's crimson Trafalgar chair. "You're out of sorts, old man, fuddled with exhaustion like you always are after leaning over green baize tables all night and losing." Though fashionably clad in tight buckskin trousers and navy blue frock coat, Edward's cravat was crooked, and his blond Brutus cut mussed. "It won't do to cry off Wallingford's dinner, you know. You might even enjoy it. I shall be there, and"—a sly gleam appeared in his eyes—"also Allegra, dying to capture you."

Richard grimaced. "Damnation, Edward. With all due respect to your sister—"

"Nay, spare me!" Edward lazily stretched his legs out, raising a languid palm. "I quite understand. Filled though

I may be with brotherly love for dear Allegra, I would sooner burn in hell than have her for my wife."

Having dispensed with his boots and his own wilted cravat, Richard poured two glasses of Madeira and handed one to his friend. Clasping the other, he reclined his long, lean body onto the Roman settee positioned in front of the fireplace. For a time he was silent, his hooded eyes regarding the blue-tipped flames that reflected on his lean, hawkish face. "I would rather burn in hell than have any wife."

"What's this?" Edward asked with a startled blink. "Never get married? I should think your father would have a thing or two to say about that."

"Since when does my father run my life? I have changed, Edward. To think, when I first came to London, I was one of those crass Bond Street loungers, spending my days ogling the ladies, with my share of successes, I might add. Now I cringe at the very thought."

"Indeed," Edward mocked, "how you hated all that flattery."

"Laugh if you like. But it flattered me no end when some empty-headed minx contrived to be my wife ... prodded by her scheming mother, of course."

"But what's changed? Are they not still after you?"

"Yes, God help me, but I have danced my last quadrille at Almack's. This Season is the end of it. I've only just begun to realize I disapprove heartily of marriage. I look around at this new crop of young chits looking for a husband, and am horrified. They're all so shallow, debauching their minds on lachrymose novels, sighing over love's young dream, regarding me with cakey eyes, as if I were their handsome prince come to carry them off to a life of bliss."

Richard made a sweeping gesture around the dark-paneled room. "I find myself asking, why should I change? Everything I want is right here. Competent servants ... comfortable lodgings ... shelves of books stacked high—scads of poetry! ... warm fire in the fireplace . . . I ride Thunder in Hyde Park any time I please, drop by Tattersall's to inspect the finest cattle, go for enlightened conversation to my club. Add an occasional night at the theater, a bit of grouse shooting up in Scotland, and I am complete. With the exception of these blasted London Seasons, I live a life of sheer perfection."

"Don't forget your lady birds," Edward jibed. He scratched his head in jest. "Damme, I forget your latest, there've been so many."

"Clarice," supplied Richard with a sniff, "the giggly one."

"I vow, you go through mistresses like Thunder goes through horseshoes."

"Pray, leave my horse out of it," Richard answered, smiling wryly. "Thunder is smart, loyal, courageous, and thoroughly dependable. I've yet to meet a woman who possesses even one of those qualities." He thought a moment, his expression softening. "With the exception of my mother, of course, and yours."

"What a low opinion you have of the fairer sex!"

"Can you blame me? Every mistress I ever kept has milked me for all the blunt she could."

"But what do you want in a woman?" Edward inquired. "In a prospective wife I mean, not one of the demimonde."

"My tastes are simple. I prefer my ladies to be seen and not heard, but there is more. I might admire a woman for her charm and beauty, but find it splendid if she aspires to some sort of intellectual achievement."

"Uh-oh, that lets Allegra out." Edward shook his head with mock sadness. "Alas, not only can she make no claim to even the most rudimentary intellectual achievement, 'twould be folly to suggest she could ever bring herself to keep her mouth shut."

One corner of Richard's mouth twitched slightly. "What a pity. It does appear your sister is doubly disqualified."

Edward grew silent and gazed thoughtfully at his friend. "May I speak seriously a moment?"

"By all means, if you feel you must be serious even as the cock crows."

"We grew up neighbors. We're close in age—"

"Not really. I am thirty, going on ninety. You are twenty-eight, going on ten."

Edward sniffed appreciatively. "Seriously, what I want to say is, I had three older brothers when I was growing up, so who cared whom I married? 'Tis different now, with William dying young and Rawdon dead at Waterloo."

"But Thomas is still the heir apparent, is he not?"

"Thomas is such an odd duck—self-absorbed, head buried in a book most of the time. He is still at Oxford, as you know, still a fellow, a professor of ancient history. Fellows cannot marry, of course. And I doubt he ever will." Edward emitted a reflective sigh. "With William and Rawdon gone . . . Thomas sequestered at Oxford . . . poor Father worries about an heir."

"But what about you, Edward?" Richard inquired laconically. "Surely you intend to succumb to Cupid's arrow someday."

"Like you, I have no desire to change my way of life. Single I am, and likely to remain so. But the point is, I have always thought—Father had always thought—and indeed *your* father has always *expected*—that someday you would marry Allegra."

"Impossible!"

"It would bring our two great houses together. You know how such a marriage would please your father, as well as mine. So why can you not—?"

"I hardly know Allegra," Richard replied with an arched glance. "For that matter, I hardly know my father anymore. You know we never got along. I do us both a favor by staying as far away from Hartwick House as possible. Not only that, did I not just tell you I disapprove of marriage?"

"Confound it all!" Edward looked ready to smash his glass against the wall. "Marriage is an institution, not a proper place for passion. You talk of marriage as if it were a trap, which it is not. Your father is deeply troubled by your continued bachelor status. So why not marry Allegra? Think of the dowry! Think of the blissful conjoining of two great estates! Share her bed long enough to breed an heir. 'Tis all Society demands, all your father expects. After that, you can go your separate way and live as you always have. Keep a dozen mistresses at once, for all anybody cares. I warrant Allegra will live her own life as she sees fit, and the two of you shall live happily ever after."

"Prittle prattle! Have you forgotten my brother? Henry can carry on the family dynasty, for all I care."

Edward snorted. "Are you daft? *You* are the elder, as well as the responsible one, whereas Henry is a drunken ne'er-do-well. I hear his gambling debts grow ever higher."

Richard sighed and nodded. " 'Tis only a matter of time before he's compelled to flee to the Continent."

"There, you see?"

"I cannot argue," Richard said regretfully, "but as far as my taking a wife, it will never happen, so let us get on to other things." Richard cocked his head to one side. "How soon do you think we can politely leave this wretched dinner party at Wallingford's? Where shall we go after? Whites? The Guards?"

"Blast it! Don't change the subject." Edward wagged a warning finger. "A pox on your complacency! I know you. You're more of a romantic than you think. Someday you're going to fall in love—madly, agonizingly, totally in love. When you do, you'll look back upon this conversation and realize you sounded like a jackass."

"Good try, Edward." Lord Beaumont awarded his friend an indulgent smile. "I'm happy as I am, a bachelor. As for love, 'tis but a myth, women's treasured fantasy. There's not a woman in this world with whom I could ever fall in love."

He sighed again. "Damme! How I loathe the thought of Wallingford's dinner party."

Chapter 2

Meg Quincy, lady's maid to Lady Caroline, daughter of the Earl of Wallingford, hurried up the back staircase of the earl's Park Lane town house, a slight frown creasing her fair young forehead. Time had slipped away. She should know by now it always did when she was reading poetry. Already it was late afternoon, and Lady Caroline and her stepmother would soon be returning from their Hyde Park carriage ride. *I should not have kept a rendezvous with Lord Byron,* Meg chided herself, at the same time wondering how she could ever resist the lure of slipping into his lordship's library whenever she could do so unobserved. *Someday I shall have my own books . . .* her well-molded chin nodded with resolve . . . *and time to read them.*

But for now . . . to work, to work! Meg ordered herself. This morning she had awakened with the larks to light the dressing-room fire, lay out clothes, haul hot water up steep stairs. And the day had hardly begun. Lady Caroline, nearly finished with her first London Season, was constantly on the go. All day Meg had assisted her mistress in dressing, undressing, and dressing again. She combed her hair and tidied up, then accompanied her on a walk in Green Park, finding time in between to iron, mend, and sew. Tonight Caroline would attend the dance at Almack's. These next few hours Meg would be working slavishly hard. First, the blue satin-and-net ball gown must be ironed into a state of unwrinkled perfection. Then came the most consequential challenge of the day: dressing Caroline for the dance and creating her coiffure. Perhaps the new *à la Venus* would be suitable for tonight, she mused idly, and then, afterward . . .

Meg's frown disappeared as her fingers brushed the pocket of her apron wherein a small book of Robert Burns's poems lay tucked deep inside. She would read it tonight while waiting up for Lady Caroline, in those silent, lonely hours when there was no one to talk to and nothing left to do. Tomorrow she would return it, of course, as she had done with all his lordship's books she had secretly "borrowed" from his library.

"Well, well! Damme, if 'tisn't little Meg."

Meg halted abruptly. On the narrow landing one step up, Algernon, the bacon-faced son of the new countess, stood resplendent in biscuit-colored pantaloons, gray waistcoat, and stiff collar. What was he doing on the servants' stairway? This was the second time today he had appeared out of nowhere for the sole purpose, it appeared, of leering at her. She stifled an amused smile. Algernon's "perfect *orientale*" cravat was tied so tightly around his neck his eyes bulged. In truth, he appeared half strangled. Worse, he was puffing himself up like a bullfrog, an effect which made his eyes bulge even more.

"Sir, may I pass?" She tried to squeeze by him, but he shifted his excessive bulk so that it blocked most of the landing, effectively barring her path.

"Not so fast." His gaze swept her up and down. "'Pon my soul, you are a pretty little thing, despite your affliction."

She curbed her irritation with his unctuous manner and said politely, "Sir, you block my way."

"Do tell." His eyes brightened with a lecherous gleam as they traveled over her, from her high-crowned cap of white gauze, down her long gray dress and apron, to the tips of her sturdy black shoes. Sniggering, he tugged at a curl that had escaped her cap. "How old are you, my pet?"

She answered reluctantly, "Eighteen."

"Ah, eighteen"—Algernon nodded sagely—"a good age." *You nodcock,* she thought, for he himself was all of twenty-two. "A ripe age," he continued with an obscenely raised eyebrow, "ripe, like a juicy plum waiting to be picked." He bent over her, nostrils flaring. "Or have you been picked already, Meg my girl?"

"Allow me to pass, m'lord." Again she tried to squeeze by but failed. She frowned at him. "I do not recall inviting your attention."

"Why fly into a miff? You should be grateful I am partial to guinea-gold blondes with deep blue eyes." He gazed down his nose at her. "Even though you are far beneath my touch. But never fear, my sweet, I can be the soul of charity."

Meg felt an urge to slap his silly face. But much as he deserved it, she knew better than to insult this pompous young lord. Instead, she calmly tucked the errant curl beneath her cap and backed a step down. "Lady Caroline will be home shortly, and I must—"

"Must what? Come, now, you are not all that busy. A word to the wise—a smart little abigail would be a lot more friendly."

"You heard what I said! Lady Caroline—"

"Pox on Caroline!" Algernon poked his index finger at the book in her pocket, his thick lips pulling into a taunting smile. "You sneaked a book. I saw you. 'Tis hid in there." He bent so close his snuff-scented breath nearly gagged her. "Give us a kiss, and we won't tell."

She tried to retreat, but he grabbed her upper arms in an ironlike vise. She could have been a feather the way he pulled her toward him, lifting her feet clear off the step. Before she could stop him, his mouth came down forcefully on hers, planting a wet kiss full on her lips.

Ugg! Her stomach wrenched. She struggled wildly, kicking at him, continuing until he let loose. Fury almost choked her as her feet touched the step again. Her thoughts in disarray, she swept her arm back, brought it around, and slapped him with such force an angry red welt arose instantly upon his ruddy cheek.

Gasping in disbelief, Algernon backed off, raising his palm to rub the stinging spot. "How dare you strike me!"

His bulging eyes reminded her of the dead cod Mrs. Randall the cook had laid out for dinner. Coolly she advised, "You should not have kissed me, sir."

He stood blinking furiously, near paralyzed by astonishment. "Do you realize you have struck a marquess?"

She tipped her head back and looked him in the eye. "I would not care if you were the Prince Regent himself. You keep your hands off me."

"Why, you . . . you . . . ungrateful . . ." Quivering with indignation, Algernon dropped his gaze to the outline of the book in her pocket. His upper lip curled in a sneer. "You stole that book. You do it all the time. 'Tis my duty to inform Mama you are nothing but a common thief."

"Tell her what you please," Meg responded confidently. "I have worked in this household all my life. The first Lady Wallingford trusted me implicitly. She—"

"*That* Lady Wallingford is dead," Algernon interrupted mockingly. "My mother is countess now. A good thing, too. 'Tis beyond my comprehension how the earl could have abided the looseness with which *your* Lady Wallingford ran this household."

His contemptuous tone rekindled her anger. "What are you implying? Her ladyship was most generous. She—"

"She was far too lenient with the servants. Take you, for instance." His scornful gaze swept her up and down, warning her that further vitriol was about to drip from his lips. " 'Tis clearly the will of God that servants are of an inferior status. Yet for reasons I cannot begin to fathom, the first countess allowed you to learn to read and write, thereby stuffing your simple servant's head with excessive amounts of unnecessary knowledge. Why, I have even seen you with a sketch pad and watercolors."

"What's wrong with that?"

"A total waste, as far as I am concerned. Servants

should serve, and nothing more. But *you*"—he glared at her accusingly—"you do not sound like a servant, nor do you act like one."

How she longed to slap him one more time! But her anger had quickly ebbed, leaving reason in charge of her head again. "I am not an object to be mauled," she informed him firmly, "and furthermore, what's *stuffed* in my head is none of your concern. What should be your concern, sir, is that if you touch me one more time, you may expect dire consequences." What she meant by that she wasn't sure, but it shouldn't be too difficult to out-bluff this ninny.

While Algernon sputtered for an answer she marveled at what an immature oaf he was. But how could he be otherwise? His smug statements simply mirrored the views of his priggish, narrow-minded mother. What a tragedy the first Lady Wallingford had died! Meg would never forget her shock of two years ago, when that stern but kindly woman slipped away only hours after bearing her eleventh child. To compound the tragedy, the countess was hardly cold in her grave before the earl took the devout, self-righteous Evelyn Ada as his bride. She, too, had been married before, to a gouty old marquess who had left her with a tidy sum and Algernon, her insufferable son.

Algernon's face had grown tight with anger, his watery blue eyes like bits of stone. "Mama does not approve of your attitude. She has remarked more than once you don't know your place. God's truth, she would like to get rid of you, although naturally she feels sorry for you because of"—his voice hardened ruthlessly—"your affliction."

Twice! That made twice this ... this *fribble* had attempted to wound her with cruel words. She would sooner leap into the Thames, though, than let her feelings show. Proudly she tilted her chin. "You had better leave, sir. I don't wish to hear another word from you, unless you care to offer an apology."

"*I?* Apologize to a servant?" Algernon drew himself up, his several chins quivering. "Mama shall hear of this." With a haughty sniff he pushed past her and stomped down the stairs. At the bottom he turned and pointed an accusing finger toward her apron pocket. "You stole that book. Lord Wallingford does not tolerate thieves. The household will be well rid of you."

Despite her resolve, Meg clutched at her pocket. "You know full well I did not steal it, I borrowed it. You cannot—"

"I *cannot?*" He was yelling now. "What rights have you, you little jilt? You are naught but a scullery maid's by-blow and crippled to boot. I shall have you dismissed."

Dismissed. The word struck her like a thunderbolt. As far back as she could remember she had been a faithful employee to the Wallingfords, first at Auberry Hall, the family estate near Cambridge, and now, because of Caroline's first Season, their London town house. She had worked hard, been fiercely loyal, but would that matter? Could it possibly be that she, on the word of a fool like Algernon, was about to be turned off? Meg's knees turned to jelly as she watched Algernon award her a withering glance and disappear.

What have I done?

Sagging against the wall Meg sank to the steps and made a tight ball of herself, wrapping her arms around the long gray skirt draped over her drawn-up knees. "Oh, what *have* I done?" she moaned aloud.

"What 'ave you done indade?" From above, tiny, red-haired Polly Plummer, one of the parlor maids who had lately been assisting her, started down the stairs.

Meg looked up. "You heard?"

" 'Ow could I not 'ear, the way he was yellin' at you. An' before that, when he kissed you and you slapped him—oh, my stars! You should not 'a done that, but 'twas most satisfyin' to watch." Cap askew, carrying two empty buckets, Polly reached the landing and plopped down next to Meg. "Did he mean what he said?"

"I *hate* being a servant!" Meg burst out.

" 'E's a bad one all right," Polly replied.

" 'Tis more than fending off Algernon." Meg slammed her fist against her knee. "Must I spend a lifetime bobbing and curtsying? Hauling water buckets up the stairs? Ironing someone else's ball gowns?"

Polly flinched and looked bewildered. "But I thought you liked workin' for Lady Caroline, you and she growin' up together and bein' the same age an' all."

"That has nothing to do with it."

"Wut, then? You think you're the only one wishin' she could trade places with the ton? Wear pretty dresses an' go to balls an' such? But what choice do we 'ave?" The tiny maid's forehead furrowed in a perplexed frown. "Ain't we doin' what God laid down for us to do?"

"Oh, Polly," Meg patted the tiny maid's shoulder, "pay me no heed." She lifted her chin defiantly. "But I doubt 'tis God's plan."

"Maybe not for you," Polly replied, "you ain't like me, nor like any servant here. You're special, being's you can read an' write, an' talk like a lady, an' you know so much and are ever so smart."

"Thanks to Lady Wallingford, the *first* Lady Wallingford. Do you know she used to let me attend classes with her own children? I never knew why." Meg heaved a sigh. "But what good did all the lessons do me? I work long, hard hours at practically no pay. I bow and scrape and curtsy, and choke on 'yes, m'lord, no m'lady' all the day, and am at the mercy of the likes of Algernon. And do they care? They treat us like inferiors, Polly, when I know in my heart we're not."

"But they feed us—an' don't beat us—an' at least we 'ave a roof over our 'eads."

"Just barely." Meg pictured her tiny room up on the fourth floor under the eaves, a room not fit for a dog in summer with its sweltering heat, nor in winter with its miserable damp chill.

"But 'tis God's will—" Polly began, but the outraged expression on Meg's face caused her to fall into silence and stare back round-eyed. " 'Pon my soul, you are not yourself today. I never knew you felt this way."

"I was never threatened with being tossed out on the streets before." Meg paused. No sense upsetting Polly. She forced herself to settle down. " 'Tis no use," she whispered, more to herself than Polly. "You shall not hear me complain again. When all is done, I cannot walk away. This life is all I have."

Polly cocked her head inquisitively. "But what about yur plan? A long time ago, remember what you told me? You would not be in service all yur life, you said."

"The plan ... my dream." A burning, faraway look appeared in Meg's eyes. "Someday I shall keep apartments for gentlefolk someplace by the sea, possibly Brighton. Then I shall read all I please—collect books—sketch— write poetry—travel to Paris, Venice, everywhere!"

"Have you lost the dream, Meg?"

"I save every farthing I can."

" 'Twill still take you years an' years."

"What else do I have to look forward to? I shall always be alone, Polly, so whatever comfort I find in life, 'tis up to me." Meg's wistful smile held a touch of sadness as she added, "It gives me something to think about when I wake up in the middle of the night. . . ." *In the dark, when I lie there knowing there is nobody in the world who really loves me—nobody who really cares.*

"But you ain't alone," Polly proclaimed stoutly. "Mrs. Randall loves you, and McDarby, and, of course, me."

Meg laughed wryly. " 'Tis all well and good to have the affection of the cook, the butler, and you, dear Polly, but that's not what I had in mind. I meant a different sort of love."

"You meant the kind you had best be careful of," stated Polly, "like Mrs. Randall warns."

Seeing the funny side to their conversation, Meg shoved her gloomy thoughts away. Faking a frown, she drew in her chin, lowered her voice, and launched into an imitation of the sobersided cook. " 'Watch you don't get a big belly, my girl. You must avoid those rascally lotharios in livery who care naught for your virtue, and most especially you must avoid the young master!' "

Polly started giggling. "You sound just like 'er."

"Ah, Polly, we can be amused by Mrs. Randall's advice, but I was not referring to losing my virtue to Algernon or some scoundrel of a footman."

The tiny maid nodded resolutely. "You'll find your own true love someday, same as me."

"Not I," Meg responded quickly. From beneath her voluminous skirt she thrust out her twisted right foot in its ugly black shoe. "Not when God has gifted me with this."

After a pause, Polly said gently, "You ain't never talked about yur foot before."

"What is there to say? I have lived with this cursed clubfoot all my life, so why, pray, should I want to talk about it now?"

" 'Tis not so bad, you know. McDarby says 'e's seen far worse a limp than yours."

"There's a comfort," Meg answered dryly.

Polly went on, "I've wondered . . . thought maybe you 'ad an accident—'urt yourself when you was little."

"Fate, Polly. I was born with it."

"Then fate made a turrible mistake!" Polly declared indignantly. "How could something so cruel happen to someone as good as you?"

"Perhaps it comes from my mother . . . or my father . . . I really have no idea."

"Are they both dead?"

Meg shrugged. "My mother, yes. My father, I cannot say. I never knew my parents. My earliest memories are of growing up at Auberry Hall, cared for by the servants. When I was old enough, six I think, I was put to work cleaning candlesticks and lamp glasses, and tugging coal buckets up the stairs."

"You never asked?"

"I cannot tell you the number of times I asked Mrs. Randall and McDarby about my mother. All they ever told me was that my mother was a scullery maid named Eliza Quincy who died giving birth to me. Anything else, their mouths would tighten up, as if they were under orders not to say another word."

"And your father?"

A wistfulness stole into Meg's expression. "I knew it would be useless even to ask."

"How orful! That's all you were ever told?"

Meg nodded briefly, aware she was not being completely truthful. There was another time, that dreadful scene, but she had put that sad, troubling occasion at the back of her mind and tried not to think about it anymore.

Time was pressing. Meg arose from the step. "I had best get back to work."

Polly got up, too, shaking her head. "I wish you 'adn't slapped the young master."

"But I did, and he deserved it. What is done is done."

"Maybe you could apologize?"

"To that fop? Never. But it is of no consequence."

"Are you sure?" Polly looked doubtful.

"If Algernon tries to get rid of me, I am positive Lady Caroline will intervene, and you know how his lordship dotes on her. Now back to work. You are to assist me tonight, and you must pay attention if ever you're to become a lady's maid yourself."

Meg turned and hurried up the stairs feeling a strange anxiety. Not only had Polly's remarks raised old, unsolved questions, now other problems were even more pressing.

With a heavy heart she wondered where she would go if they actually dismissed her. She would immediately seek another position, of course. *But who would hire a cripple?*

* * *

In the wee small hours of the chilly June morning, Meg waited up for Lady Caroline. She was still unsure about Algernon. Earlier, Caroline had returned from her round of visiting, brimming with excitement. Lord Carstairs, grandson of the Duke of Hollender, was about to propose, she was sure of it! The family was ecstatic. Not only had Caroline genuinely fallen in love with the handsome young lord, he was a first son with much to recommend him, not the least of which was ten thousand pounds per annum. Meg tried to reassure herself that in all the excitement Algernon would forget his threat, yet her apprehension grew by the hour. There was nothing she could say, though. She had no intention of burdening a buoyant Caroline with the petty complaints of a servant.

Meg was proud of her mistress's success. Caroline had become one of the Season's Incomparables, not only because of her wit and charm, but because of her dress and coiffures. Meg had worked slavishly hard to make her the most beautiful ... and here came that dark thought again, creeping unbidden into her head as it often did in the middle of the night ...

Must Caroline's joys be my joys? Must Carolyn's sorrows be my sorrows? Is this all there is? I am but eighteen, yet I have no life of my own. Why have I been so loyal when I could be out on the streets tomorrow ... no place to go ... end up in the workhouse ... ?

Catching her gloomy thought, Meg forced herself to put it aside. Smoothing the figured velvet bedspread, she peered around Caroline's gold and green bedroom and nodded approvingly. Fire lit ... bucket full of coal ... nightdress laid neatly on the bed ... all lay in readiness. She sank wearily into a beech-carved armchair. Ah, so good to sit down! Still, a feeling of unease came over her. Somehow she knew Algernon had *not* forgotten.

Force yourself not to think about it. Here, in the waning midnight hours, she at last had time for herself and should not waste it fretting over the likes of Algernon. From her pocket she withdrew the book of Robert Burns's poems. Tenderly, she patted the cover, opened the book, and instantly transported herself to bonny Scotland, where she basked in the joy of Burns's poetic thoughts until the clip-clop of approaching horses announced Caroline's return.

Meg tucked her book away, stood up and squared her cap, smoothed her apron, and fixed her face into a welcoming smile.

Chapter 3

"Oh, Meg, I am betrothed!"

Trim-figured Lady Caroline, brown eyes sparkling, fair cheeks flushed with excitement, bounced into her bedchamber. She twirled around, her netted blue satin gown swirling in graceful folds about her. "Lord Carstairs has already spoken to Father. It is to be announced at our dinner party tonight." Jabbering away, she finally settled down enough to sit before her dressing table while Meg, in the familiar routine, pulled the pins from her shining chestnut hair. "But, oh"—Caroline touched the sleeve of her gown—"see here? My dress got spattered with candle fat from a chandelier. Can you repair it?"

Meg solemnly examined the several small spots. "I may have to replace the sleeve, but it can be done. I saved some of the blue satin."

Caroline gazed up at her curiously. "I own, you seem blue-deviled tonight. Is something wrong?"

"Nothing, m'lady."

Exasperated, Caroline exclaimed, "I have told you, Meg, when we're alone, there's no need to call me 'm'lady.' "

"That is easier said than done."

"Are we not friends? Did we not play together when we were little girls?"

Meg returned a wry smile. "That was before either of us realized we were not created equal."

"Bother!" Caroline threw her hands in the air. "You

know very well I never regard you as a servant. You are more like a sister to me. I love you dearly and want you to share my happiness, as would Mama"—tears sprang to her eyes—"if she were here."

Meg picked up a brush, and in long, caring strokes started brushing Caroline's hair. "You know I shall always love your mother. I'll never forget how she allowed me to sit in on your lessons with Miss Plinny, though I never knew why, my being only a servant." Mischief pooled in her eyes. "If not for Miss Plinny, I would still be dropping my h's."

Caroline let out a giggle. "Miss Plinny could not abide incorrect English. Remember how she kept after you?"

"How could I forget?" Meg stuck her nose in the air, in a fair imitation of the former governess, and mimicked, " '*Not* she is poorly, Meg! You must say, she is sickly, or in poor health. In truth, I flinch when you lapse into the language of the servants, which is why I make haste to correct those uncouth accents I hear coming from your mouth, and the dropping of h's, and that other vulgar street chaff you pick up belowstairs.' "

Caroline grinned. "She succeeded, did she not? Indeed, you polished your English until it sounds better than mine, and not the least like ... like ..." Caroline stumbled and stopped.

"Like a lowborn, ignorant servant girl," Meg finished for her. "No need to feel bad, Caroline. I accept my station in life." *Most of the time.*

"But it seems wrong somehow ..." Caroline floundered, and not knowing what else to say, groped for a change in subject. "You shall have this dress."

Meg shook her head. "I'm grateful to receive your cast-off clothes, but you know as well as I, I have no need of a fancy dress."

"Nonsense! Every girl should have one. You have avoided this long enough. I want you to try it on."

Meg shook her head. Whether or not she owned a party dress was the farthest thing from her mind. But

Caroline, heady with her own happiness, proclaimed, "I vow, I shall not go to bed until you try it."

Useless to argue. Meg pulled on the dress while Caroline, laboring to tie her up behind, laughingly asked, "Would I not make a good lady's maid?"

Meg laughed softly, then gazed at herself in the tall, gilt mirror. The high-waisted dress had a long flared skirt and deep, square-cut neckline. It consisted of two layers, transparent blue net worn over deeper blue satin, and was luxuriously embroidered in various shades of blue around the bodice, sleeves, and hemline. She could not help but see how the dress hung in graceful folds, concealing, yet revealing, her slim hips and tiny waistline. Not only that, the cut of the high waistline pushed up and exposed her full bosom in a manner she was not accustomed to. Never had she seen herself like this before. Never had she realized . . . "I feel naked," she remarked lightly, focusing on the daring décolletage. "Do you not feel a dreadful chill wearing a dress like this?"

"No, I don't, and you look positively entrancing." Caroline finished tying the dress. "Let's get that cap off your head." Before Meg could stop her, Caroline tugged at the ribbons and grabbed the cap off, allowing Meg's thick blond mane to cascade in soft curls down her back. "Ah, Meg, how lovely! Just look at yourself."

Meg looked, and almost gasped. She was accustomed to seeing herself in her modest gray servant's garb, but here, in the shimmering blue satin, with the glow of the candles casting a rosy radiance over her fair white skin, she indeed saw beauty. But only for a moment. "Until I move," she half whispered, almost to herself, "beautiful until I walk a step."

"Meg! I have never heard you talk like that before. In truth, I never see you as a . . . a . . ."

"A cripple?" Meg supplied gently.

"No!" Caroline's delicately arched eyebrows flew together in a scowl. "You are so beautiful in other ways, I never remember about your foot. From within, you are beautiful. As for the rest, your hair alone . . ." Caroline lifted Meg's heavy mane and fanned it across her shoulders. "Just think how pretty 'twould look if it were fixed atop your head with all those darling little curls, like you do mine. Oh, Meg, you need to feel pretty for a change. You *must* take the dress."

As if a dress could make a difference . . .

But Meg did not have the heart to disappoint Caroline. "All right, I shall take it, though I shall have no place to wear it."

"Nonsense! The Season's almost over. We shall be returning to Auberry Hall soon. I've noticed you always avoid the parties to which the servants are invited, but from now on, I absolutely insist you go."

The apprehension returned. Meg turned to face Caroline, knowing the time for truth was at hand. "There is a good chance I shall be dismissed tomorrow." She told Caroline about Algernon. ". . . So 'tis possible I shall never return to Auberry Hall."

Lady Caroline at first looked stunned, then quickly recovered. "But that cannot be. Papa would never allow it. He knows how much you mean to me."

"But your stepmother"—Meg searched for a delicate way to phrase it—"appears not overly fond of me. She is most strongheaded and, I have noticed, generally gets her way."

Caroline laughed lightly. "I should not be concerned. My stepmother has far more important things to do than listen to that ninny son of hers. Indeed, I can assure you all her thoughts are on dazzling the ton at her dinner party tonight. Now 'twill be even more dazzling with Papa announcing my betrothal."

"But—"

"—I must say," Caroline babbled on, "I am impressed by her guest list. She even chanced inviting the most eligible bachelor in all London. Voilà! He accepted."

Meg felt a pang of futility that Caroline could so easily ignore her fears. But how could Caroline possibly understand, given her current state of euphoria? *And why should she be burdened with my troubles?* Silently Meg decided her mistress should not be assailed by any further references to Algernon's threats. "Most eligible bachelor?" she inquired, resigning herself to the change of subject. "That would have to be Richard, Lord Beaumont, heir apparent of the Earl of Montclaire."

" 'Pon my soul," exclaimed Caroline, "even the servants have heard of him."

"Indeed! He's the main subject of juicy tittle-tattle belowstairs. They say nearly every girl in London has set her cap for him, but so far he's having none of them."

Caroline looked sheepish. "I own, when the Season started, I considered him myself. He's devilishly handsome, a bit on the dark side, with black wavy hair, and his eyes—oh! they have a gleam that's absolutely sinister. I shall never forget the first time I saw him sauntering into Almack's: He had this air of complete disdain about him, and was scanning the assembly through his quizzing glass—*deigning* to bestow his attentions only on such young ladies as caught his fancy."

"I've heard he is quite arrogant, and so rich he doesn't need to wed a fortune."

"If he cares to wed at all," affirmed Caroline. "I had a few dances with him, but had the feeling he was looking down his nose at me, as if he considered me some little country bumpkin." Caroline giggled. "Well, I am! But now I'm betrothed to Lord Carstairs, so I haven't a care."

Meg inquired, "Who else is coming to the dinner?"

"Twenty altogether, including my cousins, the Marquess and Marchioness of Semple. We hardly ever see them, but they rented a town house in London for the Season to accommodate their daughter, Allegra, who has come out." Caroline thought a moment, then frowned. "Lord Edward, their fourth son, is quite the buck, but Allegra, *mon Dieu*! She's such a horrid girl. She was presented at court the same day as I, and since then I have had to contend with her everywhere. In truth, I cannot abide her, but I must be nice because she is my cousin."

"What is wrong with her?"

"Everything! No doubt she'll be at her worst tonight, in a pet because I am betrothed, whereas she . . . well, I know for a fact she has not received one decent offer all Season, despite a dowry that's most considerable, I can assure you."

"How sad." Meg could not help feeling sorry for the poor girl, no matter how horrid she was.

"Save your sympathy," Caroline fairly snapped back. "Speaking of Lord Beaumont, Allegra keeps throwing herself at the poor man. He, of course, keeps putting her off." Caroline giggled, her irritation forgotten. "My step-mother plans to pair him with Allegra for dinner tonight. Might not that raise a breeze! If you ask me, he finds her as odious as I do, but her brother Edward is his best friend, so he, too, must be nice." Caroline's expression brightened. "Edward's all right, though a bit of a rascal. Allegra's mother, Lady Charlotte Semple, is a shy, timid little thing. So timid, in fact, I am hard put to understand how she could possibly have produced a boorish daughter like Allegra."

"So what relation is she to you?" Meg inquired.

"To me? Humm, let's see . . . Charlotte is my first cousin once removed. Not by blood, though. Her husband, Lord Semple, and his sister, Lady Lydia, are my mother's first cousins."

Charlotte—Lady Lydia. The names caused Meg a flicker of apprehension. She had briefly met Lady Lydia two years ago at Auberry Hall, on the day the first countess died. Though she had never met Caroline's Cousin Charlotte, Meg vividly recalled that the countess had mentioned a Charlotte on her deathbed, during that dreadful scene.

Stop thinking about it, Meg scolded herself. She had more important items to fret over, such as getting dismissed. This very day she could be thrown out of the only home she had ever known, onto the hard, unforgiving streets of London.

"Good morning, Papa, everyone." Lady Caroline bounced into the morning room. "Is not this a glorious day?"

"Hurumph," replied the stout, balding Earl of Wallingford from behind his newspaper. Deep in conversation, Algernon and his mother either ignored her or failed to hear.

Undaunted, Caroline took her place at the breakfast room table, her exuberance tempered only slightly by the unusual presence of Algernon, who usually slept till noon. Too bad. In her private opinion, the less she saw of her overbearing, overstuffed stepbrother, the better. Sipping her orange juice, she observed that whatever Algernon was relating to his mother must be of a serious nature, judging from their earnest frowns.

The earl peered around his newspaper. "You are up early for one who danced the night away, Caroline."

"I know," she mumbled, only half paying attention. What devilment was Algernon up to?

Thin, slightly horse-faced Evelyn Ada was nodding her head vigorously at whatever Algernon was whispering in her ear. "Just as I suspected"—Caroline heard her say—"that scheming light-skirt is after you."

"What is this?" demanded the earl, lowering his paper.

The countless scowled. "That little baggage, that Meg."

"The little lame wench?" asked the earl. He added with a knowing glance, "The one at which Algernon continually casts sheep's eyes?"

The countess awarded him a look layered in blackness. "Surely you jest, sir! Algernon would not lower himself. What I cannot understand is how you could have abided that impertinent cripple all these years."

The earl appeared taken aback. "But, my dear, the first countess considered her a family treasure."

"You have missed the point." Evelyn Ada compressed her lips into one thin, disapproving line. " 'Tis obvious God is displeased with Meg Quincy. Why else would He have cursed her with that ghastly clubfoot? But Meg does not understand that. She *refuses* to be humble, which I find intolerable. And not only that"—Evelyn Ada bent forward, as if she were about to impart a great secret. "The girl has no shame. Just yesterday, she made bold advances toward Algernon."

"Nonsense!" the earl protested, "Meg has always been a good girl and hard worker. Why, Elinore always—"

"Elinore?" the countess interrupted, fairly spitting the name out. "I cannot fathom why your first wife favored Meg, considering the girl's lowly status and unsightly limp. Now we discover she's a thief besides. Tell him, Algernon."

All eagerness, Algernon proceeded to recount to the earl what he had discovered concerning Meg's "thefts" from the library. Caroline listened confidently. Papa would surely see Algernon's accusations were arrant nonsense, and would award him with a good set-down. She would enjoy seeing her stepbrother humbled as he deserved.

To her surprise, though, a troubled frown rested on Papa's brow when Algernon finished his diatribe. He remained strangely silent instead of rebuking his stepson.

"Well?" demanded Evelyn Ada. "Will you allow a thief to remain in the house?"

"Do whatever you wish, my dear," replied the earl. In no way did he wish to displease his new bride. She might be a bit of a shrew, but had proved not the least displeasing in his bed.

The new countess made no effort to hide her smug smile. "Then, she shall be let go."

Stung by her father's perfidy, Lady Caroline cried, "But you cannot do that!"

"Indeed I can," Evelyn Ada declared. "Unlike your

mother, I shall not have an impudent, thieving servant under my roof."

Lady Caroline turned to her father, her lower lip trembling. "But I need her, Papa! Who else can dress me for riding, visiting, dances, everything? Who else can fix my curls like Meg can? And Meg is so"—desperately Caroline searched for words—"so funny, no matter how bad things get, and she's smart and loves poetry and painting, and she always knows just what to do. I vow, I cannot do without her."

Mindful of murderous looks being cast his way from the countess, the earl held his ground. "Nonsense, Caroline. Now you have found yourself a husband, you no longer have need of such a fancy lady's maid. Meg will be dismissed, but I should not worry if I were you. We shall give her a good character. I doubt she'll have the least bit of trouble finding another position."

"She shall *not* have a character!" Evelyn Ada decreed.

" 'Pon my soul, madam, why not?"

"How can we, in good conscience, vouch for a thief?"

"But that's cruel, Father," protested Caroline. "We cannot just throw Meg out on the streets. She's crippled! No one but us knows what a pearl of a lady's maid she is. What if no one wants to hire—?"

"Enough!" thundered the earl. Snapping his newspaper, he decreed, "I do not wish to hear another word on the subject from any of you."

Recognizing defeat, Caroline pleaded, "Papa, may I at least have Meg for the rest of the Season before she—" Her voice broke. In a broken whisper she continued, "—before she goes?"

"One more night," decreed Evelyn Ada. She turned to her husband. "I must confess 'twould be most inconvenient if we let her go before this evening's dinner party."

"But, no!" Caroline cried.

"But, yes!" countered a triumphant Evelyn Ada. "Just one more night. And furthermore, you are not to inform the girl of any of this. You know how servants are. She is bound to be useless once she knows she's being dismissed."

Caroline opened her mouth to speak, but before she could, her father spoke again. "That is our final word on the subject, Caroline. Meg stays one more night. She goes tomorrow, without fail."

Only minutes later, Meg was mysteriously summoned to the kitchen, where gray-haired Mrs. Randall, the eternally gloomy cook, held reign. When she arrived, she discovered not only Mrs. Randall, but McDarby, the butler, was there as well. Apprehension knotted inside her when she saw how solemn-faced they both were.

"Sit down, my gel," said McDarby.

Meg sank into a chair, her anxiety mounting. McDarby wasted no time in hiding the truth.

"Ye've been dismissed, Meg, by her ladyship."

Meg felt the blood drain from her face. "Her ladyship dismissed me?" she repeated softly. She gave a choked, desperate laugh. "Algernon." A sinking feeling enveloped her from head to toe. "How do you know?"

Mrs. Randall patted her shoulder. "James the footman heard 'em talking at breakfast just now. Mind you, Lady Caroline stood up for you best that she could, but Herself was not about to take no for an answer, and that Algernon—humph!"

Meg sat in a daze, shaking her head. "I haven't the faintest notion what I shall do."

"Oh, my gel," said McDarby, eyes filled with concern.

"That Algernon, there's wickedness for you!" proclaimed Mrs. Randall. "And that hen-witted countess! The first countess would never have—"

"Now, now," hastily interrupted McDarby, "it does no good to speak of our employers in such a fashion. There's naught we can do except help Meg find a new position." He picked up his copy of the *Morning Post*. "I shall go through the classifieds—"

" 'Twon't be easy, not with her affliction." Mrs. Randall, not generally known for her great tact, continued, "Mayhap she could try one of those servant registries."

McDarby drew himself up. "Over my dead body! Those offices have a bad reputation for victimizing servant girls. They take fees under false pretenses, and they"—McDarby paused, appearing uncomfortable—"and that is not all."

"Tell me all of it," said Meg, "I must know."

The butler hesitated before continuing, "You're too sheltered to hear such things, but I can see that for your own protection, you must be made aware. The worst of those registries are chiefly interested in the procurement of young girls for prostitution. There's the odd honest one, but most are markets for pimps and procurers."

Meg bit her lip. "I've only a little money. What would you suggest I do?"

McDarby appeared deep in thought. "Hmmm . . . ah, yes! The Dowager Duchess of Brambleshire might be looking for a lady's maid. I was talking to her coachman only yesterday."

Mrs. Randall scowled. "But that won't do! I heard him, too, McDarby! He said the duchess needs a new lady's maid because the last one died of pneumonia, contracted at that drafty, cold castle of hers up in the wilds of Scotland. Why that 'ud be a turrible place for a young girl!"

"Beggars cannot be choosers, Mrs. Randall."

"Meg can do better than that!"

McDarby turned to Meg. "Best keep it in mind. Meanwhile, I shall look through the classifieds, and also make inquiries."

"We must find you a position soon, girl!" Mrs. Randall said. "Or you could easily end up in some vile lodging house, packed in a filthy bed with other out-of-work servants, vermin plopping from the ceiling onto your head!"

Hearing such a dire prediction, Meg wanted to clap her hands to her ears, yet she knew in her heart that both Mrs. Randall and McDarby were only trying to help. She stood, squared her shoulders, and managed a smile. "Mr. McDarby, if you should find a suitable advertisement, please be so kind as to inform me. Meanwhile, perhaps I shall find a way to contact the Dowager Duch-ess of Brambleshire. As you said, beggars cannot be choosers."

Meg left the kitchen with her head held high. But once outside, she had to fight back tears. She paused, fists clenched, to take a ragged breath. Where would she go? What would she do? Fear and uncertainty engulfed her, then anger. She had spent her entire life working for this family. Why did she have to hear of her dismissal from the servants? Didn't the Earl and Countess of Walling-ford care enough to give her even one day's notice? Such injustice was not to be endured! Throwing all caution to the winds, she made her way to the drawing room. When she entered, she found the countess alone, sitting ramrod-straight behind her Carlton House desk, busily scratching a letter with her carmine-plumed quill pen.

Speaking in as reasonable a voice as she could manage, Meg said, "There has been a rumor—"

"You are dismissed, Meg." The countess did not bother to lift her gaze.

Meg felt her knees shaking underneath her skirt. She was mortified to find she was near tears again, and made a valiant effort to keep her voice from shaking. "I demand to know why."

After moments of ominous silence, Lady Wallingford lifted her gaze. Stony-faced, she examined Meg care-fully. "*Demand?* It is for that precise reason you are being dismissed, girl, for being insolent. Aside, of course, from your worse transgression—stealing books from his lordship's library."

"But—" Meg stopped short, suddenly feeling total futility, knowing it was useless to argue. Instead, she looked her employer square in the eye. "I trust I shall receive my full twenty guineas before I go, and, of course, a character."

The countess's nostrils quivered. "You shall have your twenty guineas, but not the character."

How unfair—how cruel! Meg recognized instantly that because she was a servant, there was nothing she could say that would matter a wit to this cold, selfish woman. Full of fury, she gritted her teeth and silently vowed she would rather die than give the countess the satisfaction of hearing her beg.

"You may stay until tomorrow." Evelyn Ada's lips spread into the tightest of smiles. "Lady Caroline will be needing you one more night."

The gall! How Meg yearned to inform her ladyship she would depart this very minute, dinner party be damned, but she could not hurt Caroline, so instead she bit her tongue. "Tomorrow," she said curtly, whirled and left the room, omitting, for one of the rare times in her life, her usual curtsy.

Once outside, she realized that never before had she felt such abject humiliation. Hurrying down the hallway, she saw Caroline standing in the doorway of the dining room. When Caroline turned and saw her, her face fell.

"Meg, you look terrible!"

"I have reason."

An involuntary gasp escaped Caroline's lips. "You heard?"

"Of course," Meg snapped, " 'tis time you learned the walls have ears."

Caroline's face clouded. "Oh, Meg, I tried!"

Meg instantly regretted her sharp words. Caroline was not to blame. Sheltered as she was, how could she possibly know how cruel and unfair life was for servants? "Don't feel bad, Caroline. I shall be fine, and meanwhile"—she managed a smile—"tonight I shall outdo myself. Your dress, your coiffure—rest assured you shall be a diamond of first water at tonight's dinner party."

Chapter 4

". . . And so, my dear Lord Beaumont, enjoy your good health while you may. As for me, just last night I was struck by the most distressing attack of the dropsy, which, mind you, comes on top of the gout that plagues me in my left big toe. . . ."

The many-chinned Dowager Duchess of Brambleshire interrupted her monologue to take a sip of claret, thus allowing a brief respite for Lord Beaumont, seated to her right. Near paralyzed with boredom, Richard gazed about the long, damask-covered table laden with twenty settings of china, silver, and glittering crystal. At the head sat the jovial Earl of Wallingford, who earlier tonight had announced his daughter Caroline's betrothal. At the foot sat his sharp-nosed countess, whose face would no doubt crack if ever she attempted a smile. Richard glanced across the center bank of flowers, peering through the many candle-bearing arms of the weighty epergne, which sat in overornamented splendor on a silver platform in the center. There sat Edward, currently acting the village idiot, captivated by the blond minx on his right, whose curls jiggled as she babbled and who displayed, for Edward's intense, bulging-eyed pleasure, a delicious décolletage. To Edward's left sat the beauteous young Caroline, cheeks flushed, eyes bright with excitement, marvelously turned out in her Grecian coiffure and lilac gauze gown.

Richard dared not look to his own right. He had been paired with that wet goose, Allegra, who was more than sufficiently bedizened this evening, having stuffed her tree-stump body into a heavily embroidered rose satin and lace gown with silver borders, set off by an obscene number of diamonds circling her plump arms and throat. All evening, her more-than-ample bosom had proved quite unnerving, threatening at any moment to spill entirely out. Her face was not so terribly unattractive, he supposed. She had plump rosy cheeks and smooth fair skin, although her nose was a touch bulbous, her eyes too close. Worst was her hair, a mishmash of curls, ringlets, flowers, and feathers, horribly overdone. If Allegra had a lady's maid, and surely she did, the wench should be sent packing. *And Father wants me to marry this woman?*

He could feel her eyes drilling into him—it was unbearable! He had already suffered through two conversations with her earlier. That was enough. Given the choice, he would prefer learning every last detail of the dowager duchess's gout. He looked to his left again. Blast! The duchess had deserted him—no more than he deserved, actually—and was now delivering her monologue to her left. An elbow jabbed his ribs. *Blast again.* All hope gone, he surrendered his attention to his right.

"Just look," Allegra loudly whispered in her annoying nasal voice. Lifting one nostril disdainfully, she peered down the table. "Lady Exeter was but a governess before she snagged the viscount, yet she goes around with her nose so *retroussé*. Did you know he gambles? He is quite dished up, according to the latest *on dit*, which I can well believe since their abode in London is only rented this Season. 'Tis quite small, I hear, hardly enough to entertain. So disgusting, these commoners with pretensions of grandeur, *n'est-ce pas*, Lord Beaumont?"

God save him from empty-headed romps who prattled French phrases they hardly understood. "I really cannot say," he answered noncommittally. So far this evening, Allegra's spiteful prittle prattle had spared no one at the table except himself. Or had it? He had to wonder what she said behind his back. *And Father wants me to marry this woman?*

Allegra edged closer, bringing her thick lips close to his ear, and pressing—accidentally?—the left side of her perilously positioned bosom against his arm. "How fortuitous that we are seated together tonight, Lord Beaumont. At home we are neighbors, yet when I was growing up, I scarcely saw you."

Richard retained his polite smile. "Ah, but I am much older than you, and I have been living in London for quite some time now."

"But now that I am out, we must become better acquainted."

"Er . . . yes."

"Much better acquainted!"

"Ahhh . . . indeed."

"Your father and my father talk occasionally. Would you care to hear the subject uppermost in their minds?"

No, he most definitely did not, particularly since he knew very well the topic was marriage. Desperately Richard gazed across the table just as Caroline looked up. *A reprieve.* He caught her eye. "You are looking especially lovely tonight, Caroline. Betrothal becomes you."

It did the trick, for Caroline captured the entire table's attention when she replied wistfully, "If I look good, I owe it to my abigail. She was the best in all the world." Caroline cast a glance at her stepmother, a daggered glance, Richard noted, barely disguised. "But now I have lost her." With a hollow laugh she added, "I shall never look the same."

"Nonsense!" the countess cut in sharply. "We shall soon find you another. The world is full of competent lady's maids."

"Not so!" sniffed the Dowager Duchess of Brambleshire. "I am searching for a good one myself. Perhaps a French one this time, since they are all the rage. I have had quite enough of those sobersided Swiss maids who are cold as stones."

"What does it matter where she comes from?" came the cold, arrogant voice of Allegra's father, Cyril, Marquess of Semple, a man Richard avoided like the plague. "As long as she tends to her duties and is honest, submissive, and discreet."

"Ah, just the qualities I would want in a wife!" put in Edward with a supercilious grin.

After the laughter died, Allegra's mother, the soft-spoken Lady Charlotte Semple, peered inquiringly at Caroline. "What is wrong with your maid?"

"I dismissed her," the countess cut in.

"But that is most surprising," declared Lady Semple. "I cannot tell you the number of times I have seen Caroline this Season and remarked to myself how perfectly turned out she was. The true sign of a pearl of a lady's maid."

"That may very well be," replied the countess, her mouth pursed like a prune, "but most unfortunately, Caroline's maid was consistently insolent and did not recognize her humble station."

"What a pity," Lady Semple said thoughtfully. "I don't agree that a good abigail is easy to find. I've been searching for a new maid for Allegra for some time now, and—"

"Mama, what are you saying?" Allegra demanded loudly, glaring at Lady Semple. "I have no need for a new one." Her gaze quickly swung to her left, to Richard. With a flutter of eyelashes, she asked, "Kindly give me your opinion, Lord Beaumont, am I not well turned out?"

Stuck, thought Richard, as conversations started buzzing around the table again, as though everyone wished to distance themselves from impending embarrassment. He thought quickly. "My dear Allegra, you look as beautiful tonight as I have ever seen you."

Pleased, Allegra laughed brashly. "Indeed? And may I say how much I admire *you*? Why, I have never seen you but what you weren't dressed bang up to the nines." She regarded him craftily. "No wonder the young chits all flock around. But you know what your father says?"

Desperately, Richard glanced to his left. The duchess was free! Turning his back on Allegra, he began, "So where did you say your gout was located, Your Grace? In your right toe or was it your left?"

The flattered duchess had just begun to set him straight when Richard felt something lightly push against his knee. At first he paid it no heed, then whatever it was pressed harder. Was some animal loose beneath the table? A dog perhaps? He could not imagine ... It pressed again. My God, a knee! Thunderstruck, he turned away from the duchess and found himself gazing into the innocently smiling countenance of Lady Allegra.

Out of the corner of his mouth, he muttered, "Whatever are you doing?"

"Getting better acquainted, m'lord," she murmured back sweetly. "Your father wants—"

"Desist at once, madam!" he whispered vehemently, so incensed he could feel a rush of blood to his face. Galling! And not only did her knee not move away, but he felt the warmth of her palm upon his thigh. Aghast, he whispered, "Stop!" and slipped his hand beneath the tablecloth to grasp her wrist. With a controlled effort, he tried to lift her hand away, but her muscles tensed, her grasp grew tighter. *God's oath*, the woman was strong as an ox! Plainly, he could not wrestle her without drawing attention to themselves. Was anyone aware? He looked around the table.

Damnation!

Across, he spied Edward curiously regarding the suspicious slant of Allegra's left arm. Suddenly a knowing look appeared in Edward's eye. "Oops!" he declared, "I have dropped my napkin." He ducked beneath the table, where he remained a suspiciously long time, finally coming up wearing a big grin. "Is something the matter,

Richard?" he called, choking back laughter. "You look positively overheated, for some reason."

Through gritted teeth Richard replied, "I have no idea what you mean, Edward. Everything is fine." He clasped Allegra's wrist tighter and tried to move her hand. Not only would it not budge, he could feel her fingers kneading into his inner thigh. "Perdition, madam," he hissed, trying to keep his lips from moving, "unhand me, or I shall—"

"Shall what?" she whispered back. Her eyes were wide and glistening. Her smile had enlarged into a big bold grin that was absolutely maddening. "Now are you ready to hear what your father says?"

He knew defeat when he saw it. Much as it galled him, he let go of her wrist. "All right, I surrender. Remove your hand. Then, if you must, proceed."

She lifted her hand away, then regarded him coyly. "It is your father's wish that we be married. I think I should like that, my dear Lord Beaumont. What do you say?"

"What do I say?" Scowling he continued, "I say, my dear Lady Allegra, that I would as lief be married to my mother's pet poodle as married to you."

He knew before the words left his mouth that his blunt insult was the wrong approach, yet he would not have changed one syllable if his life depended on it. He turned away, picked up his fork, and attempted to take a bite of his *fricandeau à l'oseille*. He could not, though, because her hostile stare was burning into him, finally compelling him to drop his fork and look back at her. Her mouth had tightened, her eyes had taken on a stony fury. Watching transfixed, he saw her gaze roam over the table until she spied her full glass of claret. She picked it up, at the same time glancing around the table. *She wasn't—oh, no, she wouldn't!*

"Allegra—!"

"Pet poodle, sir?" she hissed, and hurled the contents of the crystal goblet full in his face.

Richard leaped up, grabbing for his napkin, pushing

his chair back so swiftly it tipped over with a resounding crash. Mopping at his face, he looked down and, *damnation, blast the woman,* there were ghastly red stains on his superbly cut gray tailcoat, his fashionable buckskin trousers, and his previously snowy white cravat.

" 'Pon my word, what is it, Richard?" the earl called in alarm from the head of the table.

"Your pardon, sir," he managed, "it appears . . . that I was clumsy enough to have spilled my wine."

"On your face?" came Edward's amused observation from across the table—a remark for which he would suffer a thousand tortures later.

"See to Lord Beaumont," the Earl of Wallingford told a footman. "Take him to my valet. Dreadfully sorry, Richard. Follow my footman here. Get back soon's you can. We'll not let it spoil the evening, shall we?"

Oblivious to the muffled sounds of gaiety emitting from the dining room, Meg, carrying a slender volume of Keats's poetry, made her way along the main hallway and entered the mahogany-paneled, candlelit library. It was a handsome room, two stories high, with a gallery halfway up. Since she had come to London five months ago, this room had been her refuge. Whenever she found a spare moment, she had slipped in to browse fondly among his lordship's extensive collection of books packed into floor-to-ceiling shelves. How many times had she found a gem of a volume—something she absolutely must read—quietly borrowed it, and read it by candlelight late that night in her small room under the eaves, being careful to slip it back into its place the next day.

How she would miss these books! She crossed the room, skirting a high-backed sofa situated toward the center of the room, away from the shelves. She stepped behind it and bent to slip the book back to its place on the bottom shelf. *For the last time.* Hand still resting on the book, she reconsidered, remembering it contained

"On the Sea," one of her favorite sonnets. What would it hurt to read it one more time? *Once more, before I am out on the streets.* She sat cross-legged on the floor and placed the book in her lap. In the secluded spot, she untied the ribbons of her cap and tugged it off. Ah, how she loved the feel of freedom as her hair tumbled about her shoulders and hung loose down her back. Eagerly, she opened the book, and was just turning the first page when she heard someone enter the library and shut—nay, practically slam—the door.

"Blast!" she heard a deep male voice say. Then, "Damn the woman!" There was a sound similar to a footstool being kicked.

This must be a guest from the dinner party, obviously one who was mightily displeased, and who assumed no one else was in the room. She had better make her presence known before he further embarrassed himself. "Sir," she called, "you are not alone."

After a silence, she heard a surprised voice ask: "What the deuce? Where are you? I hear you, but I cannot see you."

"Over here. Look back of the sofa. I'm sitting on the floor in front of the shelves."

"Ah, there you are."

A tall, dark figure loomed over her. Straining her gaze upward, she encountered first an angry countenance, then observed the whole of the man, discovering that from the top of his carefully tousled dark locks to the bottoms of his glossy black boots, was one of the most devastatingly handsome men she had ever seen. He had massive broad shoulders and a rather narrow face with sharp, assessing eyes, a thin mouth with a cynical twist, a proud, aquiline nose, and a captivating cleft in his chin. He wore a beautifully cut, form-fitting gray jacket that appeared to have some damp spots on it, as if it had recently been sponged. A muscle clenched in his jaw as he stared down at her. She gave him a tentative smile. "Good evening, sir. You seem a mite chagrined."

"Chagrined!" he burst. "Now, there's an understatement by half. But I most humbly beg your—"

Richard stopped abruptly, having finally remarked the girl's gray dress and white apron. The deuce! Allegra had so unnerved him that he had almost done the unthinkable and apologized to a servant. Nonetheless, she was a pretty little chit. Never had he seen such hair, guinea gold he would call it, unfettered by a cap, streaming long and silky down her back. Hands on hips, Richard peered down into the girl's dark-lashed blue eyes. "May I ask what you are doing on the floor?"

"Returning a book of poetry."

"Ah, I see . . . for your mistress."

"For myself." She held up the small volume. "Shelly writes in anger and protest, Byron in the excitements of a passionate, combative life, but Keats?" Her eyes brightened with pleasure. "Keats writes in ecstasy, don't you agree?"

"Really!" This was most astounding. He hardly knew any servants who could read, let alone any who were partial to poetry. Moreover, this one was not acting in the manner maids were supposed to act. No leaping to her feet all agog, curtsying and apologizing for the very existence of her inferior self. No indeed, this one simply looked up at him, book in her hand, with a cool directness in her gaze. She did not even appear flustered that her cap was lying on the floor when it should most properly have been covering her head.

"And what are *you* doing in the library?" she bluntly inquired. "Should you not be at the dinner table?"

Ordinarily, Richard would have informed a mere servant that her question was bold, insolent, and entirely out of order. But anger roiled inside him, he felt the need to let it out, and there was something about this girl that put him in a mood to talk. "A lady—I employ the term loosely—threw a glass of wine in my face." He gazed down at himself, scowling at the water spots. "Had to borrow one of the earl's cravats—get his valet to sponge me off. Now I must wait for the spots to dry."

"Did you deserve it?" she inquired.

"Deserve what?"

"The wine in your face."

Did she think his wits were all abroad? "I did not!" he answered vehemently. "The act was perpetrated by the most . . . the most . . . monstrous of women!"

"Do you like poetry?"

The girl's abrupt switch of subjects startled him into silence. For a moment he could do naught but stare at her. "Of course I like poetry. More than like: I find I cannot do without poetry."

The girl held up the book in her hand. "Then, listen to this and calm yourself."

"Which poem did you have in mind?"

" 'On the Sea.' Now, find a place to sit, and I shall read it to you." He watched her get up off the floor. Standing tall, she rested the slender volume on the high back of the sofa, making a sort of makeshift pulpit of it. Well, why not? The spots were not yet dry. Until they were, he would not dream of reappearing in the dining room. He retraced his steps around the sofa and sank into an armchair, stretching out his legs and gazing at her speculatively. "So begin," he said, wondering how well she could read. God grant him patience if the poor creature had to trace the words with her finger.

"Now, close your eyes and imagine the sea," she said, "and just listen . . .

> It keeps eternal whisperings around
> Desolate shores, and with its mighty spell
> Gluts twice ten thousand caverns . . ."

Her melodious voice washed over him, warm and soothing. How could a servant have learned such perfect diction? And project words so soft, yet firm . . . full of enchantment. He listened, totally engrossed, and before the poem was done, his rage and anger drained away and he felt calm again. Why, just to be in her presence was soothing. . . .

When she finished all of Keats's composition, he clapped his hands together and proclaimed, "Splendid! I have never heard it read as well. In truth, it is one of my favorite sonnets."

She looked pleased. "Mine, too."

"You read with such feeling. You must have spent much time by the sea."

"I have never seen it."

That surprised him. Remembering his many excursions to Brighton, and of course, his two grand tours, it was inconceivable that any Englishman, or woman, might not have seen the sea. Of course, she was but a servant. Strange, he had never considered it before, but there must be many a servant who had never had the chance to travel, who had never seen the sea.

"So are you over your pique?" she inquired.

He frowned. "I, in a pique? Never."

"Indeed?" There was teasing laughter in her eyes. "Have you so soon forgotten that odious woman who threw wine in your face?" She lowered her voice an octave and imitated perfectly, "The act was perpetrated by the most . . . the most . . . monstrous of women!"

Disarmed, Richard could not suppress a smile. "Damme, I believe I do feel better." He gazed long at her. Standing behind the couch as she was, holding the book, that pale, shining hair falling about her shoulders, she looked beautiful, not like any serving girl he had ever seen. "Come out from behind the couch and sit down."

"I am happy where I am, sir," she said shortly, clearly not inviting further argument. She bent and retrieved her cap. "Such disarray!" she exclaimed as she placed it on her head. "I must apologize to your lordship."

"Your lordship? Then you must know who I am." He watched, fascinated, as her arms lifted gracefully to tuck her hair beneath the cap. Her bosom lifted, too. Though he could barely discern it beneath her white starched apron, the sight caused a sudden, unexpected tug, deep within himself, that made him catch his breath.

Strange. Only minutes ago he had been adrift in a veritable sea of powdered, perfumed bosoms—some practically shoved in his face—and felt nothing. Yet just now, the mere hint of a breast under this servant girl's prim uniform had affected him inordinately.

She was saying, "I can hazard a guess as to who you are. Are you Lord Beaumont?"

"How did you know?"

"Your reputation precedes you," she answered lightly. "The most lowly slavey in the house has heard of the handsome Lord Beaumont."

He could not resist asking, "Is that good or bad?"

She gave a slight shrug. "That depends. If your aim is to be the most devilish rake in all London, who has broken at least a dozen hearts, then 'tis good. If you want the world to know you discard your mistresses as you would your cravats, then 'tis good. Why, even we servants have heard—"

"That is quite enough," he said shortly. Though she was quite correct, and he had not minded in the least the *on dit* about his reputation, it somehow sounded different coming from the ruby lips of this young girl. It made him sound selfish . . . unfeeling.

The door opened, and Edward stuck his head in. "Ah, Richard, there you are! You've missed dessert, but you must come back for your after-dinner port. And if you're worried about Allegra, the ladies have withdrawn."

So Allegra was the culprit! Meg noted. Lady Caroline's "odious" cousin.

Not waiting for a response, Edward shut the door. Richard loathed being rushed and sank deeper in his chair. Besides, he was still intrigued by this forward baggage of a servant. "You know my name," he said, "so tell me yours."

"Meg Quincy," she answered, "I am Lady Caroline's

lady's maid, or . . . that is . . ." she stopped, and for the first time appeared flustered, biting her lip as if she had just remembered something. "Her former lady's maid. I shall be leaving tomorrow."

"Ah, so you're the one!" he exclaimed, remembering Caroline's lament at dinner.

"The one *what*, sir?"

"The servant who is not humble."

She smiled wryly. "That must be I."

He examined her carefully. "I trust you have obtained another position."

She seemed to stiffen. "It is of no consequence. Do not trouble yourself." She had lifted her chin in a most defiant manner.

She was right. Why should he give one extra thought to this saucy chit who liked poetry? He glanced down and noted the spots were gone. "Then, I most certainly shall not trouble myself," he replied, and rose and went to the door. "May good fortune follow you, Meg Quincy." He held the door open and regarded her inquisitively. "Well, are you coming?"

She bent and replaced the book, then seemed to hesitate, as if she were rooted to that spot behind the sofa and wished to remain so. Her brow furrowed, as if she were making some momentous decision. "Yes, indeed, m'lord."

He stood watching as she circled around the couch. How unexpected that a mere serving maid possessed such patrician features! Such a delicate nose—slender white neck—temptingly curved mouth—and the fairest skin that made her cheeks look as if they had been softly brushed with rose-and-white pearl. She had a well-molded chin, tilted up at the moment, giving her the appearance of iron determination. Interesting, how even that drab gown and starched apron could not hide the nubile curves beneath, nor that incredibly tiny waist, nor . . . She was halfway across the carpet when he realized, *God's blood, she has a limp.*

A strange feeling gripped his heart, caused by shock, not pity. He found himself hard put to keep his expression impassive as the realization dawned on him that this fair-haired girl with the fine, patrician face and the body of a temptress was a cripple. He could not prevent his gaze from shifting downward to discover why she limped, but nothing was visible below her long gray skirt.

She was passing him now, not slowly. " 'Tis a clubfoot, my lord," she said, smiling at him faintly, as if she knew exactly what was in his head. Devil take it, she did. He tried to form an answer, but before he could reply, she had passed him and started down the hall. Not a bad limp, really—he had seen worse—but a limp, nonetheless. She was about to disappear. A kind of consternation surged through him. He did not want to see her go. "Where will you go tomorrow?" he called after her.

She stopped and turned. "Do not trouble yourself, your lordship," she called, "I shall find a place." A playful smile curved her mouth. "Perhaps I shall become an orange girl. Or there's always the workhouse. Just think, I could spend my time picking oakum and breaking stones." She started up a far stairway and was gone.

Edward appeared in the hallway again. "Whatever is keeping you, Richard? I told you—"

"How deucedly unfair!" Richard exclaimed, his gaze still fixed on the spot where she disappeared. "Tell me, Edward, what do servants do when they are suddenly dismissed?"

"How should I know? Why should I care? Really, Richard, why concern yourself with such trivia?"

Richard returned his reluctant attention to his friend. "I have just been talking to Lady Caroline's lady's maid. They are practically throwing her out on the street tomorrow, which I consider an absolute disgrace. Something should be done."

"Come, Richard," Edward answered soothingly. "No

need to fly into the boughs. Good God, man, she is, after all, only a servant, and since when—?"

Richard drew himself up, regaining his composure as he flicked an imaginary piece of lint from his sleeve. Edward was quite correct. "She was a pretty little chit, but as you say, only a servant. Shall we get back to the dining room? I should wager the gentlemen are well into their cups by now."

"That's the spirit!" Edward clapped him on the back. "Don't trouble yourself about Allegra. I daresay you will survive, if you're quick enough to duck next time."

Chapter 5

Despite his reassurances to Edward, try as Lord Beaumont might, he could not stop thinking about the blond little maidservant he had met in the library.

Whereas he always enjoyed the men-only, after-dinner ceremony of port, tobacco, and lively discussion, tonight he was hard put to keep his mind upon the conversation. Talk heated up around him, but for once he did not care a groat if Napoleon escaped from St. Helena, formed an army, and marched on England once again. Instead, he kept seeing that delicately constructed face, stunning figure, and the most perceptive blue eyes he had ever peered into.

"You seem distracted," Edward commented after noticing the distant look in his friend's eye.

"If you must know, I cannot keep from thinking of that maidservant I met in the library," Richard snapped back. "Damme, despite what you say, someone ought to help her find another position."

Edward looked at him askance. "Whatever has got into you? I would have thought you were far above dabbling in domestic matters."

"It is simply that I pity the poor creature."

"Do tell," commented Edward, obviously trying not to smile.

Ignoring his mockery, Richard continued, "As a matter of fact, an idea has occurred to me. I shall have a word with Lady Semple as soon as we join the ladies."

"Watch out for Allegra," Edward slyly commented, still trying to quell his amusement.

"Allegra be damned. All I care about is speaking to her mother."

When the gentlemen finally adjourned, Richard was one of the first in the drawing room. Allegra, thank God, was engaged in conversation in a far corner. To his relief, he saw that Lady Semple was by herself at the moment, seated on an Egyptian-style ottoman. *She's a handsome woman still,* he thought, as he gazed upon the quiet, gracious lady who had lived in the neighboring mansion all his life. Quickly Richard approached and gave a slight bow. "Ah, Lady Semple, how fortuitous I have found you alone. May I sit down?"

"Please do, Richard." Charlotte smiled her shy smile and patted the cushion beside her. "As a matter of fact, I've been wanting to talk to you. We're having a dinner and ball at Pentworth Park a fortnight from now. I am so hoping you can come."

And be at the mercy of Allegra? With a gracious nod he answered, "Thank you for your kind invitation. I shall be there if I can, but as you know, I have not been home in quite some time now, and am not certain of my plans." Desirous of a swift change of subject, he inquired, "And how is Thomas?"

Her fleeting expression of chagrin told him nothing concerning her third son had changed. "Regretfully, Thomas is still at Oxford. Poor Cyril, now that William is gone, and Rawdon killed at Waterloo, his hopes are pinned on Thomas, though he's beginning to despair that Thomas will ever marry." Charlotte eyed him sadly. "That leaves Edward, who appears to adore his life of dissipation in London and shows no sign of settling down." With a sigh, Lady Semple snapped open her mother-of-pearl fan. "Who would have thought we would not have been blessed with one single grandchild by now, nor one in sight? I have begun to think Allegra is our only hope."

Her comment gave Richard the perfect opportunity to introduce a topic foremost on his mind. "You mentioned at dinner that Allegra is in need of a lady's maid."

A frown creased Charlotte's brow. "Allegra has a lady's maid, a sweet young thing, but, as you know, Allegra is quite strong-minded. The maid cannot stand up to her, so Allegra wears what she pleases with what are sometimes, I fear, less-than-suitable results."

Such as looking like a trollop on the streets, thought Richard. "At dinner, Lady Caroline mentioned her own lady's maid."

"Ah, yes, the one dismissed." Charlotte shook her head. "Such a pity. She is highly skilled, obviously, judging from young Caroline's impeccable appearance. I do wonder what is wrong with her."

"Nothing!" Richard blurted, then vowed to contain himself. "Although I'm sure the countess has her own good reasons to say what she said. Be that as it may, I happen to have met the young woman in the library a short time ago. Pleasant little creature. Appears quite competent."

"But was she humble?" asked Charlotte, a glint of humor in her eye.

Richard frowned, wrestling with the truth. "Not exactly humble, but—"

"Pray, do not trouble yourself, Lord Beaumont," Charlotte said. " 'Tis quite all right. 'Humble' may be a requirement of the countess, but as for me, I am more concerned with what kind of work she's capable of. And judging from the simply ravishing manner in which Caroline is turned out . . ." She regarded him appraisingly. "I must say, I am impressed at your kindness, taking an interest in this poor servant girl."

Richard returned a saintly smile. "We do what we can, do we not, Lady Semple, for the unfortunates of the world?" He risked a quick glance around. He would never hear the end of it if Edward had overheard such blather.

Charlotte folded her fan and tapped it thoughtfully on her chin. "I shall be in London a few more days. Perhaps—"

"She's to be tossed onto the streets tomorrow," Richard interjected hastily.

"Indeed? Then I had better see her tonight."

Filled with curiosity, Meg entered the empty library. A footman had summoned her there without telling her why. Wondering who wished to see her, Meg pushed aside the crimson velvet curtain covering the long, bow window that faced the gaslit street. Gazing idly at the line of waiting carriages and coachmen lounging at the curb, she saw a ragged waif dart up to the coachman begging alms. He—or was it she?—was cursed and chased away. Meg felt a shiver of dread, wondering where she herself would be tomorrow night. Though she would not be out on the street like that waif, she would be obliged to find a room somewhere. The specter of poverty haunted her. She was loath to use up the money she had so laboriously saved toward the day she could leave her life of servitude behind. It was all she lived for. How could she bear to spend even one farthing now?

Despite her apprehension, she tried to look at the bright side. Tomorrow, for the first time since she was six, she would not be working from dawn until well past midnight. She would not be dipping and curtsying, parroting "yes, m'lady, no, m'lady" all the day. A not-altogether loathsome thought, she reminded herself.

"Meg?" Caroline's voice. She had entered the room so quietly, Meg had not heard.

Meg turned from the window. "Why, m'lady! The party isn't over yet, is it?"

"No, but there's someone who wants to talk to you." Caroline hesitated, looking concerned. "Standing there, you looked so wistful."

Meg managed a brave smile. "I was just thinking that I shall be able to see London now, all those places I have missed. Astley's Royal Amphitheater in Lambeth, Covent Garden, Drury Lane. How I would love to see a Shakespearean tragedy! And Vauxhall Gardens. I hear there are thousands of little colored lamps decorating the trees, and cascades of water, and romantic, sylvan grottoes—" Meg caught herself. With whom could she ever be romantic?

Lady Caroline's face fell. "Oh, Meg, I never realized—but you're right! I've kept you so busy all Season, you never had the opportunity to get out. How inconsiderate I am! Perhaps someday I can make it up to you." Caroline's face lit in a happy smile. "I have good news. My cousin, the Marchioness of Semple, will be here shortly to talk to you. It seems her daughter is in need of a new lady's maid."

Instantly alert, Meg slanted a guarded look at Caroline. "Are you referring to your Cousin Allegra?" Caroline nodded. "The *odious* Allegra?"

"Oh, bother!" Guiltily Caroline touched her finger to her lips. "I should never have said a word. But you can handle Allegra. I know you could. Think of it! You would have a position, not be out on the streets."

Meg was not convinced. Though frivolous and naive, Caroline had a kind heart and hardly ever said a bad word about anybody. So it followed that if she loathed Allegra, and she most obviously did, then that young lady must be odious indeed. "You say her ladyship is coming here?" Meg asked cautiously.

"She shall be here any moment."

Meg thought hard. Even the best of mistresses could be taxing at times. But the worst, and surely Allegra would be the worst, would be devilishly difficult to deal with. Better to end up in the drafty old castle in Scotland. "I am sorry to disappoint you, Caroline, but I must warn you in advance—I am disinclined to consider working for her."

Caroline gasped in dismay. "But I am astounded! My Cousin Charlotte lives at Pentworth Park, which is one of the most beautiful estates in all England. You should see the exquisite furnishings! And outside? Why, the gardens are perfectly symmetrical, with peacocks strolling around the grounds. The whole countryside fights for invitations to her house parties and balls. Of course you want to work for her!"

Full of youthful exuberance, ignoring what she did not want to hear, Caroline pulled Meg onto one of two gracefully carved Thomas Sheraton corner stools and sat herself upon the other. Bending forward confidentially, she asked, "How on earth did you manage to persuade Lord Beaumont to put in a word for you? Wherever did you meet him? He could hardly wait to get Cousin Charlotte aside when the gentlemen rejoined us in the drawing room. According to her, he sung your praises highly."

"He did?" Taken by surprise, Meg shook her head. "I met Lord Beaumont only briefly in the library, where he had gone after his . . . accident with spilled wine. We talked for only a short time. I never—"

A polite knocking at the open doorway interrupted. Meg looked up to see a slender woman in her late forties, elegantly attired in a high-waisted, violet satin dress bordered around the hem with a band of rich gold and white embroidery. The lady was strikingly beautiful with blond hair piled high, exotic cheekbones, and large blue eyes. She seemed not to know it, though. Her shoulders slumped; her face had an apologetic look. Altogether, there was an aura of unsureness about her. "I do hope I have not intruded," she hesitantly began.

"Cousin Charlotte, do come in!" cried Caroline, springing from the stool. "Please sit down," she said, indicating the stool where she had been sitting. "This is Meg, my abigail. Meg, this is my cousin, Lady Semple."

Meg stood and curtsied, but before she could speak the marchioness waved her down again, declaring in a quiet, unassuming voice, "Do not trouble yourself, my dear, sit down. I wanted to talk to you because I am looking for a lady's maid for my daughter, Allegra."

In a friendly manner, she proceeded to quiz Meg concerning her qualifications. She seemed pleased when Meg described the teachings of the Incomparable Celeste, the French maid who had been her mentor.

"Celeste took me under her wing. She taught me the art of hairdressing, as well as skills in needlework, ironing, and cosmetics. In time she introduced me to various concoctions and decoctions that she mixed herself." Meg smiled. "I learned how to pound musk with amber to counterfeit Rowland's Hair Oil, and the recipe for alum water. I learned that bullock's gall is best for fading black spots and, and how sunburn can be counteracted with ass's milk . . ."

After Meg finished describing her qualifications, with Caroline chiming in enthusiastically from time to time, Lady Semple appeared pleased.

"Well, Meg, I am most favorably impressed with your qualifications and would like to hire you."

Yet Meg could not cast aside thoughts of Allegra. "I'm flattered you would consider me, your ladyship, but my mind is made up. My answer must be no."

Lady Caroline gasped aloud in dismay. "How could you refuse such an offer?"

Meg hated to disappoint a lady as kind as Lady Semple, but it would never do to let her know that her daughter's reputation for obnoxiousness and bad behavior was her main reason for refusing. "Thank you, Lady Caroline, for your concern. I am indeed aware of my predicament, but I wish to remain in London. For me to accept a position at Pentworth Park is to be buried in the country. I could grow old there—die there—and never see London again. 'Tis such an exciting city! I want to see it while I can." There, that was truthful enough, and would spare Lady Semple's feelings.

"Are you sure you wish to remain in London?" Lady

Semple inquired. "Surely you're aware it's full of dangerous pitfalls for young, innocent girls like you."

"She's right, Meg," Caroline eagerly broke in. "I should not rest knowing you are out on the streets somewhere. Or living over some gin shop, or—" Hampered by her limited knowledge of London's dark side, she concluded lamely, "—or heavens knows where."

"You must not worry, m'lady." Meg switched her gaze back to the marchioness. "My answer still must be no."

While Lady Caroline continued to sputter, Lady Semple took Meg's hand and murmured softly, "Of course, my dear, I do understand. You are a charming young girl, and I wish you the very best of everything. Perhaps the day will come when you won't mind being"—the corners of her eyes crinkled with amusement—"buried in the country. If such is ever the case, you must get in touch with me."

Meg caught the sincerity in Lady Semple's voice. For a moment she was tempted . . . but no! She would not mind working for this lady, but never her daughter. She gave her thanks to Lady Semple, arose, gave a curtsy, and started away.

Halfway cross the library, she heard a gasp behind her. "That limp!" cried the marchioness.

Meg squeezed her eyes shut in chagrin. *Twice in one night.* First she had been obliged to explain her cursed limp to Lord Beaumont. Now again. At least his lordship had possessed the decency not to comment, but her ladyship? Hoping she would not be showered with sympathy, Meg slowly turned. Her head held high, she replied, "It appears you have noticed my limp, your ladyship. It is caused by the clubfoot I was born with. I pay it no heed, however, and I manage quite tolerably."

To Meg's surprise, the marchioness had not only turned pale, she was wide-eyed, hand pressed over her heart, as if she were about to faint. "Tell me, Meg," she asked in a strangely tremulous voice, "what is your last name?"

"Quincy, your ladyship."

Intense astonishment touched the blanched face of Lady Semple. She gasped and half stood. But then her knees buckled under her, and with a moan, she started to collapse. She would have crumpled to the floor had not Lady Caroline on one side and Meg on the other caught her between them and helped her back to the stool.

"Cousin Charlotte, whatever is amiss?" cried Caroline.

Meg picked up her ladyship's fan and started vigorously fanning. "Are you all right, m'lady?"

"I . . . I shall be fine."

Meg smiled in sympathy. "You appeared distraught."

"Why, I . . . I . . ." For a time Lady Semple was silent, as if she was trying to formulate a reply. "Forgive me," she finally said in a voice little above a whisper, "but I am so distressed. You cannot imagine . . . my beloved Allegra has so many good qualities that I was sure a competent lady's maid could bring out. Caroline, I had so counted on Meg to help us that I was overcome with disappointment when she said no." Meg started to speak, but Charlotte patted her hand and continued, "No, no! 'Tis quite all right, my dear. You must do what suits you." Charlotte gazed bleakly into Meg's concerned eyes. "Of course, I would have seen that you got to London from time to time. You would not, as you claim, have been buried in the country, but"—sadly she sighed—"it is too late now. As for Allegra, not one acceptable offer the whole Season! I vow, I am in despair." Tears filled her eyes. "I don't know what to do."

"Oh, m'lady!" Meg could not stand to see this lovely lady in tears. "Perhaps I spoke too hastily. If you need me that badly—"

"I do, I do!"

"She does, she does!" Caroline joined in enthusiastically.

Meg continued, "I've been training Polly to be a lady's maid. May she come along?"

"Yes! That is, if Lord Wallingford agrees."

"Then . . . I shall accept the position. I shall be Allegra's lady's maid."

Joyously Caroline clapped her hands. "Wonderful! You will never regret it, Cousin Charlotte. Meg is a true gem."

Already regretful, Meg tried to swallow the expanding lump in her throat. Why, oh, why had she not refused? But she knew the answer. Lady Semple's near collapse had stirred such sympathy in her heart that against her better judgment she'd said yes.

There was something else, too, that was bothersome. Why had Lady Semple collapsed? True, she was concerned about her daughter, but it did not seem reasonable that Allegra's lack of proposals could make her mother swoon.

Meg had an uneasy feeling that something wasn't right, though she had no idea what it could be. Already she suspected she had made a terrible mistake, but she forced a smile, deciding she would not allow herself to dwell on the possibilities of dire consequences.

Chapter 6

When Meg emerged from the library, a group of departing guests stood chatting by the front entryway. Aware, as always, that servants should remain invisible, she hurried in the other direction toward the back staircase. As she reached the first step, she felt a tap on her shoulder. She spun around and was startled to find herself gazing into the somber, dark eyes of Lord Beaumont.

"Well, Meg," he inquired solicitously, "did you accept the position?"

Suddenly she remembered: This arrogant lord had actually done her a favor, or so he thought. His interest seemed genuine, but since when did a noble the likes of this one take notice of a humble maid? Surely he had a hidden motive, and if he expected her to get on her knees with gratitude, he was much mistaken. Meg lifted her chin and met him with a cool gaze. "Yes, I have accepted a position with the Marchioness of Semple to be Lady Allegra's abigail. But I have no recollection of asking you to intercede on my behalf, sir."

Lord Beaumont frowned in puzzlement. "But are you not pleased?"

"To be obliged to work for such a—" She clamped her lips. She had almost said "hoity-toity," and thus would have defamed one of his own. Why could he not have left her alone? If her bitterness was evident, so be it. "If ever the occasion arises again, I would appreciate your not interfering."

"Indeed?" Lord Beaumont returned an arched glance.

"There's gratitude for you. Rest assured, I shall not interfere again."

"Rest assured," she flung back, "I'm quite capable of finding my own position."

"But of course." He appeared calm, even slightly detached, but sharp observer that she was, she caught a slight twitch at the corner of his mouth that gave his discomfit away. He drew back a step, his disdainful expression softened by a touch of genuine regret. "Hartwick House, my estate, lies but three miles from Pentworth Park. Perhaps we shall meet again."

Whatever did he mean? she wondered. Such a strange man. "Our lives run on different paths, sir. Three miles? It might as well be three million miles."

He did not immediately reply, but stood solemnly regarding her with a look that signaled he would like to say more. But finally he smiled, if faintly and wryly, and said, "Different paths. You are right, of course."

She relaxed, her irritation melting away. Perhaps she was mistaken. Perhaps, despite his being one of the ton, he had harbored a genuine desire to help. "On second thought, it appears I have been remiss. I"—the words did not come easily—"I wish to thank you for your help. Were it not for you, I could very well have been out on the streets, or catching pneumonia in some drafty Scottish castle."

"You are quite welcome, Meg. Good night," he said with a frosty smile, and walked away.

A few days later, in the drawing room at Pentworth Park, Lady Semple's sister-in-law, Lady Lydia, her face reddening with anger, set teacup to saucer with a clatter and asked, "Have you gone mad?"

Charlotte remained calm, musing that the years had not been kind to her spinster sister-in-law. Still, some of it was Lydia's own doing; those deep-cut wrinkles on her forehead were caused by a permanent scowl. "I am not daft," she told Lydia. "I cannot tell you how delighted I am to have Meg here, if only in my employ."

"I shall not have this!" Lydia looked as if she might have a tantrum. "It is quite unconscionable that after all these years you should bring this . . . this . . . trollop to live under the same roof as Allegra. You cannot do this to Cyril! You cannot do this to Allegra!"

"Please, Lydia, help me. I know 'tis awkward, but—"

"Help you?" Lydia cut in, laughing bitterly. "Why should I? I, who have been nothing more than a toad eater to your high-and-mighty ladyship all these years!"

Inside, Charlotte seethed. Lydia was one of those unfortunates of the world: an older, unmarried female with no status and no power. She had lived at Pentworth Park all her life, first at the sufferance of her father, now her brother Cyril. At times Charlotte found her priggishness well-nigh intolerable, yet she had always treated her sister-in-law with the utmost courtesy—had, in fact, allowed Lydia to practically run the household. And all for naught, she reflected bitterly.

Charlotte was not accustomed to defying Lydia; however, in this instance she had no intention of backing down. Trying to appease, she said, "No one, other than you and I, shall know. Certainly not Cyril. As for Allegra, do not concern yourself. Her chances will not be risked in the slightest."

"So you say now, Charlotte." Lydia's lips pinched tight. Though obviously trying to control herself, she succumbed to an angry burst of words. "Who knows what disasters you have wrought with your foolishness? Why could you not have left well enough alone? What will you do with the chit? Are you planning to tell her?"

Charlotte felt herself close to tears. She *hated* anger and criticism, hated scenes. "One question at a time, please, Lydia," she answered with a timid smile. "I have wrought no disasters. You see, now that I have found Meg, I want her here. I can see no harm in allowing her to continue as Allegra's lady's maid, and no, I don't plan to tell her."

As Charlotte expected, Lydia was not the least assuaged. "Mark my word, Meg will bring nothing but trouble to this household."

Charlotte's back stiffened. "Meg is here, and here she remains. That's all I care to say on the subject." Hoping to lure her sister-in-law into safer topics, she picked up her embroidery and casually remarked, "While in London I saw Lord Beaumont at Wallingford's dinner party. I invited him to our ball, but he declined to give me either a yes or no."

"But he *must* come! It means everything to Allegra." Lydia picked up her own hoop of embroidery and jammed the needle into the cloth.

Her vexation was not totally unexpected. Of all the family, Lydia was Allegra's most staunch supporter— sometimes her only supporter, considering that Allegra's coarse, selfish behavior would have tried the patience of God, let alone her family. "I want Lord Beaumont to attend as much as you do, Lydia, although how Allegra plans to snare him after that debacle in London remains to be seen."

Lydia shrugged. "A splash of wine in his face is nothing. Allegra will find a way. Besides, Richard will have a hard time disregarding Cyril's increase in Allegra's dowry. Not only that, Richard's father is dead set on this match."

"Two definite enticements, I agree, although bear in mind Lord Beaumont does as he pleases." Charlotte paused, wishing to address Lydia on a certain delicate matter. "Lydia, you seem to have more influence on Allegra than I. I do believe she would have more of a chance with Richard if she would tone down her . . . er, enthusiasm."

As expected, Lydia immediately bristled. "Whatever do you mean?"

"On several occasions I have caught her casting flirtatious glances at the footmen, but the worst is when that rakehell Henry comes to call. Then she outdoes herself in being bold and provocative."

"Nonsense!" Lydia's narrow nose twitched with irritation. "Allegra is high-spirited, that's all."

Coarse, not high-spirited, Charlotte thought, then scolded herself. She must not have such wicked thoughts about a daughter.

"Although I do agree," Lydia continued, "that the less we see of Henry, the better."

Charlotte nodded with a sigh. "Henry is a drunk, a gambler, and a disgrace to the family, but what are we to do? He is Richard's younger brother, after all."

"We dare not be rude."

For a time they both stitched in silence until Charlotte casually remarked, "Speaking of Richard, I hear something strange is going on at Hartwick House. Quarreling servants . . . rumors of illness."

Lydia answered, "So I have heard. Apparently young Henry takes no interest. What they need is for Richard to come home."

"He claims he is happy where he is."

"Nonsense!" Lydia took on her usual pursed-lip expression of disapproval. " 'Tis absolutely imperative that Richard give up his dissolute life in London. He must come home, marry Allegra, and settle down." She set her embroidery aside and stood, smoothing her plain, mud-colored gown. "Where is Meg?"

"Upstairs in Allegra's chambers, I suppose, but why—?"

"I have not seen the girl since she arrived. I must have a word with her."

"I see no need," Lady Semple said cautiously.

"Well, I do," Lady Lydia replied with an emphatic bob of her sharp chin.

Meg was alone in the dressing room, mixing vinegar and lemon juice to be employed on Allegra's freckles, when Lady Lydia walked in and said, "So I see you have arrived."

Meg was so startled, she nearly dropped the jar. "Lady Lydia! Why, I remember you from your visit to Auberry Hall when the countess died. I remember—"

"You shall *not* remember!" the older woman commanded. "Bad enough you're here, but I wish to make it clear you are not to say a word about your life at Auberry Hall, nor Lady Elinore, especially anything she said on the day she died. Is that clear?"

Meg's mind was churning, but she had presence of mind enough to murmur a quick, "Yes, ma'am."

"See that you don't. If you do"—Lady Lydia fairly hissed—"you shall suffer the consequences, which shall be most unpalatable, I can assure you."

After Lady Lydia swept away, Meg sat stunned for a time. Not remember her life at Auberry Hall? Nor Lady Elinore? Nor, most especially, what Lady Elinore said to her on the last day of her life? Meg gazed into space, her thoughts flying back to two years ago, when she was sixteen, and what had occurred only hours before the first countess died . . .

Confused and mystified, young Meg had been summoned into the countess's bedchamber. Shocked at the desperately ill appearance of the countess, Meg could only look on silently until the countess, in a voice barely audible, summoned her to her bed.

"Ah, my little Meg," she whispered, weakly grasping Meg's hand. "How pretty you have grown. I summoned you . . . because I have decided you have a right to know . . . a secret kept from you all these years."

What secret could the exalted Countess of Wallingford possibly reveal to a lowly servant? Totally perplexed, grieved at the knowledge the good countess lay dying, Meg knelt by the bed, still clasping the countess's hand. "What do you wish to tell me, your ladyship?"

"You were told lies . . . told your mother was a

scullery maid. Such a wicked deception! But it was not my doing, 'twas my cousins, Lydia and Charlotte. I only agreed to such a scheme because ..." The countess's voice grew faint. She closed her eyes, appearing to drift away.

Overwhelmed by curiosity, Meg fought the impulse to shake the countess awake. Instead, after a quick intake of breath she asked gently, "Yes, m'lady? You were about to say ... ?"

The countess's eyelids flickered open. She was fading fast, but managed to whisper, "Your mother ... 'tis time you knew your mother was not a scullery maid."

Meg's heart leaped. Holding her breath, she asked, "Then tell me who my mother was, Lady Wallingford."

"Your mother—"

"Enough!" a sharp voice interrupted. Meg looked up to see Lady Wallingford's pinch-faced spinster cousin, Lady Lydia, who was visiting from her brother's home at Pentworth Park. Lips pressed tight, towering over the bed, Lydia stabbed her folded silk fan toward Meg and commanded, "Get back to your work, girl." In a gentler tone she addressed the dying countess. "Old secrets are best never revealed, no matter how much time has passed or how much our conscience hurts us."

"But 'tis so unfair ..." Lady Wallingford had to fight for breath. "... keeping Meg in the dark all these years." Her eyelids closed. Again she drifted.

Lady Lydia scowled at Meg, still kneeling by the bed. "Did you not hear me? Leave now!"

Meg rose to her feet. "But, m'lady, she was about to reveal the truth about my mother. I wanted—"

"A pox on what you want. You will never mention this incident again, do you understand?"

Meg recalled how she had clamped her lips shut that day, knowing any attempt to defy Lady Lydia would be sheer folly. Sour and spiteful, Lady Lydia was easily capable of making her life a good deal more difficult.

But Meg had never forgotten. In truth, not a day had

since passed that she hadn't thought about Lady Elinore's astounding revelation that sad day, that she was *not* the daughter of a scullery maid.

"I shan't wear that drab, dull atrocity!" Allegra, her lower lip stuck out in a pout, flung aside the visiting gown of dove-gray jaconet that Meg had laid out. "Fetch my lavender crepe."

Meg bent to pick up the discarded dress, aware her new mistress was even more insufferable than she had ever imagined. Though she had been at Pentworth Park only a week, it was abundantly clear already that Lady Caroline's "odious" was an adjective that hardly began to describe Allegra. "It is only ten o'clock in the morning, m'lady. The lavender crepe is evening wear. Are you sure—?"

"Fetch it," Allegra muttered petulantly. "I vow, I shall not have a mere servant tell me what to do." She was only half paying attention, being more engrossed in her image in a full-length mirror, her fingers trailing lovingly over herself, from the square-necked top of her fine cotton chemise, to the large fabric roses fastened on the garters that secured her stockings. "Today I want you to put my hair up and lace it with those purple plumes. I shall look most elegant when Edward and I go calling this afternoon."

"Yes, m'lady." Meg went quickly to the wardrobe to retrieve the lavender crepe, reflecting upon the good advice the French maid Celeste had given her so long ago: *Never let your emotions show.* But it was hard. She had spent the week struggling to fit into her new situation, but still felt strange. The servants were friendly enough, and Lady Semple had been all kindness, even allowing her to bring Polly along. But all the kindness in the world would not make up for the misery of working for Allegra. *Nothing* could make up for Allegra.

At least Caroline had been right about one thing: Pentworth Park was a delight with its lush green acres of trees, strolling peacocks, and flower gardens. But thus far Meg had only been able to view them from her window. Allegra had allowed her no time to explore the grounds.

After Allegra was finally dressed, Meg sat in a corner mending when a knock sounded on the door.

"Good morning, sister dear." Edward slung himself onto a chaise. "What's this I hear? Mama informs me you are planning a ball?"

Allegra, still preening in front of the mirror, answered over her shoulder, "Indeed. We are inviting the cream of the countryside."

"You seem particularly keen this time; what's the occasion?"

"Silly boy, don't you know?" Allegra turned to face him, her expression resembling a cat stalking its prey. "Richard must come. The ball will give us a chance to get better acquainted." Her eyes hardened. "He *is* going to marry me. *C'est fait accompli.*"

Edward burst into hearty laughter. "Pray, do not waste your fancy French phrases on me. I am not impressed. And may I ask, how can you be so sure? Last I heard, Richard was wiping the wine off his face, vowing *not* to marry anybody."

Allegra glared at her brother. "He shall marry me, and no mistake. In case you doubt it, his father is my ally. Papa, too, and why shouldn't he be? Thomas will never marry, and you, Edward, are nothing but a wastrel, destined never to marry, let alone produce an heir. So *I* am the one most likely to carry on family tradition. Father would dearly love to see me marry Richard and join our two estates. And have you heard? Papa has increased my dowry."

"I would advise you not to get your hopes up. Richard is not in need of money."

"*Mon Dieu!* Even his high-and-mighty lordship won't turn up his nose at this amount."

Edward appeared puzzled. "Why do you want him,

Allegra? I've never seen any indication you were madly in love with Richard. So why—?"

"Who said I was in love?" Allegra snapped.

A glimmer of revelation appeared in Edward's eye. "Aha! I remember when you were little, Allegra, and threw temper tantrums when you didn't get your way. You *always* wanted what you couldn't have. Now you want Richard. Could it be because so far he's done an excellent job of ignoring you?"

"Nonsense!" Allegra protested, rather feebly.

Edward inquired, "How do you know Richard would be willing to leave his beloved London to come to this party of yours? He avoids his father like the plague—hasn't even been home for at least a year."

Allegra grasped her brother's arm with a grip like iron. "He shall come because you are his best friend, Edward, and when you return to London tomorrow, you will use your friendship to get him to accept the invitation."

Edward shrugged. "I shall see what I can do, but bear in mind, Richard is his own man."

Allegra's jaw clamped determinedly. "He'll be *my* man soon. Just see to it that he comes."

"Perdition, Allegra! I—" Edward stopped suddenly, having spotted Meg in the far corner. "Well, well, the new lady's maid," he said in a softer tone. "Meg, is it not? I have heard about you."

"Good morning, sir." Meg stood and curtsied, feeling Edward's gaze upon her, warm, admiring.

Edward got up off the chaise and walked over to her. He scanned her critically, beaming approval. "Yes, you are as pretty as Lord Beaumont said you were."

Meg felt her heart jump at the sound of his name. *Now how could that be?* she wondered. Before she could reply, Allegra inquired sharply, "Lord Beaumont knows you?"

"We met only briefly, m'lady, in the library, the night of the Earl of Wallingford's dinner party."

Edward looked amused. "The memorable night of the

wine toss, gentle sister." He immediately turned his attention back to Meg, where his gaze lingered.

Meg remained impassive beneath his gaze, thinking he had not seen her walk yet. When he did, how quickly his opinion would change! In fact, she hoped it *would* change. If it did not, then she would have to contend with yet another young lord of the manor breathing hot and heavy after her. Not that Edward was without a certain charm. She rather liked his warm and friendly manner. True, he was brash, but in a manner different as night and day from his sister.

". . . And besides, Richard had ought to come home," Allegra was saying. "The latest *on dit* has it that his father's gout is so bad, he's confined to his room. And his mother, from what I hear, is quite ill."

"Good Lord!" exclaimed Edward, "why hasn't Richard been informed?"

"You know his mother. From what I hear, she's very proud and does not want him to know. I really think you ought to tell him." Allegra's lips twisted into a crafty smile. "If nothing else, that will surely bring him home."

Chapter 7

Meg had a headache.

Without doubt, it was occasioned by Allegra, whose demands had been excessive even for her this afternoon. Dressing for a round of visiting, the foolish girl could not make up her mind. One gown was *du vieux temps*, another, *mal à propos*. Discarded gowns, shoes, bonnets, stockings were scattered everywhere, like the aftermath of a whirlwind. In the end, thanks to Meg's persistent guidance, Allegra appeared well turned out in an afternoon dress of bishop's blue silk, flowered bonnet, and heelless white kid shoes trimmed with blue silk ruche and ties that wrapped around her ankles. Now, Meg helping, she was tugging on white kid gloves printed with a pattern of small black diamonds.

"*Mon Dieu*, such a mess!" Allegra exclaimed as she glanced around. "After you clean it up, you can catch up on your mending. When that is done, you may re-iron my green-sprigged muslin. When that is done, I don't expect to find you idle upon my return. Find something useful to do."

"Yes, m'lady." Meg kept her head bent low over the glove, clenching her teeth in order to curb her tongue.

As directed, she finished all her chores with time to spare, but after contemplating Allegra's command to "find something useful to do," she decided that considering her headache and the arduous hours she had already worked today, the most "useful" thing she could do would be to allot some time to herself. She had not even seen the grounds of the estate yet, or the river.

Sketch pad in hand, she slipped from the house and hurried across the wide flagstone steps of the library terrace. Had anyone seen her from the windows? A quick check told her she was safe, so she continued on through her ladyship's rose garden, past clipped yew hedges, to where the woods bordered the yews. From there, it was but a short trip through the woods to a path that followed the river. She was out of sight of the house now, free! Her headache started to ease as she slowed her pace, and for a time strolled along the path, catching glimpses of the swiftly flowing stream through tangled hedgerows and thick growths of alder, birch, elm, and hornbeam trees. Wanting to get closer, she cut away from the path when she spied a trail, only faintly discernible, that wound through tall trees, by huckleberries in a hollow, by light purple heath with bees humming dreamily about the blooms. Finally she reached the river's edge and to her delight and surprise, found herself in a spot that resembled a glade in fairyland.

Above, the interlaced branches of tall oak trees formed a canopy; underneath, the ground was carpeted with a tangle of rich green grass, blue forget-me-nots, yellow primroses, and purple violets nestled against mossy stones. There was even a little stream meandering through, gurgling its last before disappearing into the River Wey. Her heart lifted. Here was her own private spot, the perfect place to be alone. She could even forget Allegra in a setting this beautiful! Savoring a sniff of fresh air, she dropped down beside a clump of forget-me-nots, slipped off her shoes and stockings, and dangled her feet in the tiny stream. Her headache had disappeared.

How she needed just to have some time alone!

But settling back, contemplating her life, and Allegra, Meg soon became enveloped in gloom. How long must she be harassed by that shallow girl? Was this to be her existence from now on? She felt the emptiness again—

that hollow feeling that occasionally crept over her when she wondered who she was, where she came from, and, most important, where she would end. Surely not here. Pentworth Park might be beautiful, yet for her it was simply another prison, like the London town house and Auberry Hall. If only she had wings! If she did, this would be the moment she would spread them wide and fly—to anywhere away from here.

It was time to remind herself she would not be a servant forever. She *would* travel, *would* have a good life. Perhaps she would even find someone who would love her, whom she could love. But how could she find him? He would have to be a man of at least moderate circumstances, who loved music, art, and poetry as much as she. Generous and kind, of course, with a sense of humor. That surely disqualified all the male servants. All were uneducated. Most couldn't even read.

Finally, aware of the futility of her thoughts, Meg shook her head and shoved them aside. *Don't wish for the moon, silly Meg.* Laughing at herself, she laid her sketch pad on her lap and started to draw the forget-me-nots.

As she worked, she started thinking about Edward and Allegra's conversation this morning. Though she tried never to pry, her ears had perked up at the very mention of Lord Beaumont. So Allegra had set her cap for him! She had not realized.

Strange, but since that night she had met Lord Beaumont and engaged in that conversation, he had been on her mind. Exactly why, she wasn't clear, except that despite his lofty manner she found him oddly appealing. But for what reason? With his impeccable clothes, his wealth, his attitude, he placed himself among the pink of the ton, and thus was not one wit better than the rest of the dandies. And yet, there was a depth to him— she could see it in his eyes—which put him in a class by himself.

She remembered the manner in which he had listened

attentively while she read Keats's poem, obviously loving the poem himself, and, it appeared, the way she read it. Or had he only been impressed that a servant could read? His compliment afterward seemed sincere . . . yes, she was sure he *had* approved of her reading! But then again . . . was her vanity playing tricks on her? Perhaps she had simply gotten carried away by flattery. Why was she thinking of him so much? And why, when Allegra announced she was determined to marry him, had she felt a small stab of pain?

Idly, Meg bent forward and trailed her hand through the cool water as it bubbled past. *Absolutely ridiculous!* Like a dog baying for the moon. How could she, a lowly servant, have the audacity even to dream of a man like Lord Beaumont? A serving girl's folly indeed! As if she could ever *want* a man as arrogant as he.

It was time. She picked up her things and started back, thinking she would return here again and again. It was comforting to think of this fairyland glade as *her* spot, to which no one but she would ever come.

When Lord Edward arrived at the London lodgings of his friend Lord Beaumont, he was a bit apprehensive. Settled with a glass of port in his favorite Trafalgar chair, he chatted of this and that, waiting for precisely the right moment in which to extend Allegra's invitation.

Naturally, Richard would immediately say no. But Edward had armed himself with an array of arguments designed to make his friend change his mind—indeed, anything to make Richard attend Lady Semple's ball! Not so much because of his sister, who was as helpless as a python and could take care of herself. Edward's concern was for his mother. Pity the woman whose only daughter has gone through one whole Season and not received one single acceptable offer! At this point, Mama was most anxious—nay, beyond anxious, closer to desperate. Damme! He would give anything to remove that look of anxiety from his mother's eyes.

There were limits to which Edward would go, however. Despite Allegra's crafty plan, he would not deign to inform Richard his mother was ill. If Countess Montclaire did not want her son aware of her condition, far be it from Edward to tell.

At last, a lull in the conversation arrived. "I say, Richard, my family's giving a ball next weekend and would like you to attend. Will you come?" Having said that, Edward slouched in his chair, expression impassive, bracing himself for a fight, or, at the very least, a burst of derision.

To his surprise, Richard remained silent, engrossed in the solemn contemplation of the tips of his boots. "Your mother mentioned it," he finally answered softly. He quirked an eyebrow. "Allegra's idea?"

"Of course." No sense lying, especially to Richard, whom he could not fool anyway. "This doesn't mean you have to marry the girl, just come to the party."

"I see."

Silence again. Edward could not abide it. "So you'll come?"

With an effort, Richard bestirred himself long enough to pour another glass of port. *What is wrong with me?* he wondered. Under ordinary circumstances, he would have parried with Edward immediately, lashed out with some brilliant riposte concerning his opinion of Allegra's invitation. But this past week, ever since Wallingford's dinner party, some kind of indefinable malaise had overtaken him. He had not gone riding on Thunder, not even once. Nor had he gone to White's. Even worse, he had been obliged to prod himself to visit Clarice. A disaster when he did, as it turned out. For some obscure reason, they had quarreled. The whole visit had fallen flat. He left without touching her—truly a phenomenon, considering the blissful transports that lively lady had caused his libido to reach but a short time ago.

"Well, Richard? Time to get out of the city, don't you agree? Visit your parents? It has been a while."

Silently Richard sipped his wine. *Mama* . . . yes, it had been a while, actually nearly a year since he had visited. Lately he had felt a yearning to see her again. That would mean seeing his father, of course, a burden to which he had subjected himself as little as possible in recent years.

Richard always cringed inside when he remembered that stern cold face, a face he identified with the sound of a swishing birch limb, followed by a cutting sting, then his mother calling, "He is only a boy, m'lord! Please, no more!" And always after that, the cold, dark attic where he was sent without supper, and the words, oft-repeated, "Cease your whimpering, Richard. Be a man."

Perhaps he should accept the invitation, though if he did, he must contend with Allegra's blatant pursuit. Not that he couldn't handle her . . . and there was another reason to go: *Meg*. His thoughts had strayed to her often this past week. She might be a mere maidservant, crippled at that, but how many times had he laughed, remembering how she had most decidedly put him in his place? So amusing, the way she acted, as if she had no realization of her humble position in life.

Come to think of it, it was almost as though it was Meg who was causing his strange mood. Preposterous, of course. And yet . . . he wanted to see her again. He *would* see her again. But if he did, what could he possibly do with her? He was not truly into shallow debauchery, and the thought of giving her a quick tumble simply did not sit well, although she would not be the first serving girl . . .

Damme, I don't know what I would do with her, but I want to see her just the same. "All right, Edward. I accept Allegra's invitation, but I warn you, as God is my witness, your sister is not going to trap me. Now, when is this to be? Next weekend?"

The next weekend, by coach, phaeton, barouche, and horseback, the guests, some of whom would spend the night, began to arrive at Pentworth Park.

"Me achin' back!" cried Polly. "Scrubbin' floors . . . emptyin' grates . . . where's the end of it?" Laden with buckets of warm water, the petite housemaid made her arduous way up the back staircase. "Is the 'ole world takin' a bath?"

Meg, coming up behind her, took up a pail. "Here, let me help."

"Ooo, don't you 'av to." Polly lowered her voice. "You've enough on your 'ands, what with Lady Allegra."

Meg silently agreed. She had been up and running to fulfill Lady Allegra's demands since dawn.

A footman approached. "Lady Allegra is at the front entrance and would like her shawl."

Meg sped to the bedchamber, scooped up Allegra's pinecone-patterned Indian shawl, and hurried downstairs to the main entrance, where guests who had already been greeted milled about. Allegra, flushed with excitement, was straining her eyes as she looked down the long driveway. "He must be coming soon," she cried out as Meg handed her the shawl, which she took, of course, without a glance of thanks. Meg started to withdraw, but before she could, a coach turned into the drive. "Here he is!" cried Allegra.

All eyes turned to watch a shiny black coach roll up the driveway, brass gleaming, harness shining, pulled by a perfectly matched, high-stepping pair of matched grays, with a spirited black horse tethered behind. When the coach stopped by the broad front steps, a smiling Edward stepped to the ground. Allegra affixed a quick peck on his cheek, then aimed her questioning gaze beyond him and gave a squeal of delight as the raven's-wing hair and broad shoulders of Lord Beaumont emerged. Meg stood transfixed as he made a lithe and graceful descent. How handsome he looked! How much the perfect dandy in his superbly cut gray waistcoat and tight-fitting doeskin trousers. Although maintaining a lofty expression, he was even smiling. It was a guarded smile, of course, as his perceptive, slightly amused dark eyes took in the guests and family swarming to greet him. From the top of the front entrance steps, Meg watched as Richard directed his gaze over the heads of the crowd. It was almost as if he were searching for somebody. Almost as if . . .

Their eyes locked. She could not move, let alone drag her gaze away. He, too, seemed utterly immobile. Then, for a brief moment, something jolting passed between them. They stared at each other—Meg was not sure how long—until Lady Lydia cried, "Meg! Why are you standing there? Get back to your work!"

Meg felt her face flush as both she and Lord Beaumont broke the spell and glanced away. But he looked back again, as did she. A tiny gleam of devilment appeared in his eyes. He nodded briefly, so imperceptibly that only she could see, before he resumed his lofty expression and turned his attention to the marchioness.

"I shall not come in now, Lady Semple. I am only dropping Edward off, then I shall be on my way home to Hartwick House. But rest assured I shall return this evening for dinner and the ball."

He's coming back, Meg thought, her spirits rising. Then she remembered the ridiculousness, the futility, of a lowly servant hungering after a lofty lord. *But you don't feel like a lowly servant,* protested a little voice within her. *And you don't have the time to think about it,* a more practical voice informed her. She hurried toward the servants' staircase.

By the time she resumed her duties, she had convinced herself Lord Beaumont's lingering look had been meant for someone else, not her at all.

"On to Hartwick House, Bingham," Lord Beaumont called to his coachman. Leaning back against the squabs, Richard let out an astounded, "Damme!"

"Something wrong, m'lord?" inquired Richard's valet.

"Er . . . nothing, Cummings." Richard had almost become undone back there. The sight of the little crippled servant girl standing on the steps had shaken him down to his Wellingtons. But why? She was only a servant, an inferior being like all the rest, even if she could read poetry. She dressed as servants dressed. She acted as servants acted. God's blood! She had even made a silly little curtsy, bobbing her white-capped head, before she scurried—*limped*—away.

And yet . . . that moment when he had caught her gaze he felt as if a stallion had bucked its hind legs and struck him in the chest. He allowed himself a wry laugh. Back in his callow, randy youth he had tumbled a willing scullery maid or two—or three or four—but it had been many a year since Richard, Viscount Beaumont, proud heir apparent of the Earl of Montclaire, had consorted with servant girls. He had matured. His taste ran to fine Cyprians now, of which Clarice was a diamond of the first water.

Clarice . . .

Upon reflection, he had to admit that on that last visit he had treated her abominably. He would make amends. Upon his return to London, he would send her a huge bouquet of roses, with, perhaps, a pearl necklace tucked amid the blooms. Indeed, he would turn himself around when he returned to London: start riding Thunder again, show his face at Whites. Life would be good again, in fact better than before, just as soon as he got through this miserable weekend. His spirits lifted. *Enamored of a crippled little chit of a serving girl? Damme, no!*

Pleased with himself, he knew he was over his mysterious funk. He looked forward to visiting his mother. As for Father, well, he was out of the old boy's clutches now. Perhaps he could tolerate even his father, if only for a little while . . .

Something was wrong.

Richard knew it the second the coach turned into the long curved drive that led to the grand entrance of

Hartwick House, his childhood home. The drive had always been perfectly groomed with nary a leaf, weed, or twig marring its graveled surface. The boxwood bushes lining the road had always been trimmed within an inch of their lives. Never had a single branch from an oak or a willow tree been allowed to hang too low, but not anymore. Now the hedges were unkempt, shaggy. Low-hanging branches dragged across the top of the coach while the wheels rolled through dirty piles of leaves and other debris.

"Faster, Bingham," Richard called through the coach window. Suddenly he was most anxious to be home.

Chapter 8

"We did not expect you, m'lord."

As he stepped past Vickers, Richard could hardly suppress his shock at the shoddy condition of the vast entry hall. Pictures askew . . . scuffed floor . . . dusty tapestries . . . as far back as he could remember, a finely carved antique vase by Gibbons had stood by the main staircase. Now it was gone.

And Vickers! Both in manner and dress he had always been the perfect butler, but today his expression was just this side of surly, his breeches wrinkled, his linen none too clean. The man hardly looked himself. He was heavier-jowled than a year ago, and his face was flushed by an unhealthy ruddy red, which, come to think of it, was the color one associated with drink. *And speaking of drink, what is that on his breath?* Richard took a discreet sniff. Gin! God's blood, this was unbelievable! What was Papa thinking of?

"I wish to see my father immediately, Vickers. Is he in?"

"In, but resting, sir." The butler studied a spot on the floor. "He left orders not to be disturbed."

"My brother, Henry?"

The butler glanced toward the ceiling and rolled his eyes. "Master Henry has gone out, m'lord."

Which meant Henry was ensconced in the nearest tavern, hastening his demise. "Then, I would like to see my mother. I trust the countess is in?"

"She is in her room, but she also—"

"I'm going up." What was this shifty-eyed butler trying to conceal? Without another word, Richard charged up the broad staircase to his mother's bedchamber. He knocked and waited. Hearing a faint, "Enter," he opened the door and entered. His mother lay asleep in her four-poster bed. An old man, head bowed, sat beside her. Richard was halfway across the room before he realized the identity of this fragile figure. "Papa, is that you?"

Wearily the Earl of Montclaire raised his head to peer at Richard. "So you have finally come home, son."

At least the voice was recognizable—the rest was unimaginable. His father had always been so strong, so robust! The shock rendered Richard nearly immobile. Unable to speak, he drew close to the bed, noticing at once that his mother's breathing was shallow.

His father spoke again. "Your mother is . . . your mother is not well."

Richard took a closer look. This sweet, gentle woman had always been so lively. He could hardly remember her ever sitting quietly, unless with a piece of embroidery in her hand. But now her hair had turned entirely white, and she was, in truth, emaciated and obviously very ill. "Mama," he called softly, dropping to his knees. She did not respond. He looked into his father's grieving face and asked, "What is wrong with her?"

" 'Tis a peccant humor in her stomach. Started a few months ago—keeps getting worse."

Richard recalled the many little notes his mother had sent him—one just last week, in fact—always indicating all was well. "Why didn't she tell me?"

"She had no wish to disturb you." An accusatory glint crept into his father's eyes. "You lead such a busy life in London, much too busy to come home."

"What in blazes—?" Richard blinked, bitterness welling up within him. On another day, he would have liked to let his father know exactly why he avoided coming home. But not today. His mother stirred. He touched her arm. "Mama, can you hear me?"

"Leave her alone for now, son. We gave her a dose of laudanum not long ago. Come back in an hour or two. She should be awake by then."

Richard watched in growing consternation as his father slowly rose, gripping a cane, and made his way painfully toward the door. Despite his rancor, it was disturbing to see his once-invincible father hobbling, wincing with every step. "Papa, what is wrong with you?"

" 'Tis nothing, merely a touch of gout. I shall be better soon." Shoulders held back proudly, his father limped from the room.

Richard left his mother's bedchamber shortly after, feeling drained, numb with shock. Papa ill, Mama dying, good God! He must get away—at least for a while until his mother awakened—but where? Ah, yes, the river! When he was a small boy, no matter how deep his misery, he could always find solace by the river. He would ride Thunder to his favorite spot, try to put aside his grief for a while. *As if that were possible.*

In the late afternoon Meg contracted another headache. It had been the most difficult of days, with Allegra acting even more insufferable. *Beyond insufferable.* Could she steal a few moments for herself? Meg peeped through the door of Allegra's bedchamber. Her mistress lay fast asleep and gently snoring. Many of the guests were catching naps in preparation for tonight's dinner and ball, so for the moment there was nothing pressing for Meg to do. Should she dare steal off for one tiny hour at the river? Allegra would disapprove, of course, but with a little luck she would not have to know.

Meg raced up to her room and picked up her brushes, paints, sketch pad, and small volume of Keats's poems. Her luck held. She met not a soul as she slipped down the back stairs, out the servants' exit, down the path to her secret glade beside the River Wey. Once there, her spirits lifted as she thought, *mine alone, one whole hour!* She pulled off her cap, shoes, and stockings, and sank down upon a clump of grass next to the tiny stream. Soon she spied a green hairstreak butterfly, its exquisite pink and turquoise wings fluttering over a stalk of purple clover. She grabbed up her brush and began to sketch, so concentrated on her work that she forgot her disgust with Allegra. Here, in this lovely spot, she felt peace and serenity until—oh, drat!—the butterfly flitted away.

Tossing sketch pad and brush aside, she started after it, all the while softly crooning, "Come back, butterfly, please don't fly away!" The butterfly flitted from flower, to tree limb, to flower again. As she chased it, she knotted her skirt up in front so she could move more freely. How delicious to run through the tall grass in the warm sunshine, barefoot, hair streaming loose behind! She became so concentrated on her chase, she failed to notice that she had reached the path again and that a man on horseback approached at a trot. Still calling, "Here, butterfly!" Meg barely missed crashing into the horse's side. It shied, rearing its front legs high. Neighing in protest, it plunged down, then up again. The man in the saddle remained calm, exuding a mixture of power and competency as he fought for control, and in no time brought the horse to a complete stop.

Meg stared up at the rider. Lord Beaumont! He was dressed not in his formal attire, but instead wore riding pants tucked into sturdy boots and a plain white linen shirt open enough at the collar to reveal crisp brown hair. After her initial shock, her first thought was to note how handsome he looked astride his spirited black mount. Her second, to inform herself she did not give a fig if he was handsome or not.

"My apologies, m'lord. It was not my intention to startle your horse."

He leaned over and inquired, "Are you hurt?"

"Not a bit, just rather surprised to see you here."

Assured she wasn't injured, he looked past her, and replied in a hollow, offhand manner, "Surprised? But I am on my own property."

"This is your land? I thought—"

"It is a common misconception that this part of the river is part of Pentworth Park. 'Tis not. It belongs to Hartwick House."

How distant he was acting! But what else could she expect when she was only a servant, not worth his time. Obviously 'twas true the lingering look she imagined he gave her this morning was meant for someone else. A curse on all nobles! Allegra treated her with complete disdain, now this arrogant lord seated high above her on his equally arrogant horse was talking down to her both figuratively and literally. She stepped back and regarded him candidly. "I shall leave immediately."

"You need not leave on my account."

"This is *your* land, sir, as you just pointed out."

As he continued to gaze down at her, his expression softened, as if her words had just sunk in. "Meg, you don't have to leave. That was not at all my intent."

"Then, what *did* you mean?"

He had the decency to return a puzzled frown. "Obviously I have offended you, but I've not the faintest notion why. Perhaps you could enlighten me?"

There was something curiously different about him, Meg thought. Where was his lofty smile? Indeed, now that she looked closer, she observed a look of strained near whiteness around his mouth, and a remote sadness in his eyes.

"You haven't offended me, but—" She hesitated, aware she had no business speaking to a noble this way, but he looked so strange. "Lord Beaumont, is something wrong?"

Richard stared down, unsmiling. Then, with a fluid motion, he was off his horse and confronting her face-to-face. "Why do you think that?"

His expression was so unreadable, she couldn't tell if

he was angry or not, but she had gone this far and would not back down. "You have a strange look about you, as if you had just experienced a shock."

He was silent for so long, she decided she had mightily displeased him and felt the urge to back away and run. "How perceptive of you," he answered finally. "My apologies if I offended you. My only excuse is that I received some bad news just now that has left me rather shaken." She opened her mouth to answer, but he waved a hand of dismissal and continued, "Nothing I cannot handle." He gestured toward the river. "So what brings you here?"

"I came to sketch and read poetry. Now and again, I feel the need to get away."

"From Allegra," he said flatly.

"Your words, sir, not mine."

Finally he smiled, a wistful, charming smile, despite the sadness that curved its edges. "At any rate, here we are, and I must admit, I would like to hear more from the little maid who chases butterflies."

Meg felt herself blush to the very roots of her hair. Not only had he witnessed her foolishness, he was treating her as if she were slightly bird-witted! In her defense, she replied, "It was not just an ordinary butterfly, but a green hairstreak."

He raised an eyebrow. "You know butterflies, too, as well as poetry?"

She nodded. "I know them all. An old gardener taught me when I lived at Auberry Hall."

"Now I'm doubly impressed."

"Thank you. Still, I must be getting back." She started to turn away. "I shall collect my things and go."

"You needn't leave. I used to come here all the time when I was a little boy. There's a small glade down there worth viewing, with a running brook, mossy rocks, and blue and yellow forget-me-nots—quite beautiful."

Without thinking, she eagerly replied, " 'Tis my favorite spot!" then corrected herself. "It *was* my favorite spot. You may rest assured, I shan't tread upon your property again."

"That won't be necessary. You have my permission to come anytime you want. Did you bring along a book?"

She nodded. "Keats."

"I remember your reading Keats's poem that evening in the library. Would you read it again, Meg? At the glade? Today I could use a bit of poetry."

She considered the impropriety of sitting in a hidden glade with the heir apparent of the Earl of Montclaire. "It would not look seemly, m'lord. I must decline, for your sake, as well as my own."

He laughed lightly, appearing more amused than offended. "I shall be the judge of that. You don't fear me, do you?"

" 'Tis not you I fear, Lord Beaumont. The danger lies in wagging tongues, as you well know."

"I assure you, no one ever comes here."

What he failed to realize was that she didn't care if he now wanted to be friendly. She did *not* desire any favors and wanted only to escape. "I must go." She reached to adjust her cap, but to her chagrin suddenly realized it was not atop her head. Her gaze dropped to her feet. Oh, no! Not only was her head uncovered, she was barefoot and her skirt knotted up like a hoyden's. Never, not since she was able to dress herself, had she allowed anyone to see her twisted foot. Quickly, almost without thinking, she drew it behind the other.

"Too late," he remarked.

She bent to unknot her skirt, her long hair falling forward around her face and shoulders. "What do you mean, *too late*?"

"No sense hiding your foot."

"I was not—"

"You were, but to no avail. I have already seen it, and I must say—"

"You must *not* say!" she retorted sharply as she finished untying the knot. The skirt dropped down. She straightened and looked him in the eye. "Do you take pleasure in making fun of cripples, sir?"

"It was not my intention to poke fun at you, as surely you must know. Had you heard me out, I meant to tell you—"

"I don't wish to hear it!" So hurt that tears stung her eyes, Meg turned away and hurried back to the glade. She sank down beside the brook and hastily began to pull on her shoes and stockings, resolving that next she would retrieve her book and sketching things and immediately go. Anxiously she waited to hear the thud of horse's hooves retreating down the path. *Be gone!* she thought fiercely. *I don't want to see the conceited likes of you when I come back, Lord Nose-in-the-Air Beaumont.*

Jolted, Richard had watched her leave. He had only meant to tell her how much he admired her courage. He couldn't let her go this upset. With a quick twist, he tied Thunder's reins to a tree and started through the bushes to his well-remembered spot.

"Meg?"

She was seated by the brook, pulling on a stocking, her skin flushed warm pink. At that moment, a beam of sunlight penetrated the lacy cover of the trees, highlighting her long golden hair as it tumbled carelessly down the back of her simple gray dress. She looked so lovely that before he spoke, he had to clear his throat and catch his breath. Again in command of himself, he continued, "You must not feel self-conscious about your foot. I am positive no one gives a thought to it once they see what a lovely girl you are."

"How kind of you, m'lord," she answered mockingly, with barely a glance. She finished putting on her shoes and stockings, and replaced her cap. An escaping curl fell across her forehead. He wanted very much to touch it— push it back. He fought to keep his wits about him, for there, sitting among the flowers with the sunlight on her hair, was quite the most beautiful girl he had ever met, servant or no.

He sank down beside her. "Again, my apologies if I offended you." He spied her book. "Ah, the Keats. Would you read to me, Meg?"

She appeared torn for a moment, poised to flee, yet he could see she wanted to stay. Finally, to his great relief, she acquiesced. "All right," she said, opened the book, and in that soft, soothing voice of hers began, "A thing of beauty is a joy forever . . ."

Eyes closed, leaning back against an oak tree, he listened intently, arm resting on raised knee. When she finished, he felt peaceful again, and wished he would never have to leave.

"Another?" she asked.

He shook his head. "Most regretfully, 'tis time for me to go. We shall meet again, though."

"I should imagine so," she replied solemnly, "now that you are courting Allegra."

"What!" he exclaimed. "Courting Allegra?" He threw his head back and burst into laughter. "The day I marry Allegra will be the day the sun doesn't rise—the birds fail to sing, the . . . the . . ."

"River runs dry?" she supplied with answering laughter. "Apparently I was mistaken."

"You have my word on that."

"I see." *But surely Allegra does not,* Meg thought, remembering Allegra's declaration to Edward that she indeed planned to marry Lord Beaumont.

Richard took up her hand. "This has been most enjoyable." He bent over her hand, examining it intimately. *So perfectly formed, so tiny, so white.* He brought it to his lips and kissed the back gently, catching his breath as he felt the smoothness of her skin. God, how he hated to leave! "Meet me here tomorrow." He could hardly believe the words that had just flown from his mouth. And then, to his further disbelief, he found himself bending even closer and brushing her lips with his in a sweet, brief kiss.

She pulled her hand back and gave him a glance of utter disbelief. "Oh, no, sir, you must not kiss me! And meeting again is not a good idea, for you or me."

He quickly got hold of himself and returned an absolutely wicked grin. "You are quite right, Meg, but let's do it anyway. I guarantee, all I want is to listen to you read poetry."

She raised an eyebrow. "Truly?"

"Yes, truly," he replied, wondering if, in his heart, he was lying. In truth, he had no idea. The only thing he was sure of was that he wanted to see her again.

"Oh, my son, you are finally here," his mother murmured in a voice so faint he could barely hear. She opened her eyes and gazed up at him. "So wonderful to have you home!"

He covered her birdlike hands with his own. "Why didn't you tell me you were ill?"

Her gentle sigh caused his heart to wrench. " 'Tis better you remained away, for I cannot bear it when you and your father argue. I love you both so much, it tears me apart."

He leaned forward and kissed her on the forehead. "Well, I am home now, so you need not worry. We shall have you well again in no time."

Sadness filled her eyes. "No, son, I shall not be well again. It is only a matter of time."

Terrible regrets assailed him. Oh, why had he not come home sooner! "Is there nothing I can do?"

Deep in thought, she was silent for a time. Finally she whispered, "Yes, Richard, there is something you can do. I want three promises from you."

"Just tell me what they are," he said, his voice unsteady as grief near overwhelmed him.

"I want you to promise . . ." She had to pause to gather strength.

"Promise what, Mama?"

". . . That you will make up with your father. He's a good man. Much too harsh, but he always did what he thought best for you. Your father isn't well. His gout is an agony. He suffers terrible pain and must stay in bed most of the time. Promise you will make up with him! Only then can I die with a peaceful heart."

"Say no more," he reassured her. "I suppose deep down I love Papa, too. You needn't worry. I shall speak to him this very day. From here on, there shall be no more bitterness between us."

Her eyes lit with happiness. "Oh, Richard! You have no idea what this means to me."

"Perhaps I do," he replied. "Now, what is the second promise?"

"I want you to come home."

"To stay?" he blurted, shocked in spite of himself.

"The estate is going to rack and ruin."

"There I must agree. I was appalled seeing the condition of the drive, the mansion, Vickers—"

" 'Tis horrible. Only a month ago our estate manager ran off with some of our funds. And the servants are becoming more and more bold and insubordinate with no one to oversee them."

"What about Henry?"

Despite her condition, his mother managed a pained laugh. "Your ne'er-do-well brother appears totally consumed with two occupations: gambling and drinking himself to death."

"I shall have a talk with him."

"Do as you please, but rest assured your father needs *you*, not Henry, though he's much too proud to ask." She clutched his wrist. "Richard, will you stay?"

A taunting vision of his comfortable rooms in London flashed through his mind. His books . . . his paneled walls . . . his cozy fireplace . . . but what else could he do?

"All right, I promise I shall return home and stay as

long as you and Papa need me. You can stop worrying on that score. Now, what else?"

As he waited for her to speak, a feeling of dread crept over him. *Mother, please don't ask me what I think you're going to ask.*

"One more promise . . ."

He braced himself. "Go ahead."

"It is your father's fondest wish that you marry Allegra."

His heart sank. "Mama, I cannot. I do not love Allegra."

"Your father will die happy only if he knows our two estates are conjoined. Please, Richard, you are the elder son. In fact, 'tis almost as if you are the only son, considering Henry's depravity." His mother's anguished eyes met his own. "I haven't asked you for much over the years, but this promise I want from you—for your own sake, and your father's, as well as my own. It's time, Richard—time you settled down."

His mind raced back through the years, to his terrible earaches when he was little and how she sat by his bedside to comfort him all the night through, to the times she risked her own safety to protect him from his father, to the countless books she read him, games she played with him, the selfless manner in which she had always looked out for him . . .

Though he could scarcely endure the thought, he knew there was only one answer he could give. He squeezed his eyes shut a moment, gathering his strength, his misery so acute it was like a physical pain.

"All right, I shall marry Allegra."

"Oh, Richard!" Her face lit with a smile. "You have made me very happy."

Richard smiled back and touched a finger to her cheek. "Then, I'm very glad."

"You'll ask for her hand at the ball at Pentworth Park tonight?"

His throat tightened. He could hardly get the words out. "Yes, Mama, I shall ask her tonight."

"You'll not regret it."

"No, Mama." Not regret marrying Allegra? He regretted it already, regretted it before he had even uttered the words. But there was no backing out now. He was destined to marry that odious girl because he had promised his mother, and because he was, God help him, an honorable man.

"Tonight! Richard will propose tonight, Mama, I know he will!" Sitting at her dressing table, Allegra bobbed her head with sheer exuberance, causing Meg to suspend her task of pinning roses into Allegra's dark curls.

"M'lady, I cannot fix your hair when you move. If you will but hold your head still?"

"Bother!"

"Now, Allegra," implored Lady Semple. Seated near-by, she was nervously overseeing Allegra's complicated toilette. "Hold still as Meg asks. Otherwise, how can you look beautiful tonight?" She gave a knowing smile. "Especially for Lord Beaumont."

"Bother," Allegra muttered again, but remained quiet.

Meg continued fixing her mistress's curls, pulling them high atop Allegra's head and fastening them with a rope of pearls. As always, she kept her face blank, but inside, she was fighting a personal battle of restraint. *Why do you think he wants to marry you?* she wanted to inquire of Allegra. *I'm the one whose lips he brushed with a kiss this afternoon, not you!*

She had returned from the river hours ago, but her head was still full of him—every gesture he'd made, every word he'd spoken. He had looked at her bare, twisted foot and not been appalled. No man had ever kissed her hand before, either, let alone pressed it in such a meaningful way whilst gazing into her eyes with such longing. Her heart swelled when she thought of it. Oh, the warmth of his lips! And that little extra breath he'd taken when he had cradled her hand in his, as if it were some precious jewel. Oh, the exhilarating feeling that had rushed through her! Oh, the—

"Ouch, Meg! You're pulling my hair."

"Sorry, m'lady." If Allegra only knew! Not that Meg cared much what her reaction would be. But Lady Semple was a different matter. Meg felt a tinge of disloyalty, thinking she'd be mortified if her ladyship discovered her newly hired lady's maid had been dallying at the river with Allegra's future fiancé.

No, *not* future fiancé! He had made it plain he would never marry Allegra. But what, Meg asked herself coolly, did it matter? She could never have him for herself. Still, she knew this day would remain in her memory forever. It was a day full of the stuff which daydreams were built on, daydreams that for a crippled girl like her, whose chances for love were nil, might have to last a lifetime. She laughed to herself. *All thanks to that conceited man.*

Yes, he was conceited and yet . . . she perceived him as an honorable man, one who could never be so shallow as to act as he did toward her at the river today, then propose to Allegra the very same night.

How deceitful that would be!

Chapter 9

Would this evening ever end?

It was after midnight, and Meg, curled on the settee in Allegra's bedchamber, gazed at the plaster roses on the ceiling while she half listened to the faint strains of a lively waltz emanating from the ballroom below.

Polly popped her head in. "Ain't you goin' to peek? 'Tis ever so excitin', with the dancin' and the tableaux and the lords and ladies in their fancy clothes."

"Not interested, Polly."

Polly entered and sank to a chair in a weary heap. " 'Pon my soul, I'm so tired I could go to sleep this very minute. Why won't you watch?"

Meg shrugged. "When I was little, I spent whole evenings watching the fancy balls at Auberry Hall. I would huddle on the staircase and peek through the railings with breathless awe. Such sumptuous banquets! Such glittering ladies in their beautiful dresses and jewels!"

"How the rich live, oh!" Polly chimed.

"Yes, at our expense," Meg said flatly. "For me, the thrill is gone."

"Lor', Meg, the things you say!" Polly regarded her appraisingly. "You see things differnt from the rest of us."

"I see things as they are." Meg felt a leaden sluggishness creep over her, reminding her she had been up since before dawn. "All I want now is to go to bed."

"You ain't the only one." Polly yawned and rubbed her eyes. "We'll get precious little sleep tonight."

Meg nodded. "Allegra will no doubt dance 'til dawn."

Polly cast a sly look. "Guess what 'andsome gent is down there dancin' the night away."

"Who?" Meg asked, although she knew full well whom Polly had in mind.

"Lord Beaumont! I 'ave never seen a man so 'and-some! You should see 'im—"

"Acting his most noble, charming self." Meg could not help adding with a touch of irony, "No doubt he intends to captivate the hearts of all the ladies before the night is over. I am certain he will."

"You talk like you know 'im."

"I do." Meg hesitated, not sure she should go on. She was bursting to talk, though, and if there was anyone she could trust, it was Polly. "We met accidentally at the river this afternoon. I . . . read him some poetry."

Polly's mouth dropped open. "Oh, my stars! Did he . . . I mean, did he try to . . . ?"

"He kissed my hand and . . . a little more. You are never, never to tell."

"But I thought you 'ated all them fancy lords. You said—"

"He is not as bad as some, although I can assure you, there's the end of it. Nothing else happened. Nothing else is going to happen."

"No, no, of course! But, Meg, does this mean . . . does he *like* you?"

"Does it matter if he likes me or not?"

"Well, nooo . . . I guess not, 'im bein' a lord and you a servant, but still"—Polly's eyes sparkled—"think of it! What if Lord Beaumont fell madly in love with you? What if—?"

" 'What if' indeed! Do you take me for the village idiot?"

"Hear me out!" Polly clasped her hands and eagerly continued, "I can see it 'appenin'! Lord Beaumont asks you to meet him at the river again, and when you do, 'e declares 'e's fallen mad in love with you, so desprit to possess you, 'e threatens to kill 'isself if you don't run off with 'im to Gretna Green this very instant! 'E vows to marry you, Society be damned!"

Meg burst into laughter. "What imagination! Indeed, it happens all the time. Impoverished, crippled maid-servants are always marrying rich, handsome noblemen."

Polly looked wounded. "Well, it could 'appen."

Meg sobered and shook her head. "I would be a candidate for Bedlam if I dared imagine that the heir apparent of the Earl of Montclaire could fall madly in love with Meg Quincy, lady's maid."

"Ah, well." Polly shrugged and looked regretful. "But 'tis somethin' to dream about, ain't it?"

"All we have is dreams."

"Will he marry Allegra?"

"She wishes! But absolutely not. He told me so."

"Does he like you, Meg? I mean, especially?"

"Of course not. Our meeting was quite accidental. He enjoyed my reading of poetry and that is all." Meg felt a quiver, remembering that moment when his lips brushed hers, beholding again the heartrending tenderness of his gaze. But the moment had no meaning. Not to her, surely. For him, it must be of no import at all.

The door flew open. Into the chamber burst Allegra, followed by her mother. Flush-faced, eyes bright with triumph, Allegra twirled, clasped hands to her bosom, danced a pirouette around the room. "He is mine, Mama! Mine!"

Lady Semple's usual timid expression had been replaced by beaming triumph. To Meg and Polly she said, "Such wonderful news! Lord Beaumont has proposed."

After a startled silence, Polly echoed, "Yes, indade, wonderful news, m'lady." Meg stayed quiet, finding she could not talk over the sudden swelling in her throat.

". . . But I fear in her exuberance," Lady Semple continued, "Allegra has torn her gown."

Allegra stopped her dance and pointed to a foot-long piece of lace drooping from her hem. "Get your thread and needle, Meg. Be quick! Papa's making the announcement soon." Her face glowed with smug satisfaction. "Do you realize, Mama, I have caught a future earl? I shall be a countess!"

"I shall get my sewing kit. Come and help me, Polly." Meg spoke the words by rote, striving to conceal her shock.

Out of hearing in the dressing room, Polly whispered, "I thought you said—"

"That liar!"

"The scoundrel! Why did Lord Beaumont lie to you like that? 'Ow could he marry her? He's not in need of money, or so I 'ave been told."

"Greed, Polly," Meg answered as she jerked the sewing kit from a shelf. "Sheer avarice and greed, and lack of honor."

" 'As 'e broken yur 'eart?"

"Hardly!" Meg willed the swelling in her throat to go away, but it would not. "The only emotions I feel right now are pity and contempt. What a weakling he is!"

"Must be." Polly's voice dropped to a whisper. "Otherwise, 'ow could 'e let 'isself get in the clutches of that turrible girl?"

Meg returned with her sewing kit and knelt to fix the hem. Fingers flying, stoically enduring Allegra's excited babbling, she mended the torn lace. The instant she finished, Allegra popped from her chair and pulled on her mother's arm. "Come, I want Papa to make the announcement right now."

"No need to rush." Lady Semple appeared faintly amused. "Unless you fear Richard might change his mind."

Allegra tossed her curls. Her voice grew unpleasantly shrill as she answered, "Certainly not! But I want everyone to know because then I shall be the object of envy among all my unbetrothed friends."

"Not a laudable ambition, my dear," Lady Semple reproved, then turned to Meg and Polly. "Do come downstairs with us. His lordship will be making the announcement soon, in the ballroom. Such grand news! All the servants will want to be there."

"Of course, m'lady," Meg replied, biting off her words. She and Polly followed the two ladies belowstairs. Little did they know how reluctant she was, how disgusted with this sham. And how shocked they'd be if they knew that only hours ago, their precious Lord Beaumont was kissing the hand of Allegra's lady's maid, gazing deeply into her eyes, tenderly brushing his lips across hers!

The dancers were performing the complex maneuvers of a country-dance when Cyril, Lord Semple, stepped upon the platform and waved the orchestra silent. Richard stood beside Allegra, rigid, unsmiling. This is a bad dream, he kept thinking, from which he would soon awaken, relieved and thankful. He forced a wooden smile, willing himself not to move when Allegra, already pressed against his side, squeezed his hand and shoved herself closer.

Must she look so smug?

He recalled his hours of agony as he searched for the fortitude to choke out a fitting proposal. Time and again he concluded he couldn't go through with it, then reminded himself of his promise to his dying mother. Finally he had likened proposing to Allegra to swallowing those spoonfuls of castor oil his mother gave him when he was little—an odious chore from which there was no escape, best to be got through as quickly as possible. He could not mention love. Faults he had aplenty, but he was not a liar. He could offer her his name, his title, and his fortune, but not his heart—not now, not ever. Allegra would understand, though. Thick-skinned creature that she was, she would not expect or desire anything more.

He was wrong. When the dreaded moment finally arrived, and he, nearly gagging, managed to inquire, "May I have your hand in marriage?" a beam of triumph flashed through her eyes.

"I knew I would win!" she responded. She cocked her head to one side. "And never fear, my dearest Lord Beaumont, I shall make you love me!"

What could he say? Blame it on a selfish, immature eighteen-year-old's natural exuberance, he supposed. She would soon grow wiser.

Obligatory gasps of delight now filled the air as Lord Semple made the announcement in his aloof, ascetic manner. It was followed by titters behind fans, looks of surprise, and joyous applause. Yes, joyous, Richard noted sourly, especially among his bachelor friends. Allegra was finally off the market. No wonder they were wild with delight, applauding mightily.

"Congratulations!" Henry, already cup-shot, was grinning at him from ear to ear. "Lucky fellow!"

"Yes, you would think so, wouldn't you?" Richard replied cynically, regarding his younger brother with disdain. There was no resemblance between them, he thought idly; Henry was shorter than he, fair-haired, with a rather slender build. They were different in manner, with Richard by far the more outspoken, Henry possessing a quiet, almost sly way about him.

"But of course I would think you lucky!" Henry continued stoutly, "Allegra is a gem, an absolute prize."

He means it! Richard realized, fighting to keep from laughing. Come to think of it, Henry had always had an eye for Allegra, though why, he would never know.

When the dancing commenced again, Edward approached. "So you shall be my brother now," he announced with a jovial clap on the back, obviously not so much for Richard's benefit as for those around. Then he drew Richard aside. Expecting mockery, Richard dreaded looking his future brother-in-law straight in the eye. When he finally did, he beheld not derision but concern.

"Whatever have you done?" Edward inquired softly.

"Are you not delighted?" Richard murmured back. "Why aren't you rejoicing with the rest of your family that Allegra is at last off your hands? God knows, this is what you've been hounding me about."

"Only at Mama's request," Edward returned fiercely. "I never dreamed . . . ah, Richard, this is devilish queer."

"What's this?" Richard asked airily with a mock frown. "You should be happy I have taken your excellent persuasions to heart. As you pointed out, her dowry will most certainly ease the pain. And in your great wisdom you also pointed out that in no time she will be leading her own life, and I shall be leading mine . . ." He had meant to say more, but despite himself, his eyes kept returning toward the back of the room where the servants stood. Was that a small white cap and flash of gray gown he saw in the crowd?

"What are you looking for?" Edward inquired, following his gaze, "But of course! 'Tis that little chit of a lady's maid, isn't it? Can't keep your mind off her, can you? Even now—"

"Dear boy, 'tis not like that at all. In truth, I fear I may have been a trifle too friendly toward her when I met her, quite by accident, at the river this afternoon." Seeing Edward's expression, Richard raised a protesting hand. "Nothing like that, I assure you. We talked. Then I went perhaps a step too far. I . . . well, really, what's in a stolen kiss? But you know how servants are. No doubt she's a trifle hurt, and who could blame her? Wrong of me, of course. Time I realized simple servants can take even the most meaningless gesture to heart."

Edward raised a skeptical eyebrow. "Whom are you trying to deceive, Richard, me or yourself?"

"You're being ridiculous."

Despite Edward's mockery, Richard still could not keep his eyes off the small white cap that was now bobbing through the crowd toward the entryway. She was leaving! At the door she turned. He caught her eye and nodded. She nodded back, her lips curving into a smile, peering at him with ... the devil! It appeared to be amusement, as if the very idea of his marrying Allegra was the cause, not of concern or sadness, but of great merriment. She was laughing at him! He could feel her derision clear across the ballroom.

"Indeed, Richard, she appears quite brokenhearted," Edward dryly commented, following his gaze. "No doubt the poor creature's about to creep up to her room and slash her wrists."

"Hold your tongue, Edward," Richard murmured through clenched teeth. *How galling!* He lost the wooden smile he'd been maintaining upon the contemplation that Meg Quincy, lady's maid, was laughing at him. Had that moment at the river meant nothing to her? Obviously, it had not. Still, what difference did it make? As Edward said, she was only a servant. Her opinion did not count. *But if that is so, why do I feel like such a scapegrace?*

Allegra, still looking the triumphant cat, glided to his side. "Smile, my pet," she muttered from the corner of her mouth. She tugged on his arm. "You should be looking deliriously happy."

Meg was disappearing through the door. Allegra's hand dug into his arm. He clasped it tightly and pulled it away. "I shall return in a moment," he said, and left Allegra standing alone as he headed toward the entryway.

Meg hurried along the great hall, anxious to escape the crowd. Then she heard a voice call, "Where are you off to?"

Richard. Though her heart picked up its beat, she turned as slowly as she dared, an expression of puzzled unconcern affixed upon her face. "Why, m'lord, I confess I am astonished! How could you have deserted your beloved at such an exhilarating moment?"

He stopped short and drew himself up in his usual haughty fashion, although she noticed his eyes held a questioning look. "I shall be back by her side shortly," he began offhandedly, "but I felt the need to assure myself you did not think ill of me after what occurred this afternoon."

"What occurred?" she asked innocently. She glanced around. Mercifully, they were alone, a circumstance that could not last long. "Are you referring to your remark about never marrying Allegra?"

"In part."

"Why should that bother you?" she inquired sweetly. "What matters what a servant thinks?"

He managed an elaborate shrug. "I apologize for possibly misleading you."

"Do not apologize. Why you told me such a lie, I cannot imagine, but that's your affair, not mine. You're not obliged to make amends."

"That's devilish good of you," he said, "but there is also the matter of . . ."

"The kiss?" she interrupted boldly. She raised her eyebrows in mock enlightenment, and continued scornfully, "Ah, now I understand! You were afraid you might have broken this poor, pitiful, servant girl's heart."

At her tone, he pulled himself to full height and gave her a frosty smile. "After our meeting at the river today, I was concerned, naturally. Obviously, I worried for naught. 'Tis clear I haven't shocked you. As for my betrothal, it was not my intent at the time, but circumstances change."

Resentment boiled within her as she gazed up at this elegant nobleman with the haughty, higher-than-thou expression who had lied to her. The scoundrel! Although she knew she should turn her back, walk away, she was helpless to prevent the surge of recklessness that swept over her, driving her to an overwhelming urge to speak her mind. She should not, of course. Her frankness—*unhumbleness!*—had gotten her in trouble before, and probably would again, but for the life of her, she could not submerge her feelings.

"You have not shocked me in the least," she replied with a slight smile of defiance. "After all, you belong to the nobility, so what else would I expect?"

"Indeed?" he asked in feigned amazement. "Well, then, I am all eagerness to hear what belonging to the nobility has to do with this."

"You want my opinion of the nobility?" Beyond all caring now, she jammed her fists against her hips. "I cannot abide those vain, empty-headed London dandies who care only for themselves and crave nothing more in life than Society's approval."

"Now, see here! Are you implying that I—?"

"Indeed, I am implying," she answered, having thrown temperance and moderation to the winds. "You live a life of dissipation, sir, just like the rest of them. You possess not the slightest understanding of servants and the miserable lives they must lead."

He looked at her askance. "Well, dish me! And here I thought I treated my servants rather well."

"Not as well as you do your horse, I wager."

He started to speak again, then stopped abruptly, seeming to rethink his words. "They warned me. They said you were not humble."

"They were right."

Annoyance hovered in his eyes. "For a servant, you are being quite outrageous, you know."

"But you won't tell."

"Am I to take that as a compliment?"

"That you're not a talebearer?" She considered, then gave a shrug. "I suppose so."

"Aha!" he proclaimed dramatically. "It appears I possess at least one redeeming quality."

"You're not all bad," she conceded. "But still"—she leveled a cool gaze into his proud dark eyes—"you're a noble, are you not? You're born into a privileged world of richness and splendor where you lead a shallow, indolent, selfish existence and haven't a care that your servants are overworked and underpaid and subject to dismissal at the slightest whim. Indeed, it is your God-given *right* to own and abuse as many servants as you please!"

Though his only physical reaction appeared to be nothing more than a slightly raised eyebrow, she knew she had reached him. Surely no one of her station had ever spoken to him in this manner before.

He began, "Oh, come now—" but she quickly silenced him.

"You look past us as if we were not there, you . . . you master of idleness! You, who have no idea what goes on outside your snobbish little world!"

Again he attempted to speak, but she raised her hand. "I haven't finished!" She took a deep breath and glanced around quickly, to ensure herself they were still alone. "But don't concern yourself I might wish you ill, my dear Lord Beaumont. Why should I? Marriage to Allegra will be punishment enough."

Now that her words were out, Meg yearned only for a quick retreat. In fairness, though, she forced herself to stand and wait for his reaction. Would he turn nasty and cut her down? Simply walk away? Or perhaps he would run to Lord Semple and demand she be dismissed. No, not the last. Richard was no Algernon. She would wager a month's pay, he was man enough to solve his own problems and would never sneak behind her back.

"Are you quite finished?" he inquired finally, in a voice so still it signaled danger.

"Yes." Already she was regretting her last remark, although not the rest of it. "About Lady Allegra, I—"

"Hush!" He held his hand up and was about to speak again when Lady Lydia approached, it seemed from out of nowhere, her eyebrows pulled together in a fierce scowl.

"Meg! I have been listening from the doorway. I own, I am completely shocked!"

"M'lady, I—"

"How dare you speak to Lord Beaumont in such a fashion! What colossal cheek!"

"I was not—"

"I shall speak to Lord Semple and inform him you should be sent packing immediately. Now, get yourself upstairs to the servant's quarters, where you belong!"

Cheeks flushed with humiliation, Meg did not have the heart to even glance at Lord Beaumont, who stood silently by. "I've no wish to remain here," she said to Lydia in a low, trembling voice. "I shall be on the mail coach to London tomorrow."

Without another word, she whirled around and hurried toward the servants' stairway.

Chapter 10

Meg had fled halfway up the servants' staircase when Polly encountered her.

"Meg, you look orful! Pale as a ghost! Wha's wrong?"

"Nothing, beyond the fact I have just roundly insulted Lord Beaumont, and Lady Lydia overheard and wants me dismissed." Meg's knees felt weak. She sank to the step and squeezed her eyes shut a moment, as if to obliterate the spectacle of Lydia's hate-twisted face. "I've never felt so humiliated in my life. How utterly degrading! To be humbled before a man I . . ." She bit her lip.

"Admire?"

"No, detest!"

"Oh, Meg, does that mean—?"

"She told me she would go straight to his lordship, and I'm sure she will." Meg related a brief version of her argument with Lord Beaumont, followed by the terrible tongue-lashing she had received from Lady Lydia.

"That's turrible!"

"Better I starve on the streets of London than work here another day."

"Aw, you don' mean it." Polly sank down beside her and clumsily patted her shoulder. "Per'aps Lady Lydia will forget about it."

"Not likely. She heartily dislikes me."

"But, Meg, you are such a pearl of a lady's maid! Surely they will let you stay."

"A pearl of a lady's maid knows how to keep her mouth shut, whereas I . . . oh, why did I not?"

"Why indade? You certainly should 'av."

"I said terrible things to Lord Beaumont—ripped him to shreds."

"You knew what 'e was like—wut they're all like—wut good to blow your cork like you did?"

"I could not help it! That liar!"

"Wut 'ave we here?" Polly leaned back with a knowing gleam in her eye. Using Meg's own words, she mocked, "'He enjoyed my reading of poetry and that was all.' Really! 'Tis plain you have fallen for 'im."

"I wouldn't give a groat for his high-and-mighty lordship," Meg denied vehemently. "I cannot abide deceit."

Polly cocked her head. "If you care naught for 'im, why should just one lie out of his mouth make you so chagrined?"

Meg felt disinclined to answer, suspecting Polly was more right than she cared to admit. "Oh, Polly, I died a thousand deaths when Lady Lydia demeaned me in his presence."

"How orful."

"It *was* awful. To be disgraced in front of an enemy is far worse than being disgraced in front of a friend."

Polly looked puzzled. "Lord Beaumont is an enemy?"

"Yes . . . no . . . oh, I don't know!" Meg got to her feet. "In any case, I shall not waste any more time thinking about him. I had best get started making plans."

"I shud think so."

"Tomorrow I shall return to London. Then I shall be obliged to swallow my pride and plead with the Dowager Duchess of Brambleshire to take me on, provided she's still in town and hasn't filled the position."

"How orful."

"Quit saying that," Meg snapped, then was instantly sorry. "Forgive me, Polly, but the thought of being forced to move again makes me ill."

"Look at the bright side! You won't 'ave to put up with Allegra anymore."

"I shan't miss her ordering me about. And I shan't be obliged to witness her gloating smile when she gazes upon her new fiancé as if she had just bagged a priceless trophy." Meg made a face and muttered, "Some priceless trophy *he!*"

Polly held in a snicker. "I see we are back to Lord Beaumont again."

Not hearing, Meg continued, "Nor shall I be forced to endure the disgusting spectacle of the Master of Idleness fawning over the Mistress of Coarseness. How I misjudged him! How happy I shall be never to lay eyes on that perfidious face again."

"Plain to see you cannot stand the sight of the man."

"I mean it, Polly!"

Once back in her room, Meg threw herself on the bed and fought back tears as she bleakly contemplated what her loss of temper had accomplished. A timid knock sounded on her door. When she opened it, she was astounded to discover Lady Semple standing in the doorway, eyes beseeching, hands pressed together, as if in prayer.

"M'lady!"

"May I come in, Meg? I must talk to you."

Meg had never seen the lady of the manor visit the servants' quarters before—not at Auberry Hall, the London town house, or here. So startled she forgot to curtsy, she invited Lady Semple in and waved her to be seated upon her one wooden chair. She closed the door, and at her ladyship's direction, sat down stiffly opposite on the only other seating available, the bed. "What is it, your ladyship? I must say, I find it strange to see you here."

"Oh, Meg"—Lady Semple's voice was strained—"is it true? Did you really have a confrontation with Lord Beaumont? Are you really planning to seek employment elsewhere?"

"You know already?" Meg asked with disbelief.

"Strange, is it not, how fast rumors travel in these huge households? There's no such thing as a secret, what with servants' keen ears at every door"—she managed a wry smile—"and apparently every staircase."

"I agree," Lady Semple replied, "but this time such is not the case. Lord Beaumont went to Lord Semple immediately after the, er, incident and apprised him of what had occurred. The man seemed quite concerned. He came to your defense and claimed your conversation was of no consequence, that he was not the least insulted and that Lady Lydia had misunderstood."

"How terribly kind of him," Meg answered dryly. "But the truth is, I *did* insult him, most explicitly. He couldn't help but know it."

Lady Semple took on a pained expression. "Oh, Meg, must you be so honest?"

"Yes, I fear I must, although I'm well aware I would be better off if I were not."

"I came to inform you Lord Beaumont was successful," Lady Semple continued. "His lordship has agreed that you may stay, provided, of course, there are no further . . . shall we say, incidents? I most heartily agree. Staying here is by far the best thing for you."

Meg bristled. "If I did what was best for me, I would keep my mouth shut and my eyes to the ground." She could hear the bitter edge in her voice but was powerless to alter it. "I would strip myself of feeling, and never worry beyond where my next meal was coming from and where to lay my head each night."

Tears welled in Lady Semple's eyes. "You don't still plan on leaving?"

Had she not controlled them, Meg might have had tears welling in her eyes, too. "I . . . I am not sure what to do."

Lady Semple heaved a deep sigh. " 'Tis Allegra, is it not?"

"In part," Meg reluctantly replied. Difficult, discussing a daughter like Allegra with a mother so gentle and kind.

107

"But 'tis not only Allegra," Meg continued. "There are other things, too, that perforce I cannot explain. And then there's Lady Lydia's attitude, as if she hates me. And then you . . . forgive me, ma'am, but ever since we met, I've felt you were keeping something from me."

"Oh, Meg . . ." Lady Semple's voice broke as she suddenly bent her forehead into the palm of her hand. "There are certain happenings you're not aware of, happenings that . . . that—"

"That what? Why all the secrecy? Whatever you have to say to me, can you not simply say it?"

"I have done you a monstrous disservice," Lady Semple whispered into her lace handkerchief, her eyes focused on the floor, "but I cannot tell you, however much I might want to. I simply cannot—"

"If you cannot tell me, then, do not," Meg broke in firmly. She couldn't understand such wobbling. "Truly, I am beginning to think I really should return to London, despite the uncertainties. I feel I belong there, much more than here."

"But you do not!" her ladyship blurted. "Your place is here, at Pentworth Park."

"But why?"

"Because you were born here!" Lady Semple replied, twisting her handkerchief, her tears spilling over. "I . . ." She tried to choke out words, but they refused to come. ". . . Because this is your home," she finished lamely.

"I was born here?" Meg asked, stabbing a finger at her chest. Once again, she recalled with stunning clarity that day when Lady Elinore lay dying. Heart pounding, Meg directed a searching gaze into her ladyship's eyes. "Whatever your secret, your cousin, Lady Elinore, knew it, too, did she not?"

"What do you mean?" gasped Lady Semple, growing even paler.

"I mean that only hours before the first countess died, she informed me my mother was not a scullery maid. She mentioned your name, as well as Lady Lydia's. Unfortunately for me, Lady Lydia was there and stopped her from saying more. So the secret died with the countess, m'lady. I can assure you, though, that not a day has since passed, I have not thought of it."

Lady Semple had sat, pale and totally attentive, listening to Meg. Now, unexpectedly, she buried her head in her hands again.

Meg implored, "Can you not give me the answer, m'lady? Was this the reason Lady Wallingford allowed me to attend class with her own children? Surely it was, for no other scullery maid in the household was ever allowed to absorb lessons in French, art, deportment, music—all subjects—like I was. And what other servant was trained in the arts of being a lady's maid from such an early age? No servant but me, and I would like to know why."

Pale and shaken, her ladyship gazed up at her. "So you've been looking for an answer ever since?"

"Of course! How could I put the countess's revelations totally to rest?" Meg found herself floundering in an agonizing maelstrom. "Why do you remain silent? What's so terrible you cannot say?"

"I must go!" Charlotte cried in a low, tormented voice, her expression one of mute wretchedness. With a choked, desperate laugh, she stumbled toward the door. "I am not myself . . . I should not have come here. Forget this, Meg."

"No!" Moving swiftly, Meg slipped in front of the door, barring Lady Semple's way. "You cannot leave in this condition, m'lady," she said softly. With a touch of irony, she added, "What would the servants say?"

"Oh, dear, you're right." Lady Semple returned to her chair.

Disturbed by her distress, Meg decided to let a few barriers slip away. "May I speak honestly?" she inquired, bending forward earnestly. "Not as servant to mistress, but just this once, simply as a friend?"

Charlotte dabbed her eyes. "Please do."

"What are you afraid of? If you wish to keep your secret, then do so. But is it worth tormenting yourself? How can you live this way? Have you ever thought to face whatever it is head-on, and the devil be damned?"

Lady Semple thought a moment, then sadly shook her head. "It is easy enough for you to say, Meg, you with your courage and your strength. How I admire you for it! But as for me, I'm not nearly as strong. Lord Semple looks at me, I crumble. Lady Lydia looks at me, I crumble. Oh, no! I shall never have your pluck." She paused, then made a valiant attempt to stop her tears. "I've said too much. I must go."

Meg found herself fighting off her own frustration. First Lady Wallingford, now Lady Semple. What was this terrible secret that neither could tell? She was born in this house? Then, she wanted desperately to ask, *Who was my mother? Who was my father?* But Lady Semple, mouth set in a sad line, obviously had no desire to be questioned further.

Without another word, Meg opened the door and allowed Lady Semple to pass through. "Will you be all right?" she called after her.

Charlotte turned, desolation in her eyes. "I wish I had half your courage, Meg."

"But you do! More than you think, m'lady!"

"You are too kind."

"I mean it. You *do* have the courage to look your troubles in the eye, whatever they are. Try it just once—I implore you."

"Oh, Meg, I shall ask you one more time—will you stay?" Lady Semple's voice was fragile and shaking. "If you say yes, I promise you that when Allegra marries, you shall not accompany her to Hartwick House but shall stay with me. You may be assured I shall endeavor to do all in my power to straighten out . . . to tell you . . ."

"Very well, m'lady," Meg broke in, unable to endure her ladyship's despair a moment longer. "I shall think on it and give you my decision in the morning."

* * *

Charlotte descended the staircase chastising herself for her weakness. How she wished she could summon up the courage to tell Meg the truth, but if she did, a Pandora's box of problems would surely open. Cyril, her husband, might find out. Worse, snake-tongued Lydia would make her life unendurable.

It was quite late. The guests had either departed or turned into bed. Most of the servants had retired also, after clearing and cleaning, she noticed, in a most haphazard fashion. She must speak to them in the morning. Deciding she had better check the state of the dining room, she swung the wide door open and started inside. Suddenly she froze. Before her was a sight so shocking she gasped and clutched her palm to her chest.

There swayed Allegra, half lying in the bend of Henry's arm. He was kissing her, and with his other hand . . . "Allegra! Whatever are you doing?"

The two jumped apart so fast Henry nearly dropped Allegra on the floor. She quickly recovered herself, smoothed her hair, and with an easy smirk replied, "Mama, why are you shouting?"

"Why, good evening, Lady Semple," Henry remarked with a slight bow, not a trace of embarrassment showing in his weak blue eyes.

"Leave us, Henry," Charlotte commanded with all the authority she could muster, "and shut the door."

Henry offered no argument. Charlotte waited in stony silence until he had left the room. Before she could speak again, Allegra shrugged, remarking, "Really, Mama, such a to-do about nothing. We were not doing anything wrong."

Emotion was not seemly, no matter what the cause, so Charlotte choked back her anger, just as she always had. When she could trust herself to speak again, she replied, "I am shocked at your behavior. That I should catch a daughter of mine in such an intimate pose, and you just betrothed, and with your fiancé's very own brother, of all things!"

"Don't be a goose, Mama, you must be going blind. Henry was not even close to me. We were simply standing here talking, discussing my wedding plans."

Allegra reached leisurely for the silver ladle in the punch bowl. With maddening calm, she poured herself a cup of mulled wine. "Some wine, Mama?"

"Certainly not!" Charlotte was appalled. "How can you calmly stand there when—?"

"You say you are shocked at my behavior?" Allegra interrupted. "Well, I am shocked at yours." With great deliberation she scooped up a handful of crumbs from the near-empty cake plate. "Really, Mama, we are all worried about you. You are *so* forgetful, and you keep seeing things that aren't there." She stuffed the crumbs into her mouth, licked her fingers, and casually went about selecting more.

Charlotte stood silent, not sure what to do. Allegra had been churlish before, many times, but this mocking, scornful attitude was something new. She was at a loss what to do until suddenly she remembered Meg's words: *You* do *have the courage to look your troubles in the eye, whatever they are.*

Charlotte hated a scene, hated it so much she felt an overwhelming desire to turn around right now and leave—go up to her room, and lock the door so that she would not have to confront one single soul.

But on the other hand . . .

She had allowed Allegra to do what she pleased all her life. The girl needed a lesson. *Look your troubles in the eye.* A spark of courage shot through her.

"Allegra, put that cake down!"

"What?" Allegra stopped her chewing.

"You heard me." Charlotte watched as Allegra, eyes widening with curiosity, dropped her handful of crumbs. "You are never to talk that way to me again," Charlotte went on, pleased at the manner in which her voice rang with authority. "I know what I saw, and it was you, supposedly a lady, lowering yourself like some common scullery maid, allowing disgraceful liberties from your fiancé's own brother."

Allegra's mouth dropped open. "You cannot speak to me like that. I shall tell Aunt Lydia!"

"Do so." It felt good, letting the words tumble out without examining each one carefully. It felt good, too, seeing Allegra with mouth gaped open in astonishment. "And while you are about it, tell her about the liberties Henry was taking. And tell her about the uncivil, rude, totally unacceptable way you have addressed your mother. If there is anyone here who is losing their mind, it is *you*, Allegra. You, risking the most shocking scandal, jeopardizing your marriage to Richard by playing fast and loose with Henry."

Allegra actually paled. "Mama, you don't sound yourself. I've never seen you act this way."

"That's entirely beside the point, daughter. Mark what I said."

Lady Lydia entered the room, frowning with curiosity. After one look at her niece, she remarked, "Tears, Allegra? Whatever has your mother said to you?"

"Oh, Aunt Lydia!" Allegra hurled herself into her aunt's arms. "Mama is simply not herself!" She went on to sob out her mother's accusations. "And I was *not* kissing Henry! Mama's being mean to me—blaming me for things I didn't do."

Lydia turned accusing eyes on Charlotte. "What have you done to this poor child?"

Suddenly, in the face of Lydia's self-possessed affront, Charlotte's bravery collapsed. Her burst of courage and self-confidence was gone. "I . . . you do not know the facts, Lydia."

"I have enough facts to know you are tormenting my niece unnecessarily."

"I have nothing more to say." Charlotte's shoulders

sagged. She did not bother to straighten them again. "It is late. I am going to bed."

"Do that, Charlotte. And let us hope that by morning you will have come to your senses."

Charlotte crept up to her bedchamber. There, sinking onto the bed, she acknowledged that her little foray into standing up for herself had been fine for a time, but had ended in total disaster.

And yet, thanks to Meg, she *had* stood firm, at least for a little while. She was still afraid of Lydia, petrified of Cyril, had not yet come even close to what would have to be the great confrontation. *Look your troubles in the eye.* Well, there might be some hope for her. For Meg's sake, she would try, although she doubted she would ever possess enough courage.

Chapter 11

"God's blood, Cummings! Watch that blade. You nicked me again."

"Sorry, m'lord." Not missing a stroke, Richard's valet gave him a look which clearly indicated that if Richard hadn't moved he would not have gotten nicked. As Cummings finished the morning shaving ritual, a sunbeam broke through the window. It had the gall to catch Richard directly in the eye.

"God's blood!" Richard exclaimed again, squinting, shifting quickly in his chair. As he searched for a reason to blame Cummings again, he finally recognized the reason behind the foul mood in which he had awakened. No sense blaming his valet. No sense blaming anyone except himself for this rotten, inextricable mess into which he had gotten himself. Richard threw aside the towel and strode to the window. "That will do, Cummings," he absentmindedly decreed. Below lay the gardens of Hartwick House, a view he had cherished since childhood. The gardens were straggling and unkempt now, but lavish green still. Beyond, past the far row of birch trees, lay a ribbon of river half-hidden by tall willow trees.

Meg came the thought, unbidden, to his mind. He could see her by the river, golden hair hanging wild and free, dancing after the butterfly. Would she leave today? Last night, after the incident in the hallway, he had gone to Cyril immediately to plead Meg's case.

"I was not offended in the least," he had lied. "Your maidservant—Meg is her name?—is a lively little creature. It was simply her manner of speaking, which is, sir, rather, er . . . lively."

"Lively?" Lord Semple had peered down his nose in that superior manner that was always so annoying. "According to my sister, she ripped you up one side and down the other."

"Not a'tall," Richard heartily exclaimed. "Much ado about nothing. You're noted for your kindness, sir"—another lie—"so I pray you will extend that kindness and allow the girl to stay."

In deep thought, Lord Semple tapped his lip with his finger. "If 'twere I alone, I could forgive her. After all, what is she but a poor crippled serving girl? But still, Lydia was adamant. I shall have to think on it."

Meg a poor crippled serving girl? Richard had been hard put to keep from punching the Marquess of Semple right on his snobby, aristocratic nose. But he had managed to control himself quite well. For Meg's sake he had bit his tongue and humbly bowed his way out with a gracious "thank you."

Still gazing out the window, Richard assured himself he had done his best. Still, that shrew Lydia wanted her gone, and Lydia ruled Cyril. Only God knew what was happening at Pentworth Park today.

But even if I did persuade Cyril, what of Meg? Last night she stated she was leaving. *Then, I shall take the mail coach to London tomorrow!* She was angry, though, not thinking clearly. Would that stubborn little chit change her mind?

Life is full of quirks, Richard reflected bleakly. Only yesterday he had been an elegant Man of the Town. But in the course of twenty-four hours, he had discovered Mama dying, Papa pain-racked and frail, his beloved Hartwick House falling apart, and worst of all, he had, of his own free will, betrothed himself to a girl he could never love, let alone like, or even respect.

Not only that, he found himself besotted with thoughts of a maidservant! Not your ordinary, meek, subservient maidservant, but a spirited lass who last night had roundly rebuked him. That *he*, Lord Beaumont, heir apparent of an earl, should be set-down by one Meg Quincy, lady's maid, was unconscionable. No servant had ever dared censure him before.

The strange part was, instead of feeling indignant, or irate, or at the very least piqued, all he felt was an overwhelming urge to see her again. For what reason, he could not fathom. In London, when he went to visit his romps, he surely knew the reason why. But with Meg there was decidedly something more than a desire to satisfy his libido. Perhaps if Lady Lydia had not appeared, he would have had the opportunity to defend himself against Meg's ridiculous charges, thus clearing her out of his mind. Yes, he was sure of it. *Could have done it, too,* he thought, recalling how Meg had stood firm after delivering her barbed remarks, had squared those small, staunch shoulders, tilted that well-molded little head back, bravely waiting for him to reply.

Could her charges in any way be true? Was he shallow? . . . indolent? He shook his head swiftly, as if to clear the doubts out. Ridiculous!

"Shall you be going out today, sir?"

"Of course," Richard replied without turning. A dull, empty ache welled inside him as he asked himself, where? They would be expecting him at Pentworth Park, no doubt, but that was the last place on earth he wished to go. In truth, he would much prefer to mount Thunder and gallop back to his comfortable existence with his books and friends in London. Never had he appreciated his life there more than now. But he must stay, forced to see this travesty through to the bitter end. He must marry Allegra, share her bed, wrap his arms around that unappetizing body, endure the gloating smile she would no doubt be wearing on her smug, victorious face.

*Total darkness—that is what I shall need in order to
. . . damnation! 'Tis Meg I want, not Allegra!*

There he went again. All he could think of was Meg.
But he *must* put her out of his mind.

"God's blood!" he proclaimed yet again.

"Eh, Richard? Oaths already and the day hardly
begun?"

Edward's voice. Richard turned reluctantly to greet his
old friend and now future brother-in-law. "Must you be
so cheerful?"

Edward, maddeningly buoyant, came beaming into
Richard's bedchamber. "Why the foul mood?" His eyes
twinkled mischievously. "You look downright haggard
this morning. Can't imagine why. Have you forgotten
your betrothal to Allegra? I should think you would be
dancing with delight."

Richard scowled. "Say another word and I shall—"

"*If* you will recall, I expressed my true feelings last
night." Edward had the decency to remove his silly
smirk. "I shall never understand—"

"It is not required you understand," Richard snapped,
and was immediately sorry. Edward was, after all, his
dearest friend. "Sit down. Actually, I'm glad you came."

"So am I. Anything to get away from Pentworth Park
this morning. Allegra is driving us all mad, thanks to
you. She keeps skittering about, goading Papa about
drawing up the wedding settlement and Mama about a
white wedding gown. She demands your presence for
dinner tonight, which is officially why I'm here, to invite
you, although I own I was overjoyed to remove myself
from her . . . er, exuberance."

Richard emitted a long and weary sigh. Wordlessly, he
turned to stare out the window again. He was concerned
about Meg, longed to ask about her, but dared not risk
Edward's jibes. Before long he felt his friend's hand on
his shoulder. "Why, Richard?" Edward softly inquired.
"Damme, can you not tell me why?"

Richard pondered upon whether or not to tell Edward

the truth and finally concluded, what good would it do? He would, however, inform Edward of his mother's illness. "Mama . . ." He had not yet said the words aloud. To his surprise, he had to pause until his voice would not catch. He turned to face Edward. "My mother is dying."

Edward caught his breath. "Damme, I did not know! Although we have long suspected something was not right at Hartwick House. Ah, Richard, I am so sorry. Such a fine woman! She"—slowly his eyebrows raised— "ah, I see it all now! She has extracted a deathbed promise from you, has she not? 'Tis your father's wish you marry Allegra . . . join our two estates . . . etcetera, etcetera. That's the truth of it, is it not, Richard? Tell me I'm wrong!"

"So you guessed the truth," Richard replied wearily. "I have no wish to discuss it. Suffice to say, I made a promise. Several, actually. I shall make up with my father. I shall give up my rooms in London and move home."

"And marry Allegra, too? What insanity!" Edward stood there, amazed and shaken. "I cannot but admire your loyalty to your mother, Richard, but this is your life! Marry my hoyden sister? How could you?"

"Changed your tune, have you not?" Richard cut in bitterly. "As I recall, you were all for it. How you did babble on about the blissful conjoining of two great estates. 'Share her bed long enough to breed an heir,' you said, and after that, 'go your separate way and live as you always have. Keep a dozen mistresses at once,' you said, 'for all anybody cares.' "

Edward had the decency to look nonplussed. "As I told you last night, I was only doing Mama's bidding. Never crossed my mind you would actually propose. But look at the bright side. Think of the dowry! Think of—"

"How can I bed Allegra even once?" Richard burst out, pure agony in his voice. "Especially when—" He stopped abruptly, bit his lip, mouthed a silent oath.

Perplexed, Edward asked, "Especially when what?"

"Never mind. I hardly know myself." *Meg.* He knew very well it was Meg who made him answer as he did. Had he finished his sentence, he would have said, *especially when it is thoughts of Meg I have been besotted with since I met her. Good God! I'm desperate for Meg!*

He could not go on this way. Richard took a moment to collect his thoughts, then straightened himself with dignity. "As I see it, I have two ways to go. I can make myself miserable, caterwauling over my lot, or I can keep my mouth shut and make the best of it."

"So?" asked Edward.

Hearing his own words increased Richard's resolve. "My choice is that Allegra shall become my wife and I shall make the best of it."

Edward started to reply, but Richard raised a hand. "I shall be fine. Even though it might be difficult to cope with this unexpected, totally unwanted change in my life, I have the consolation of knowing I have done my duty. There is, after all, a certain sense of nobility attached to making sacrificial promises to one's dying mother."

Edward screwed up his face. "That was the most asinine statement I ever heard you make."

After a startled moment, Richard laughed in answer. "Damme, yes it was! But in what other manner can I handle this . . . this . . ."

"Monumental catastrophe?"

"Close enough. Let us go down to breakfast, shall we? I fancy coddled eggs and toast this morning, along with some kippered herring."

In the morning room, they were halfway through their meal when Edward casually remarked, "By the way, I have a bit of news concerning Allegra's lady's maid." He regarded Richard with veiled eyes. "If you have any interest, of course."

If I have any interest, Richard reflected with dark irony. Was Meg going or staying? He was so eager to find out, it was difficult to maintain an indifferent pose. "Continue, Edward," he said flatly.

Carefully choosing his words, a gleam of mischief in his eye, Edward went on, "I understand there was a bit of a flap last night. Meg, the wicked girl, delivered a good set-down to one of the guests, can't imagine who. Aunt Lydia overheard and was, shall we say, irate? Then rumor had it Meg would depart for London today to—listen to this!—go into the employ of the Dowager Duchess of Brambleshire. Fancy!" Edward shook his head in disbelief. "Who would want to work for that old harridan?"

"Who indeed?" Richard fought to control his impatience.

"But, then . . ." Edward trailed off and became totally engrossed in slathering butter on his scone.

"Then *what*, Edward?" *Damn the man!* Richard had to restrain himself from shoving the scone straight into Edward's silly face.

"She decided to stay." Edward popped the scone in his mouth and between chews continued, "Big row . . . Papa and Auntie Lydia . . . for once, Lydia didn't get her way."

Meg was staying! Richard experienced one fleeting giddy moment of delight before reality set in. So what if Meg was staying? What good would it do? All at once, he felt himself plunging back into the mood he had awakened in, which at its best could be described as only a cut above black despair.

"Is something wrong, Richard?"

"No." *Edward and his eagle eye.*

"Hmmm . . ." Edward cocked his head. "I suspected you had an eye for the wench. Could it be you have acquired a fondness for her? That would certainly explain—"

"Don't be absurd." Richard glared down his nose at his friend. "Even if I had, what would I do? Carry her off to Gretna Green? Papa would cut me off, of course, but no matter. I could rusticate in some primitive hamlet—

spend the rest of my life playing whist for a penny a point with fat country squires."

"Stranger things have happened."

Richard rolled his eyes to the ceiling and let out a derisive snort. But even as he did so, he pictured Mcg and himself driving off to Gretna Green together, she pressed adoringly against his side, laughing, excitement gleaming in those sparkling, wise blue eyes. On the way back, they would extend their tour to Brighton . . . no, Exeter would be better—smaller perhaps, but he could picture her delight when, making their way to the coast along the high road, they would crest the top of the hills and for the first time she would see below her the whole breathtaking vista of valley, river cliffs, and sea. How thrilled she would be! His spirits lifted at the thought, but quickly sank back to reality—and gloom. He had committed himself to Allegra. Even had he not, how could he possibly take up with a servant girl?

Either way, there was no way out, and he was doomed.

After breakfast, Richard said good-bye to Edward and went to visit his mother. Leaning close over her bed, he murmured his lie. "Mama, I do believe you are looking better this morning."

His mother returned a weak smile and reached out her hand. "Did you . . . ?"

He clasped her hand with both of his. "Allegra and I are betrothed."

Her eyes lit. "I am so pleased! Are you pleased, too, my son?"

He choked back pained laughter. "Delighted."

Later he visited his father's bedchamber, the very same room where as a little boy he had stood trembling at the wrath of the Godlike, all-powerful man looming over him. Now his frail, pain-racked father half lay in a chair, bandaged foot propped upon a pillow.

"You have made me very happy, son." His father's voice was reedy, tremulous. "When you were but a boy, I was hard on you, perhaps too hard. I was only trying to make sure—"

"Say no more, Papa." A line from a play popped into Richard's head. " 'Pray you now, forget and forgive.' "

"Shakespeare," his father answered with a wince of pain. "*King Lear.*"

"Ay, Papa."

"I am glad you're home, son. I need you. The servants are quite out of control . . . thievish and drunk, the lot of them"—he grimaced from pain again—"stealing from me, not attending to their duties."

"You can stop worrying, Papa, I am home."

"Vickers, what is that I see upon your linen—could it be a spot of gravy?" Richard's voice was warm as granite. "See that you dress properly in the future. And let it be known to all the servants that from now on, in dress, attitude, and work habits, they are to be exemplary. Is that clear? Because if it is not clear, you shall be dismissed at once, without, I might add, a character."

After he left Vickers trembling in his boots, Richard collected himself. He needed to talk to the tenants, organize the gardeners—a million things to do, but first, he must salvage some time for himself and come to grips with this desolate mood that enveloped him. He would go out riding, stop by the river. Meg had stated she would not be going back there, which was by far the best thing, of course. But in the remote circumstance she might be there, he would greet her coolly and be on his way. Or better yet, he would simply go the other direction if he saw her first.

Meg had awakened in the morning, knowing she was going to stay. How could she not? Curiosity alone was a driving reason, for she felt compelled to unravel Lady Semple's secret. As for the rest of it, somehow she would bring herself to endure Lady Lydia and Allegra. Lord Beaumont, as well.

So it is decided, she declared to herself as, dressed in her gray gown, she firmly tugged her cap in place and prepared to go belowstairs and inform Lady Semple of her decision. Besides, after Allegra was married, Lady Semple had promised she could remain at Pentworth Park. As for Lord Beaumont, she had had her say— nothing could hurt her now. She would avoid him as much as possible, and whenever her thoughts drifted to any of the unseemly images she had been having about him, she would simply remind herself what a liar he was, as well as selfish and unfeeling.

She had no intention of giving up her special spot at the river, though, even though she knew it was his property. In the rare circumstance they might meet there again, she would simply murmur a polite hello and be on her way.

That afternoon, sketchbook in hand, Meg sank down under the gnarled oak tree by the river. She had expected Allegra's constant demands would prevent her from visiting her favorite spot today, but she need not have worried. Bursting to vaunt her grand news, Allegra had swept off on a whirlwind round of visiting, determined, it appeared, to drop off her card at every estate in the countryside.

How peaceful here, watching the smooth, silent flow of the river, listening to the occasional whippoorwill's call, feeling the gentle warmth of the afternoon sun. Yet, despite the beauty of this spot, Meg felt eerie and unsettled, a mood that had begun during last night's strange conversation with Lady Semple. This morning it had worsened when she informed her ladyship she had decided to stay, an announcement that brought tears to her ladyship's eyes. Why had Lady Semple been so emotional? Why should such a grand lady care whether or not she lost a maid?

Yet not only was she mystified over Lady Semple's secret, she was, though she hated to admit it, troubled by the intensity of the anger she had displayed toward Lord Beaumont. Pensively, she looked out upon the river. He was only another lord, one of the many vain fops she had seen from afar all her life. Why, then, had she seethed with anger toward him? *Because I am drawn to him.* The admission to herself was dredged from a place beyond logic and reason. *I care about Lord Beaumont.*

But what a useless emotion!

Meg finally forced herself to start sketching and was deeply engrossed in her likeness of a silver-studded blue butterfly when she heard a bough crack behind her. A quick glance over her shoulder told her who it was. She quelled a foolish desire to leap up and flee. Instead, she carefully set aside sketchbook and brush, rose to her feet, and said calmly, "So 'tis you."

Only a few feet away, Lord Beaumont stood regarding her with equal aplomb, his expression still as stone. She had the fleeting impression he was about to turn and walk away, but instead he pushed a bough aside and approached. When he stood close, she caught the beginnings of a genuine smile, but he covered it quickly by a frown and lofty-cocked eyebrow. "So you have not departed for London after all," he remarked in that snobbish manner of his.

"More's the pity, m'lord," she answered airily, recalling her vow to cut him short in the remote event she should encounter him by the river again. But try as she might, she could not summon up her anger to the magnitude she had felt the night before. Quite understandable, she reasoned. After all, she'd had her say; there was nothing left to add. Now her best course was to withdraw as quickly as possible without seeming downright hostile. "I changed my mind," she continued with a shrug, "and informed Lady Semple I shall not be leaving." Reluctantly she added, "I suppose I should thank you for speaking on my behalf to Lord Semple."

Richard crossed his arms and raised a cynical eyebrow. "If you only suppose you should, then kindly do not."

"Very well. It would appear I am trespassing on your lordship's land again, so I most humbly beg your pardon," she went on, not feeling humble in the slightest. "I shall leave immediately."

She bent to pick up her sketchbook and brush, then attempted to step around him, but the path was narrow, and he, instead of stepping back, had leaned his palm straight out against an oak tree, his arm effectively blocking her path. He placed the other hand low-slung on his hip, in the process pushing his jacket back, revealing an immaculate white shirt covering his powerful set of shoulders and massive chest. Acutely aware, suddenly, of his masculine presence, she found it difficult not to draw in a sharp breath. "Allow me to pass, sir."

He bent over her, his keen brown eyes regarding her skeptically. "The countess was right. You are *not* humble. When you try, you are even worse."

"Obviously you're aggrieved because of the comments I made to you last night," she said flatly, vowing to maintain her show of unconcern.

He emitted a cynical laugh. "Simply because you accused me of being shallow? And—what was it now?—ah, yes, 'indolent' you called me, if memory serves correctly. Also, you made some mention of the fact that I prey upon the poor."

"You have forgotten 'selfish,' " she informed him evenly.

"I have not. Nor have I forgotten 'master of idleness,' nor my 'snobbish little world.' "

"Not only that, sir. I could add—"

"You aren't finished?" he interrupted in mock horror. "You have already turned me into a monster!"

She willed herself to look as stony-faced as he. "On second thought, I have nothing to add, nothing to subtract

... although perhaps my remark about Allegra was unseemly. I take it back."

"As indeed you should," he solemnly agreed. "I found your remark to be rude and thoughtless, showing complete lack of sensitivity. It cut me to the quick."

Had it really? But no, she caught a gleam of amusement in his eye. She quelled her own amusement as she answered, "Then, I apologize for saying what I said about Allegra."

"And the rest?"

"Certainly not." She lifted her chin.

Humor twitched his lips. " 'Tis obvious I had best not press my luck."

"That would be wise, sir."

"Last night I had no opportunity to defend myself."

She raised an eyebrow. "Oh? Do you wish to do so now? If so, perhaps you could start by explaining why you so adamantly declared you would never marry Allegra."

He appeared to fall into solemn thought. "No matter what I say, could I convince you I was sincere?"

"Your chances are slim, m'lord." She was beginning to enjoy herself. This was not a serious confrontation, but more of a game of words.

"In that case—"

"In that case"—she tried to slip past him—"I shall take your leave."

"I suggest you stay. Entirely up to you, of course." He pulled his arm back and without a backward glance strolled the rest of the path to the large oak tree by the water. Leaning his back against it, he propped one booted foot on the trunk and crossed his arms, regarded her amusedly. "Or are you afraid to?"

He had caught her off guard. Stay? Go? She balanced on one foot, then the other, then made her decision. "Do you have any idea how preposterous this is? Of course I shall go."

Quickly he sobered and said, "Stay, Meg. I shall make you a proposition."

She was immediately on guard. Was she being confronted by another Algernon? She should leave right now, but curiosity rooted her to the pathway. "A proposition?"

"Not the one that first comes to mind, I can assure you. Come sit down, Meg. Where you were, under the oak tree."

What could he want? Part of her said flee, but the other part was telling her she absolutely must know. Slowly, reluctantly, she followed the pathway back, and again seated herself beneath the oak tree. After she had spread her skirt and tucked her legs beneath, she inquired suspiciously, "What had you in mind?"

He dropped down beside her and gazed out at the river flowing almost at their feet. "That here we shall just be ourselves. No titles. I shall not be Lord Somebody, you shall not be . . . er . . ."

"Meg Nobody?" she asked, smiling wryly.

"You know what I mean."

An incredulous smile crossed her face. "Meg and Richard?" She was hardly able to choke the words out. "Just plain, ordinary folk?" He nodded solemnly. "But why?"

"Because you're simply not an ordinary servant. There is something about you . . . your demeanor, your words, your attitude place you far above your station. I prefer to talk to you on an equal footing, forgetting who I am, who you are. Quite frankly, I . . . enjoy your company and would like to be your friend."

"For purposes of conversation, then? And reading poetry?"

After only a slight hesitation, he smiled and said, "Yes, Meg, I like you for your poetry."

"But aren't you angry? After last night, why would you even want to talk to me?"

"I might ask the same."

" 'Twill never work."

He turned to her and gently clasped her hands. "Yes, it will. You shall not call me lord. In return, I shall not look past you as if you weren't there"—the corner of his mouth twisted wryly—"not that I ever did."

She made no effort to withdraw her hands, but gazed at him questioningly. "You realize, I don't regret most of what I said."

"That's of no consequence. I want us to be on equal footing now, in this moment, as friends." He let go her wrists, leaving her skin tingling from his firm grip. She was too close to him again, his lips and his chest only inches away, along with his brown velvet eyes that until now had held such mystery. Now, looking deep inside, she saw a man determined to get his way. She could almost, but not quite, forget his perfidy.

"Richard," she repeated, slowly, relishing his name on her tongue. "What would we talk about?"

"I want to hear about you—your life, from the beginning."

She looked him in the eye, but could discern no lechery, no mockery. Still suspicious, she replied, "Excepting Polly, no one has ever asked about my life before."

"Then, 'tis time someone did. I shall listen carefully."

"Very well," she said, finally seeing no reason for not giving in. She settled back, her fingers pulling idly at a clump of violets, and told him of the strangeness of her life at Auberry Hall: allowed to take lessons with Miss Plinny, yet slaving long hours at manual labor, and managing, with the help of Celeste, to become a lady's maid at the age of sixteen. He listened intently, eyes fixed upon her face, taking in every word.

"And your parents?" he asked when, finally, she paused.

"I never knew them."

"No idea who they were?"

She could not restrain a wistful sigh, though she had

no desire for sympathy. "It has troubled me all my life, not to know my mother, especially since I was told my mother—" She paused, remembering the countess's words on her deathbed. How tempted she was to tell all to this man, who at the moment was carefully, sympathetically listening. But she mustn't forget he was a lord, and therefore the enemy, and besides, she was accustomed to keeping everything about herself bottled up inside.

"You were about to say?" he prompted.

"Only that I wish I had known her!" she cried with heartfelt sincerity. "How I wish she could come back, if only for a little while. I should have so much to tell her! And I would want just to put my arms around her, and feel her arms around me."

"Oh, Meg"—Richard clasped her hand, and exclaimed in a voice vibrant with intensity—"if only I had it in my power to grant you a day with your mother!"

Speechless, Meg gazed at him, not so much astounded by his words as the compassion in his eyes. Where was the thoughtless, selfish lord she thought she knew? She fought back a tear. Not only was she moved thinking of her mother, she was overwhelmed that here, finally, was someone who actually cared. And a lord, no less. " 'Tis very good of you, m'lord—"

"Richard, remember?"

"Richard," she pronounced. " 'Tis difficult for me to get the name out."

"Roll it around your tongue," he suggested with sudden lightness. "You'll get used to it."

She almost giggled, suddenly lighthearted. He might be the Master of Idleness, but she was suddenly hard put to ignore those dimples that appeared in his cheeks when he had smiled just now, nor the aura of magnetism that surrounded him. No wonder all those chits were after him! *Stop what you're thinking,* she advised herself. How easy it would be to be trapped by his compelling charm. "So tell me about *you.* The real you," she added playfully, "not that stuffy lord who goes around with his nose in the air."

He settled back and told her of his childhood at Hartwick House, remembering the good things, omitting the bad. He was well into relating his comfortable life in London when suddenly she gasped and sprang to her feet. "I had forgotten the time! Lady Allegra must be back by now. You cannot imagine how testy she can be, even when I'm there to greet her. If I am not . . . I don't care even to imagine her wrath."

He stood, too, and looked down at her with an expression more relaxed than ever she had seen on his usually imperturbable face before. "I cannot tell you how much I have enjoyed this," he said.

"And I, too," Meg murmured hastily. She hated to leave, but began to edge away. Despite her resolution to rise above it all, be serene, she would as lief not be obliged to endure Allegra's wrath.

He stepped closer, scanning her critically, his gaze, soft as a caress, took in her face, her neck, then moved down her dress to the tips of her shoes. There was no way she could stop her heart from jolting. It alarmed her so much she backed a step away.

"Have no fear, Meg," he told her, appearing to read her thoughts. "No more stolen kisses."

"I should hope not," she answered, more fiercely than intended. Would she allow it if he did? No! Better to let him think she was still a trifle angry.

"Can you come again tomorrow?"

"This is not a good idea, m'lord. I risk a great deal by meeting you here. You even more."

"So I am 'm'lord' again." He stepped back casually. Taking his time, he plucked a stray leaf that had clung to his otherwise impeccable wool sleeve. "Very well, until next time, then."

Despite his attempt at nonchalance, she sensed it was a sham, that he was watching her closely. There was an intensity about him, as if he were a stealthy lion, motionless at the moment, yet poised to spring. She discerned that if she gave him the slightest encouragement, he would seize her and wrap her in a passionate embrace. And, she suddenly realized, she wanted him to! His nearness was overwhelming, causing her pulse to quicken, making her feel a strange inner excitement she had never felt before.

"Meg?" he said gently, his voice a soft caress of her name. "I must explain . . ."

Had she lost her senses? Last night had hurt her deeply. This morning the hurt had faded, leaving nothing behind but disgust—at Lydia, and at all the ton, including this charming, witty man standing in front of her, who lived a life she could never, ever have. She could *never* afford to be hurt like that again.

"Save your breath, sir. You need not explain yourself. You were born to what you are, nothing will change that. Believe me, I understand." She took a step backward, straightened her cap, smoothed her gown. "You have been most kind, but I must go, and I shall not be back. We can pretend all we want, but the fact remains, we live in two different worlds. And need I remind you of your betrothal?"

"Hardly." Whatever real emotion he had felt was quickly masked, not by his customary aloof expression, but by a tension of his jaw and a look of resignation in his eyes. "I shall not say good-bye, Meg, only farewell until tomorrow. Remember, I shall be here in case you change your mind."

"I shall not, sir. What madness!" She spun around and hurried away.

Hoisting her skirts, Meg ran as fast as she could back to the mansion, her thoughts in a turmoil. Lord Beaumont wanted her, she could tell. He did *not* find her crippled and ugly. Before her eyes, he had fought his impulse to take her in his arms. If it were not for her disillusionment with him, she might, for the first time in her life, feel desirable, alive! But he had ruined everything, that liar!

Polly met her in the hallway. "Allegra's back. Where 'ave you been?"

"At the river with Lord Beaumont," Meg told her bluntly.

Polly gasped. "You didn't!"

"Yes, and we talked."

"But did he"—Polly searched for the words—"does he want you? You know wut I mean!"

"Want me? Yes, Polly, I believe he does. But he . . . ah, I cannot think properly right now."

"Well, when reason reigns in your 'ead again, what will you say?"

Meg drew a long breath and thought a moment. "When reason reigns in my head again, I shall realize that the handsome, witty, charming Lord Beaumont undoubtedly desires me with all the prescience and depth of emotion of an Algernon. The reality is, Polly, he is simply trifling with me. Why else would he deign to speak to a lady's maid?"

Richard stood looking after Meg until she disappeared from view. Only eighteen, but what a brave, strong, charming girl she was! Her story twisted his heart. He contemplated his own childhood. How terrible it would have been had he grown up without the love of his mother to sustain him. Even his father had cared, harsh though he was. Contrast his life to Meg's, who had grown up lonely, loveless, alone. God's blood! Hauling buckets of coal when she was six! He wished he could make it up to her. If it were within his power, he would buy her gowns, shoes, bonnets, fans—all the books she wanted. He would take her on the grand tour of Europe. He would—

What utter nonsense am I thinking? She would not even be at the river tomorrow, she had told him so. And yet . . .

As Richard stalked toward his horse, he knew he would be here waiting tomorrow. His lips twisted into a cynical smile. *More the fool me.*

Chapter 12

Meg hurried up the stairs toward Allegra's bed-chamber, bracing herself for a tirade. Stepping inside, she was relieved to see both Lady Semple and Lady Lydia seated on a Georgian gilt settee sipping tea, and Allegra, dressed in stockings and chemise, seated at her dressing table. She appeared not the least angry, but was, as usual, engrossed in herself, at the moment pinching her cheeks while gazing in the mirror.

"So there you are, Meg," Allegra remarked laconically, "wherever have you been?"

Before Meg could begin to answer, Lady Lydia cast a hostile glare and demanded, "Where indeed! Explain yourself, girl."

Meg knew she ought to bob and curtsy and murmur, "Sorry, ma'am," but after last night's nastiness she could not bring herself to do so. Instead, she took a deep breath to calm herself and coolly replied, "I found myself with spare time, so I went to the river."

Lady Lydia's face filled with suspicion. "Why the river? Your duty is here, looking after your mistress."

Lady Semple lightly tapped her folded fan on the skinny arm of her sister-in-law. "Oh, come, Lydia, Meg may be our servant, but must she be available every minute of the day?"

Lady Lydia's lips thinned in irritation. "Meg, fetch Lady Allegra's jewels."

While she went into Allegra's dressing room to fetch the casket, Meg heard Lydia fairly hiss, "There! Do you see what I mean? I'll wager that wanton girl has been dallying with one of the footmen, or perhaps a stable boy."

"That should not be our concern, do you think, Lydia?" Lady Semple had reverted to her timid voice.

"Indeed it is!" Allegra interjected. "What else does she have to do? The poor, crippled creature has no life of her own, nor should she have. Her only purpose is to serve me."

How dare they talk around her as if she weren't there? Biting her lip with frustration, Meg pulled the gilt-edged, tortoiseshell casket from the commode.

When she returned with the jewels, Lydia confronted her again. "Tell the truth, girl, were you alone at the river?"

Lady Semple murmured, "Lydia, I am not certain this is our concern."

"I shall handle this, Charlotte, you need not interfere." Lady Lydia glared at Meg. "The truth! Whom are you meeting at the river?"

Meg felt such outrage she decided to say exactly what she pleased, consequences by damned. But as she opened her mouth to speak, Lady Semple, who had been closely observing her, commanded swiftly, "Enough, Lydia," almost as if she realized what Meg was about to say. " 'Tis no sin to want to spend some time by oneself. Allegra, you said you wished to wear the green gauze? Meg, kindly fetch that."

"But—" Lady Lydia began.

"Enough! This is my house, I shall hear no more of it!" Lady Semple bobbed her head with firm resolve and snapped open her fan.

"Well, I must say!" Lady Lydia exclaimed indignantly, but to Meg's great satisfaction, took to fluttering her own fan and did not open her mouth again. How refreshing, Meg reflected, that for once Lady Semple had spoken in a forthright manner, not with the fainthearted hesitation usually present in her voice. Meg wondered if she, herself, had been in any way responsible. Had that timid lady taken her advice?

After the two ladies left, Meg helped Allegra into the green gauze gown. She was at the dressing table, teasing a single brown curl to fall over Allegra's prominent forehead, when Edward, carrying an apple, strolled into the bedchamber. Arranging himself on the chaise, he regarded his sister with a jaded eye. "I spoke to Richard. He accepts your invitation for dinner tonight."

"He had better." Allegra poked out her bosom, sucked in her stomach, and ran her hands lovingly over her gown. "He will adore me in this."

Although Allegra could not see it, Meg caught the look of derision that flashed through Edward's eyes. After a scoffing guffaw, he inquired, "Why bother? You could descend the staircase buck naked, I warrant Richard would not look twice."

Allegra gave a tiny gasp, jerked her head away from Meg's fingers, and peered around. "What an infamous remark! Explain yourself!"

"You goose! Surely you're not fool enough to think he really loves you." Edward polished the apple casually on his sleeve. "So don't put on airs."

Comb in hand, Meg stood still as a statue watching Edward take a bite of apple, seeming to relish each chew while Allegra's face grew increasingly redder. "Why would you say such a beastly thing?" she finally asked in a voice deceptively calm.

"Ask his mother." Edward swung himself off the chaise and sauntered toward the door.

"Don't you dare!" Allegra sprung from her chair and grabbed her brother's arm. "You shall not go anywhere until you tell me what Richard's mother has to do with this."

With an offhand shrug of defeat, Edward returned to the chaise and again addressed Allegra, this time omitting the smirk. "Surely you're aware the Countess of Montclaire is dying."

"Really?" Not looking the least distressed, Allegra put on a pout. "Richard never told me."

"Strange he didn't." Edward frowned in reflection. "But, then, again, perhaps not. At any rate, Richard felt obliged to make her some deathbed promises, one of which, dear sister, was to marry *you*."

Allegra clenched her fists. "You lie!"

Edward rolled his eyes heaven-wise. "Dish me, if you didn't always put on such airs, I wouldn't have told you. But surely you cannot for a moment have believed Richard really cares about you."

Through clenched teeth Allegra hissed, "That's exactly what I thought."

"God's blood!" Edward flung his apple core across the room, closely missing the fireplace. "You shall have his title and his fortune, what more do you want? Women! Never satisfied, always after what they cannot have, which is particularly true with you."

Contemptuously Allegra countered with, "My, my, Edward, full of vitriol today, aren't you? And willing to tell any lie?"

"You refuse to believe me?"

"Of all the arrant nonsense!"

Edward sighed. "I might have known. Very well, perhaps 'tis better you have no idea of the truth." He left, muttering, "Poor Richard. No wonder I shall remain forever a bachelor."

Throughout the unpleasant exchange, Meg had stood transfixed, grateful, for once, that as far as Edward and Allegra were concerned she had become part of the furniture. As for Edward's revelation, she was stunned. So Richard was not the greedy, lying rascal she had thought he was! How she had misjudged him! Her heart swelled with a longing to tell him so this instant.

She looked toward Allegra. During the short time she had been in the employ of this very spoiled young lady, she had learned enough to expect, at the very least, a vase hurled against the wall, or a throw-herself-upon-the-bed temper tantrum. But such was not now the case. For the longest time, Allegra stood strangely still, apparently deep in thought, a posture which for her was most unusual.

"Are you all right, m'lady?"

Allegra turned to her with blazing eyes. "You are not to breathe a word of what you heard, do you understand?"

"That goes without saying," Meg answered quietly.

Meg spent most of the night awake. It was most urgent that she talk to Richard, tell him she knew the truth! The next afternoon, as early as she dared slip away, she headed toward the river again. He would be waiting, he had said he would, and she knew he was! She could feel he was!

But hurrying down the path, past the yew trees, the thought struck her, *Why am I doing this?*

To meet him again was absolutely insane. Not only that, she had been warned. If Lady Lydia discovered her at the river again—meeting with Lord Beaumont!—she surely would be dismissed without a character. Not even Lady Semple could save her next time.

But I have not the will to resist.

It was as if an unseen force was controlling her body, propelling her legs. A force that ignored logic, propriety, sensibility, compelling her to act like some lovesick chit of a schoolgirl. How, she asked herself, could she be so wildly reckless?

Her life stretched before her—years left yet, of back-breaking labor from dawn to midnight without a word of thanks, recognition, or gratitude.

But what did that matter now? All she cared about was that he would be there. She would fling herself into his arms. Lydia—Allegra—the world—be damned, and then . . .

And then . . . what? Why have I not thought beyond this?

Reaching the path, she saw Thunder, riderless, tied to the low bough of a willow tree. So he *had* come, and was waiting at their secret place! Hand pressed hard against her heart, she felt compelled to stop by Thunder to catch her breath. *His horse.* Lovingly, she clasped the silver-trimmed bridle, burying her head in the black shining mane.

"What foolishness possesses me, Thunder?" she asked aloud. When she looked up, she discovered the horse had turned his head and was gazing at her with a questioning eye, as if asking, *what foolishness indeed?*

Like a cold, hard slap, a sense of sanity recaptured her agitated mind. What *had* she been after? A few fumbling moments of hot passion beside the River Wey? "Oh, Thunder, what am I doing here?" she cried. "When your master can give me nothing except . . ."

Watch you don't get a big belly! The ominous words of Mrs. Randall swirled in her head.

And where would I be then?

I cannot do this. Meg closed her eyes to shut the world out, consoling herself that life had not completely passed her by. At least she now knew what it was like to want a man, and to want him with so strong a passion it made her knees weak, made her burn to be enveloped in his arms, offer herself up to his caress.

"Oh, Richard, 'twill never work!" she cried. Bowing her head, she nuzzled deep into Thunder's mane one more time, then turned her back on the river. "Love is blind," she softly whispered, remembering a favorite line from Shakespeare, "and lovers cannot see . . . the petty follies that they themselves commit."

There was only a horse to hear. Eyes filled with tears, Meg straightened her cap and, never once looking behind her, followed the pathway back to Pentworth Park.

Chapter 13

She's not coming.

He leaned against the oak tree, arms folded tight against his chest. She had said she wasn't. In truth, had announced her decision loud and clear. He had hoped she hadn't meant it. Misplaced optimism, it now appeared; he should have realized Meg was loath to say things she didn't mean.

Now the sun cast long shadows, signaling he must return to Hartwick House, ready himself for dinner tonight at Pentworth Park—*again. Only the beginning,* the dreary thought struck him. Ahead lay a lifetime of dinners with Allegra. *Good God.* Quickly he turned his thoughts to Meg. He had wanted so terribly much to see her, so he could talk to her—feel those wise blue eyes intent upon him, laughing at him, catching his every weakness, yet aware of his strengths. Richard caught himself and laughed aloud. *You arrogant jackass,* he berated himself. Indeed, he found as much pleasure, if not more, in listening to *her.* If they ever met again, he would listen as long as she wished to talk. She could tell him the parts of her life she had never shared before. He felt his jacket pocket and broke into pained laughter. He had even brought a book of poetry, Lord Byron this time, in hopes she would read to him, and he would read to her. They would be Meg and Richard, if only for a little while. And, of course, just friends.

Richard returned to the path and untied Thunder from the branch of the willow tree. With an easy swing, he settled into the saddle and nudged the horse toward home. Flicking the reins, he reflected upon his feelings. Such lies he had told himself just now! *Just friends indeed.* "Thunder, you've a fool on your back," he remarked with cynical humor, absentmindedly patting his mount's smooth mane.

He could not deceive himself. It was more than talk he wanted from the servant girl, but for some reason he would not, could not, take advantage of her, even though the very thought of touching her turned his insides to water—a new, and rather miraculous, phenomenon, he reflected, considering the most beguiling of his demi-mondes had never made him feel like this before. Of course, Edward would have the best, most simple, solution: bed the wench until she bored him—then appease her with a trinket or two and be gone. *But I couldn't do that to Meg.*

He was a fool, yes, but a fool with honor. *And what is honor, pray tell?* he asked himself ironically. Naught but a cruel vise that held him to a path from which he otherwise would happily have strayed.

In an effort to distract himself, Richard threw himself into the zest of the gallop, thrilling to the sound of Thunder's pounding hoofbeats, to the joyous feeling of oneness with his horse as it streaked down the wooded path. But however fast they traveled, and however much he might wish with all his soul to forget a maid named Meg Quincy, Richard could not leave his thoughts of her behind.

Upon his return home, he stopped in to see his mother, dropping wearily into a chair beside her bed. Her color was better this evening. Head propped higher on the pillow, she even managed a weak smile.

"Mama, it appears you have improved," he remarked, happy his words held some truth this evening.

"Would that it were so," she remarked stoically, for once not having to gasp for breath, "but at least 'tis one of my better days. But you"—she examined him quizzically—"you are pale, and I see a strain on your face. Tell me what is wrong, son."

Blast! He had not intended wearing his misery on his sleeve for the world to see. "I shall be fine, Mama." Though he was loath to burden his sick mother with his troubles, he couldn't keep himself from adding, "Though 'tis not one of *my* better days!"

She eyed him shrewdly. "You're trying to make light of it, but there's something in your face—your voice. What's troubling you?"

"Nothing," he answered sharply, chagrined with himself for letting her suspect.

"Then, talk to me," she said, wisely shying away from a direct approach, "tell me all you did and thought today." She waited serenely, knowing that he knew that *she* knew sooner or later he would reveal all.

"I shall do naught but bore you," he began, bursting to speak of the subject foremost on his mind.

"Bore me." She gave him an encouraging smile.

"Then, I must confess, I have met the most intriguing young woman . . ." He described Meg—her wit, charm, love of poetry, merry laugh, golden curls, wise blue eyes—all of it without revealing her identity.

"She sounds delightful," his mother said when he had finished, "yet I cannot place her, though I vow, I thought I was familiar with the virtues of every young lady in the countryside."

He opened his mouth to say, *she is but a servant,* but the words stuck in his throat. "She . . . is recently removed from London, currently residing at Pentworth Park."

"Do you love this girl?" Ill though she was, Richard thought he detected a gleam of humor deep in his mother's eyes.

Richard thought a moment. "Love? In truth, I don't know. But if love means . . ." He paused, unwilling to reveal the depth of his feelings, yet desperate to let it all pour out. "You wish the truth?"

"Of course."

"I think of her constantly. I wake up in a sweat in the middle of the night, wanting her there, with me. Of course you cannot possibly understand this . . . this aberration. You—"

"Aberration!" Despite her grave illness, his mother drew herself half off the pillow. "Do you think I was raised in a nunnery? Born old? That I have no knowledge of the hot blood that runs in your veins when you're young?" She regarded him thoughtfully. " 'Tis more than lust that troubles you. Indeed, Richard, 'tis clear to me you love this girl. From the way you talk, there can be no doubt."

Richard squeezed his eyes shut. "God help me if you're right."

His mother fell back on the pillow and eyed him narrowly. "What of Allegra?"

"The marriage is arranged, is it not?" Richard responded bitterly. "Never fear, I shall fulfill my obligations."

"Need I remind you, Richard, you are *not* obliged to be madly in love with your betrothed."

"Of course. Mine won't be the first loveless marriage, nor the last."

" 'Tis difficult for you, I know." Lady Montclaire sighed and reached for his hand. "Perhaps in time you'll get this 'mysterious' girl out of your head and learn to love Allegra."

"No, no, never!" It was as if a dam had burst within him. Richard leaped from the chair and began pacing the floor. " 'Tis almost beyond my endurance! Bad enough that I can barely abide the thought of . . . of performing my husbandly duties with Allegra. But worse, 'tis Meg I want, and Meg I cannot have."

"Meg?" his mother inquired gently. "I know of no Meg at Pentworth Park . . ."

"Meg is a servant," Richard flung at her bluntly, weary

of the charade. "Allegra's lady's maid." He sat down again, propped his elbows on his knees, and dropped his forehead into his open palms. "So there you have it, Mama. Before you sits the most eligible bachelor in all London"—he laughed harshly—"witty bon vivant, expert horseman, lover of books and the cultured life, indeed, master of all he surveys. And what has he done?" He raised pained eyes to stare at his mother. "Gone daft over a servant girl. Damme!" Halting abruptly, he ran his hands through his hair and resolutely pulled his shoulders back. "Beg pardon for the outburst. No doubt I've shocked you, but never fear, I shan't let it happen again."

His mother was silent for a time. When she spoke, it was in a gentle, reasonable tone. "Dear Richard, though I'm but a woman sheltered all her life, I'm not unaware of how it is with a man. Don't think for a moment I was not apprised when you cornered your first scullery maid—"

"Peggy. She was fourteen, I was sixteen. I caught her in the washroom. Oh, she was willing enough, but still . . ." Richard made a face. "I used to boast, but now I am ashamed."

"My son!" his mother protested. "You were no different than other boys your age. You had only a few unsuitable dalliances, as I recall."

"More than enough. I now regret each and every one."

"But they were only serving girls!" Richard inwardly winced. Even his dearly beloved mother was hardpressed to understand. She continued, "And why should one more servant matter? If you're that fond of this Meg, could you not just—?"

"Bed her a few times, then be on my merry way?" Richard asked boldly. He was not accustomed to talking to his mother in this fashion, but there was no other way. "No, never."

"I see." Lady Montclaire spent a time in deep thought. "Then, it appears there is only one solution."

"Which is?" he inquired, puzzled. There were no solutions.

"I release you from your promise."

"Which promise?"

"Your promise to marry Allegra," his mother softly replied. "A loveless marriage is one thing, but I cannot bear to see such pain, such bitterness. 'Tis obvious your betrothal to Allegra is tearing you apart."

"But Father—"

"Your father will be disappointed, but 'tis not the end of the world. You must be freed from your promise. I shall handle your father. As for Meg, do what you wish with the girl, short of marrying her."

Richard shook his head ruefully. "A gentleman can *never* release himself from his betrothal."

"Rules can be broken. Do you or do you not want your freedom?"

Free? Not forced to marry Allegra? Richard could not believe such sublime bliss. He must wait for the words to sink in. Then he would decide what to do.

That night Richard arrived for dinner at Pentworth Park, looking cool as always: imperturbable countenance, impeccable dress. But inside, turmoil. He must ask Edward for his help, there was no way around it.

He had decided he must see Meg—it was imperative! But *how*? To arrange a meeting had seemed simple enough, but when he had begun to think on it, a near impossibility. How could the heir apparent of the Earl of Montclaire legitimately visit Meg Quincy, lady's maid? Appear at the entrance of Pentworth Park and simply send in his card? Despite his dilemma, he had shaken with mirth picturing the expressions on the faces of Allegra and Lydia should such an event occur. Almost worth the scandal!

What, then? He had seen Meg about the mansion only twice—once at the front entrance the day of the ball, again that night when the earl announced his betrothal. But both circumstances were unusual. She lived in the background; the chances of running into her again were slim.

Seeking out her room had at first seemed a fine solution . . . until he pictured himself sneaking along the dark hall of the servants' quarters, stealthily opening each door until he found hers. He would be caught, of course, and what possible explanation could he give? What embarrassment! And there again, scandal.

Or he could ask one of the servants—a solution tantamount to shouting his message from the rooftop. No, God help him, there was but one solution to his dilemma. He pulled a sealed letter from his pocket. "Edward, would you kindly deliver this message to Meg?" He waited, feeling the complete fool, more vulnerable than he had ever felt in his life before.

Though he had known Edward all his life, he had no idea how his old friend would react. Edward could be wisely sympathetic the one minute, mockingly derisive the next. If Edward took it upon himself to scoff . . . Richard clenched his fists. Best not to contemplate dire consequences.

Surprise crossed Edward's countenance, but only for a moment. Straight-faced, he took the envelope. "Of course, Richard, but may I ask—?"

"You may not."

"When shall I—?"

Now! "Any time. After dinner will do."

"But of course, old man." Edward slipped the letter into his pocket. "By the way, we are due a treat tonight. Cook has managed to obtain some Russian caviar."

"Indeed? My favorite."

Thank God for Edward, a true friend.

"What a turrible mess!" Polly bounced about Allegra's bedchamber, picking up discarded dresses Allegra had chosen not to wear. "Thought she'd never make up 'er mind."

Meg remonstrated, " 'Tis not up to us to question—"

"Never satisfied, always with that pout," the tiny maid mumbled on. "Now, if *I* 'ad a grand, 'andsome man like Richard, Lord Beaumont, comin' to dinner, there'd be a big smile on me face."

Meg gave a noncommittal "hmmm," aware of the jump of her heart at the mention of his name. Since she had turned her back on the river—was it only hours ago?—she had found it difficult to concentrate.

Peals of laughter floated up the staircase from the dining salon below.

"They must be 'avin a good time." Polly gave a disdainful sniff. "I can just see Lord Beaumont now—sittin' amid all that glitter 'n' splendor, Lady Lydia fawning over 'im on the one side, Lady Allegra snappin' at 'im on the other."

Meg had to laugh. Polly might be only a maid, but she was observant, as well as wise.

"Ain't it strange," Polly continued. "He may live in all that luxury, and get waited on 'and 'n' foot, yet I feel sorry for 'im."

Meg sniffed. "A waste of sympathy. Lord Beaumont makes his own choices. He can look after himself."

"Hmmm, I suppose you're right," Polly answered thoughtfully. " 'N' why should I care? 'E's only two flights of stairs below, yet 'e lives in a different world, don't 'e? We might as well be separated by the whole Atlantic Ocean."

Meg answered, "Polly, that is exactly right," reflecting that indeed, she and Richard were oceans apart. How right she had been to resist temptation this afternoon and turn away from the river.

The door swung open. Edward, peering stealthily around, stepped inside.

Meg put down her mending and stood. "Why, m'lord! Is not Lady Allegra downstairs?"

Edward came swiftly across the room, reached in his pocket, and brought out a letter, which he stiffly, and somewhat uncomfortably, extended to her. "From a friend."

She took the letter, examined it, and suppressed a tiny gasp of surprise at sight of the dark green spot of sealing wax impressed with an elaborate "B."

Edward spoke again, in an uncharacteristically hesitant fashion. "Well, then, . . . must return before Allegra finds me." He threw her an odd smile. "Nothing need be said, of course. You're aware what I mean."

Edward departed, after which Polly exclaimed, "Mercy on us! Wut did he give you?"

Meg did not reply, but stood clutching the envelope, staring at the green circle of wax. " 'Tis . . . nothing."

"Don' I get to see?"

Ignoring Polly, Meg sat down, holding the letter as if it were a piece of her ladyship's finest china. "Strange," she remarked, "no one ever sent me a letter before."

" 'Ow many friends do you have wut can write?"

Meg's heart began to pound as she turned the missive over and over in her hands. *From Richard—sealed with his very own signet ring!* She felt an urge to rip it open, yet knew if she were wise, she would touch this missive to the nearest candle and burn it to an ash. *If I were wise. But I am not wise,* she thought, as impulsively she broke the seal and unfolded the letter. Inside, penned in Richard's strong fine hand, were words she recognized from Shakespeare's *Julius Caesar*:

> And whether we shall meet again, I know not;
> Therefore our everlasting farewell take.
> For ever, and for ever, farewell Cassius!
> If we do meet again, why we shall smile;
> If not, why then this parting was well made.

Afterward was written one simple sentence:

Tomorrow at the river? For a parting well made.

Beaumont

She read the missive aloud to Polly.

Polly looked at her with awe. "I knew it! I thought somethin' was goin' on."

Meg nodded. "But not what you think. Lord Beaumont and I have developed a friendship. He simply wants me to meet him at the river tomorrow, doubtless to read poetry."

Polly cocked an incredulous eyebrow. "If you believe that, you are indade the village idiot."

Polly was right. Whom was she fooling? Meg thought carefully before she answered, "Probably." She gave a choked, desperate laugh and added, " 'Twould be sheer folly for me to go."

"You 'ave that right."

"So I shall not go."

"Are you sure?"

"Indeed I am sure." Meg crumpled the note and tossed it into the fireplace. "Rest easy, Polly. I am not the village idiot."

"What is it you want, Allegra?" asked Richard. They had finished dinner. She had pulled him into the library and closed the door. "Has this anything to do with the way you have been glaring at me all evening?" At least, Richard noted, she had toned herself down of late; she looked halfway presentable this evening in a modest dress of aerophane trimmed with creamed glacé silk, with which she wore a cream-embroidered stole. All thanks to Meg, no doubt.

"I went calling on your mother late this afternoon," Allegra announced.

"Do tell." How *dare* she visit his mother without telling him! He was hard put to keep a straight face. "So what did Mama have to say that has gotten you so cross?"

Her face flushed red and her eyes bulged, an unfortunate tendency he had first noticed the night she tossed the wine in his face. In a voice loaded with enmity, she continued, "It appears you made your mother a promise—"

"Allegra, please—"

"Don't interrupt! 'Tis bad enough you made it, now your mother informs me she has given you lief to break it!"

"Allegra—!"

"Is it true, Richard?" She was bristling now, fairly trembling. "Have you decided not to marry me?"

Incredibly Richard found himself feeling a pang of sympathy for this wretched girl. If only she could see her face, the otherwise fairly presentable features twisted into ugliness by nastiness and rage!

Meg had mentioned she and Allegra were both the same age. Hard to believe. Meg possessed a hundred times the intelligence, grace, charm, and maturity.

"Allegra," he answered gently, "come sit down with me." He led her to a settee, where she sat down, he beside her. "It is quite true," he began, "my mother released me from my promise to marry you. I must confess, at first I—" He paused long enough to shake his head. "Well, no matter. What matters is, in the Society in which we live, a gentleman may not release himself from his betrothal. If he did, he would bring dishonor and disgrace on both himself and his family. I am a man of honor, Allegra. I shall keep my word. We are betrothed, you and I. And we shall marry"—there he went again, nearly choking over the word—"as soon as possible."

"I want you to love me!" she demanded, her face growing even redder.

He paused for a deep sigh. "Perhaps in time . . . we shall develop a fondness for one another."

"I don't want fondness!" She flung herself off the settee. "I want love!" Fists clenched, she glared down at him.

"Then, in time you must look for it elsewhere." Now, he supposed, was as good a time as any to lay down the law. "Mind, however, how you conduct yourself. Don't think for a moment your little flirtations with the coachman, the groom, and, most particularly, my younger brother, have gone unobserved."

"Scurrilous lies!"

"You heard me," he continued coolly. "If nothing else, my wife shall be discreet."

She glowered at him. "And what will *you* be, my dear Lord Beaumont, the rake of London, seducing every doxy on the street?"

Whatever sympathy he had felt for his intended dissipated as fast as a fox streaking across a field. With great dignity, he arose from the settee and walked to the door. "Heed what I say, Allegra. I shall be a good husband to you in all matters except love. In return, you shall not muddy my name. Do I make myself clear?"

For an answer, she grabbed up a vase and flung it at him. It barely missed, but instead struck the wall beside him, where it shattered into a hundred pieces. *What a pity,* he thought as he turned away from Allegra's enraged visage and walked out the door. He knew for a fact Lord Semple had paid a small fortune for that vase in Singapore.

Wild-eyed, Allegra charged into her bedchamber. Once inside she stood rigid, fists clenched in front of her, so saturated with anger she couldn't move.

Meg set down her mending. "What is it, m'lady?"

"He refuses to do what I want!" Allegra fairly yelled.

"You seem distressed," Meg commented smoothly, "shall I summon Lady Semple?"

"You needn't bother." Allegra appeared to try to pull herself together, but instead reddened and fairly yelled, "He shall pay for this! I shall make him pay! I shall make them *all* pay!"

Meg silently recoiled at Allegra's vengeful words and the vicious way she'd spoken them. *How will you make him pay?* she wanted to ask, but thought better of it. Best not to encourage such vitriol. "Revenge is not always the best answer," she said quietly, knowing full well she had just overstepped her servant's bounds.

A triumphant smile crossed Allegra's face, more frightening because of the anger simmering behind it. "Revenge is *my* best answer, Meg. Now, get this dress off me."

Dutifully, Meg began to pull at the ties that fastened the dress together in the back. Allegra spoke again. "By the way, I spoke to Mama. She had informed me you would not be going with me to Hartwick House once I am married. Now she's changed her mind." She flashed a smile. "Aren't you pleased?"

Meg froze in surprise. "But I thought—"

"That you would remain here, at Pentworth Park? No, indeed! I persuaded Mama otherwise. Think how lucky you are, Meg. Your position is secure for years—for life, actually. As far as I'm concerned, you shall be my maid forever. Now fetch hot water and be quick. I wish to prepare for bed."

Chapter 14

"May I have a moment of your time, m'lady?"

Meg stood poised in the entrance of Lady Semple's sitting room.

The marchioness was seated at her harlequin desk, writing a letter. At the sight of Meg, her face lit with pleasure. "Come in, Meg."

"Lady Allegra just informed me"—Meg paused, making sure she held her outrage well in hand—"that I shall be accompanying her to Hartwick House after the wedding."

"Oh, dear." The marchioness's smile faded. "I was afraid to tell you. I so wanted you to stay here, but you know Allegra. She kept insisting, and I . . . I . . ."

Had not the courage to stand up for me, Meg finished silently. "You made me a promise," she said firmly.

"Oh, I know, and I am terribly sorry!" Lady Semple looked as if she were about to cry, an expression Meg had seen before, and pitied, but not this time.

"Sorry does not help, m'lady. I am weary of Allegra's frantic demands."

The marchioness dropped her gaze, unable to look Meg square in the eye. "I am trying. Twice now, I have taken your advice and stood up for myself. But 'tis so hard! You're aware how powerless I am when it comes to Allegra. She keeps begging me, beseeching me. If I tell her no, and mean it, she throws one of her tantrums, and you *know* how distressing that can be. No one can control her, except, perhaps . . . do you suppose Lord

Beaumont?" This new idea was obviously appealing. "Yes! If anyone can control Allegra, 'tis the viscount. I shall have a word with him, tell him to tell her—"

"No!" Meg could not see the point in causing this weak, timid woman any further distress. "Don't trouble yourself, m'lady. I shall ask him myself."

"You? Address Lord Beaumont?" Lady Semple's eyes widened. "But do you think that wise? And how—?"

"I have my ways." The shadow of a smile crossed Meg's countenance as she came to a decision. " 'Tis not as difficult as you might think."

Polly stared in surprise. "But, Meg, I saw you throw his note away! You said you wasn't goin' down to the river anymore—leastways, not to meet 'is lordship."

"I shan't be long, Polly. If anyone asks, tell them I am out collecting elderberries to darken Allegra's lashes."

"But why are you meetin' with 'im when you said—?"

"I refuse to trail behind Allegra wherever she goes, like some kind of pet poodle! Since Lady Semple cannot help, I'm forced to plead my case with Lord Beaumont, no matter how distasteful that notion is to me."

"Distasteful? Are you sure, Meg, you won't be the least bit glad to meet 'im again?"

"That . . . that has nothing to do with it. In truth, I resent having to ask Richard to intercede on my behalf. *Lord Beaumont,* I mean. He's not 'Richard' today, or tomorrow, or any other day from now to eternity."

"So you don't like 'im, then?"

"I *do* like him, but my only purpose in meeting him is to beg his assistance in helping me escape the clutches of Allegra." Had she told a lie? Meg asked herself guiltily. Despite her resolution, she found herself eager to see Richard again.

When Meg reached the path, she found Thunder tied to the same willow bough as yesterday. But unlike yesterday, this time she would not turn back. She cut through the bushes toward the river. Just as the flowing ribbon of water came into view, she spied him gazing moodily out over the water, back against the tree, arms folded across his chest. She halted, lost in admiration of his dark, handsome face and lean, muscular figure. Finally she drew closer and inquired lightly, "Lord Beaumont, I presume?"

He swung around, assuming his usual implacable expression, but not before she caught an unguarded look of relief flash through his eyes. "Miss Quincy," he replied, mocking her formality, effecting a courtly bow. "I was not sure you would come."

"How could I stay away," she asked lightly, "drawn as I was by that lovely quote from Shakespeare?"

He broke into a smile warmer than ever she'd seen on his face before. Today she must be viewing him through different eyes, she decided, for he looked nothing like the arrogant lord she had, 'til lately, thoroughly despised. More than ever she was keenly aware of his lively dark eyes, so at odds with his past rigid manner.

"Ah," he said, "so you recognized the bard."

She feigned astonishment. "How utterly amazing that a poor, ignorant servant girl like myself would have the audacity to recognize Shakespeare. I *must* remember my place."

"We have already agreed you don't know your place, so kindly refrain from trying to fool me." He smiled back.

"I'm not trying to fool anyone," she said, unsmiling, abruptly ending their sparring game. She was suddenly aware she had been so intent on her quest to escape Allegra, she had overlooked her vow of yesterday to stay away from him, and the reasons why. Those reasons now came flooding back to her. Strange that they didn't hold the same importance as before. She must keep reminding herself how easy it would be to be trapped by his compelling charm. "I have a favor to ask. 'Tis the only reason I came."

His face became unreadable again. He leaned against the tree, recrossed his arms, gazed at her thoughtfully. "You did not come to the river yesterday."

"Obviously not."

"I was expecting you."

She considered a variety of flimsy excuses. They all would be lies, though. Better stick with the truth. "I own it freely, I came as far as the path yesterday. Then I changed my mind because you ... I ... oh, Richard!" she cried in exasperation. "This is all so ridiculous!"

His stare drilled into her. "Why did you come today? Was it only for the favor?"

No, it was not! But she did not dare tell him that. It would lead to further conversation, and she knew that if she was to keep her sanity, as well as her virtue, she must flee from him as soon as possible. " 'Twas only for the favor."

What remained of the eagerness that lit his face faded away, replaced by a grim mouth and a distinct hardness around the eyes. "Of course, Meg." His voice was tight, distant. "How may I be of assistance?"

"This morning Allegra informed me ..." She laid out all facts regarding this morning's conversation, refraining from any hint of vituperation against either Allegra or Lady Semple.

Richard listened attentively, a guarded expression stealing over his face as her intent became clear. When she finished, he emitted a harsh laugh and asked amusedly, "You have no desire to live at Hartwick House? I am crushed!"

Although it was easy to discern that this laugh was only halfhearted, Meg retorted, "This is no time for shallow jokes." It seemed her sense of humor had vanished.

He too grew serious. "Cannot Lady Semple intervene?"

"She ... uh ... she simply cannot," Meg stumbled, loathe to deprecate the marchioness in any way. "I don't wish to continue working for Allegra, and I should much appreciate your making that clear to her."

"I shall have a word with her," he said in a voice so remote she could have been a stranger. "Will there be anything else?"

"No. I am most grateful." Without thinking, Meg dropped a curtsy.

"God's blood!" he exploded, black brows fierce over his dark eyes. "Don't curtsy to me!"

Startled, she recoiled. "But m'lord—"

"And don't 'm'lord' me, either."

She had never seen him so angry. But why? She cocked her head and regarded him curiously. "Why the rage over a silly curtsy? After all, I am a servant, remember? I am supposed to curtsy, although I must admit that last curtsy was from habit and not intended. When you have curtsied hundreds, no, thousands of times, you simply do it by rote without thinking about it. You—"

"Enough! I'll hear no more talk about witless curtsies," he thundered at her. "I find a maidservant's curtsies to be so . . . so . . ."

"Subservient?" she evenly supplied. "You think I enjoy it? You think I like to dip and fawn to the likes of some smelly, drunken old lord trying to ogle down my bodice?"

Richard drew himself up, his vexation evident. "Smelly? Drunken? Is that what you think of me?"

Meg jammed both hands on her hips. "I vow, you have lost your sense of humor." Hearing herself on the verge of stridency, she softened down. "What is wrong? Why are we quarreling like this?"

"Leave it at that," he snapped, his expression still clouded with anger.

He turned to leave, but in a moment of impulse she reached out and lightly gripped his sleeve. "Whatever is the matter?"

Was it her imagination or had he trembled at her touch? He yanked his arm away and whirled around. Muttering an oath she could not hear, he retraced his steps to the oak tree. There, hands jammed in his pockets, he again directed his gaze out over the river.

She waited for him to speak. When he did, he spoke quietly, still looking the other way, in a voice near hoarse with intensity.

"I tremble at your touch. I keep thinking of you. I cannot sleep, thinking of you."

A shock ran through her. Never had she thought! Frantically she searched for a proper answer. "Pray, do not think of me." He whirled to face her, wearing such a scowl it startled her, but she continued calmly, "I regret you cannot sleep, but—"

"What would you suggest?" he asked, his voice filled with cynicism. "A soupçon of laudanum?" He took a deep, shaky breath in an obvious effort to regain his composure. "You had best go, Meg. Get back to your duties."

"Indeed I shall. You are betrothed, m'lord. This is hardly appropriate."

He gave her a look so piercing her heart leaped. "Perdition! Who cares what is appropriate!"

"I care," she began, but before she could continue, he took two long, swift strides back to her, clasped her arms in a viselike grip and pulled her to him roughly, almost violently. "Never in my life have I met a woman like you," he murmured in a ragged whisper.

How could this be happening? She, who had always considered herself the mistress of her emotions. Now, despite herself, she felt her insides jangling with excitement. She should break away, turn and run—yes, flee! But it was becoming more difficult by the second to remember yesterday's reasons for staying away from him. The warmth of his arms was so male that her knees were going weak. Instead of fighting, she relaxed, sinking into his cushioning embrace, the musk of his honey-water fragrance teasing her nostrils, his breath warm and moist against her cheek. Her heart raced as, for a moment, they swayed together, her soft curves molding to the contours of his lean body. Then, just as suddenly, he broke away.

"God's oath!" he cried. "What am I thinking of?" After a silence, he appeared to pull himself together. "Ah, Meg," he began amusedly, "it appears you have bewitched me." His gaze riveted on her face, he ran his hands lightly up her arms. "Do you know how beautiful you are? How funny? How brave? When I'm away from you, I picture the way you tilt your head, the way you smile. I hear your voice, as lilting as this brook at our feet, reading me poetry with such feeling, such passion, I cannot help but crave more."

He covered her hands with his own and raised them to press tenderly against his cheek, and in a softer voice proclaimed, "I don't mean to distress you. You're so wise, I forget you're so young. Tell me, have you ever . . . ? No!" He stopped himself abruptly. " 'Tis not my place to ask. Have no fear. I wouldn't dream of hurting you."

"What do you want from me?" she asked, puzzled.
"Must I explain again? You are a noble; I am a servant. We are worlds apart and always shall be. 'Tis hopeless!"

He stood looking at her with burning eyes that held her still. Surely here was her chance to flee, but her feet refused to budge from the spot, further evidence she had lost her iron control. Worse, she knew he sensed it. "Richard, this is foolish," she exclaimed urgently.

"Are we really worlds apart, Meg?" With tender urgency, he swept her into the circle of his arms again, pulled her close, and scattered kisses on her cheeks, her forehead, and then her mouth. At first, he caressed it more than kissed it, then took it with such a savage intensity she could not help but let her body relax, cling to him, and eagerly kiss him back.

Snap!

The sharp sound of a twig breaking, followed by a shrill, agitated female voice exclaiming, "Lord Beaumont, I am shocked!" ended the passionate moment.

Meg gave a sharp gasp as they leaped apart. She spun around, as did Richard. It was Lady Lydia!

After an initial intake of breath, Richard was the first to recover. "Good afternoon, m'lady," he said coolly, bending in an exaggerated bow. "Out for a stroll? I daresay 'tis a lovely day for it."

At first the aging spinster could do nothing but sputter and glare at them with burning, reproachful eyes. "You may see fit to discuss the weather, but you do not fool me, sir," she declared forcefully. "I saw what you were doing with my own eyes!"

"What you did or didn't see, madam, is none of your affair."

"Do not concern yourself, Lord Beaumont. You may be guilty of poor judgment, but you're not the one to blame." Lydia turned venomous eyes on Meg and spat out contemptuously, " 'Tis this . . . this *trollop* who is at fault! Lord Semple shall hear of this. My mealymouthed sister-in-law may have protected you before, Meg, but I vow, this time her ladyship cannot save you." Her lip curled into a sneer. "Whatever made you think you could dillydally with Allegra's betrothed and get away with it? You, with your insolence, your haughty airs. Well, I cannot bear another day of it. I assure you, Miss High-and-Mighty, tomorrow you shall be gone."

Still seething, Lady Lydia paused to take a breath, giving Richard a chance to address her. "I suggest you leave," he said, his voice deadly calm.

"Indeed I shall," came Lydia's acid response. "Meg, I would strongly advise you cut short your . . . your cheap *tryst* and return to Pentworth Park immediately. You won't have much time to pack your box after I inform his lordship of your shameful behavior." With a final, disdainful sniff, Lady Lydia spun on her heel and strode away.

The pair stood silently watching until the figure of Lady Lydia disappeared. "Damme!" Richard exploded. "That cursed woman—are you all right?"

Meg struggled to recapture her composure. "I'm fine, considering I have just been called a trollop." She managed a weak laugh. "And dismissed besides!"

Richard took her hands. "Have no fear. I shall speak to Lord Semple and explain—"

"What is there to explain?" Meg cried out bitterly. "Lady Lydia is right, is she not? Can you deny what she saw? I *was* in your arms—you *were* kissing me."

"Lord Semple overruled Lydia once before when I asked. Surely he will again. She's nothing but a poor relation, surely not in charge."

"But she is!" Meg responded vehemently. "Lydia rules that household with an iron hand. Her brother usually lets her have her way—much easier, I can assure you, than risking her ill will. As for Lady Semple, the poor woman is so intimidated, she's afraid to stand up to Lydia. Oh, what's the use?" Meg threw up her hands and started away. "I must get home—pack my box—say my good-byes."

Richard reached for her, and though she tried to pull away, refused to let her go, clasping her upper arms firmly. "Listen to me, Meg," he commanded, a sheen of purpose in his eyes. "I'm the cause of this, and I shall not have you suffering on my account." He pulled her close, cupped the back of her head with his hand and stroked her hair. "You needn't worry, I shall take care of you. You shall come with me to London. I shall set you up in a fine house on Doughty Street. You won't want for anything. You'll have your own carriage, jewels, and new clothes. You'll—"

"Be a light-skirt?" Meg broke vehemently from his embrace feeling a blush of humiliation creep over her cheeks. "Do you think I can be bought?! Just because I am poor, sir, just because I am a servant, does not mean I have the morals of an alley cat."

"But, Meg—"

"And for how long would this arrangement last, m'lord?" she demanded with mocking sarcasm. "Until I get a big belly? What will happen to the flat, the carriage, the jewels, the fine clothes then? Well, I wager they'll go to the next demimonde on your list, and I shall end up in the workhouse!"

"Not true, Meg," he began, but she had heard enough. She turned and started running.

"Leave me alone!" she called over her shoulder. "I want nothing to do with you—ever!"

Richard stood watching her. *You idiot!* he chastised himself. In his haste, he had acted like an unthinking oaf. What had gotten into him? Any fool would have known she would be insulted, but he had been so eager to help— no, face it, so eager to *possess* her—the words had just popped out. He could go after her . . . but she was so angry right now, she would be bound to reject him. So what should he do? "Let her go," he could hear Edward advising him, " 'tis by far the easiest thing, old boy, and the logical thing to do."

But he could not be logical when it came to Meg, perhaps because each encounter with her, including this latest, had put his ordinarily well-organized thoughts into a state of turmoil. One thing he did know, he concluded, as he stood watching her figure retreat from view, was she had not seen the last of him, nor he of her.

Meg returned to the manor in such a state of devastation, she could hardly digest the significance of Richard's kiss and its distressing aftermath. She had lost her position—of that there could be no doubt. Worse, the man whose arms had encircled her, who had caused her heart to pound, her body to ache for his touch, had just grossly insulted her.

Perhaps she was acting the fool. No doubt, many a poor girl in service would think it a dream come true if asked to become the mistress of a rich, handsome, brilliant nobleman. But for her, it was the ultimate insult. How could he!

She recalled the crush of his embrace, and that fire that swelled within her when he had showered her with kisses. That rake! She choked back a sob just thinking on it. Leaving here would be a blessing, even if she really did end up in the workhouse. She would be better off never seeing him again.

For a guilty moment she saw herself through Lady Lydia's eyes—wallowing in the hot embrace of Allegra's fiancé, returning his kisses with lustful eagerness, enjoying the stolen moment as much as he. No wonder Lydia was in a rage!

But guilt was a useless emotion. Thanks to her recklessness, she now faced a bleak future.

She sped through the mansion's mahogany-paneled hallway, bent on getting to her room as soon as possible. Passing the library, she stopped short, startled by a shrill female voice that she could hear distinctly through the closed doors. Lady Lydia, of course. To whom was she speaking? Meg had never sunk to the level of the many servants who eavesdropped, but a force beyond herself compelled her to glance up and down the hallway; then, seeing no one around, she moved to the door. Listening carefully, she heard the softer, quieter voice of Lady Semple.

"My dear Lydia, surely you are mistaken."

"She was in his arms," came Lady Lydia's near-hysterical response. "I nearly fainted from the shock of it. He was smearing her with kisses, and she, the cunning baggage, was kissing him back."

Meg could almost see the self-righteous spinster, half swooning by now, collapsing upon the couch, fanning herself vigorously.

"She what, Lydia?" came Lady Semple's slightly incredulous voice.

"She was enjoying it as much as he. Disgusting! Disgraceful! She must leave, Charlotte. I want that girl out of here tomorrow. Otherwise, she will doom Allegra's chances."

After a long pause, Meg heard the marchioness reply, " 'Tis not so simple as you would suppose, Lydia. Have you forgotten Meg is my daughter?"

Meg blinked her eyes. What was this? Surely she could not have heard correctly. The words were slightly muffled through the door, so that would explain . . .

"Stop reminding me!" came Lydia's blistering response. "I am sick and tired of your whining, Charlotte. You will never acknowledge the risk I took for you when Meg was born. What would you have done if 'twere not for me? What thanks do *I* get? None! All you do is pester me, trying to make me feel guilty for a thoroughly generous act on my part; one that most assuredly needed to be done."

"Did it?" Lady Semple's voice was louder now. Meg, her heart pounding, continued to listen, nearly paralyzed with astonishment. "You will recall that at the last moment I changed my mind, and that it was then you cruelly forced my baby away from me."

"Poppycock! I did what was best for you. I . . ."

Meg could stand it no longer. So numb she hardly knew what she was doing, she pushed open the library door and nearly stumbled inside. As if at a great distance she heard her own voice addressing Lady Semple. "I was outside . . . m'lady, is it true?"

Lady Semple clasped her hand to her heart and sprang from the couch. "Oh, Meg, you heard?"

Lydia heaved herself off the couch, red with rage. "Leave us at once, Meg," she demanded. "I shall not have you—"

"Kindly lower your voice, Lydia," Lady Semple requested, her own voice low, constrained. "If you don't, we shall be the talk of the servants' quarters."

"I warned you not to bring her here," hissed Lydia. "I predicted doom and disaster, did I not? Now look what has happened."

Lady Semple's eyes locked with Meg's. "She deserves

to know the truth," she told her sister-in-law without deigning to look at her. "I must explain."

"I suppose"—Lydia paused, biting her lip as if in deep thought—"if you must assuage your guilt, what matter whether she knows or not? What could she do? I take it you have no intention of letting the whole world know, especially Cyril." Her faded blue-gray eyes gleamed with malice. "Am I correct, Charlotte?"

"Unfortunately, yes," the marchioness answered grimly. Taking Meg by the elbow, she continued, "Please come sit down, my dear, you look pale."

Indeed, Meg had felt the blood rushing from her face. Now her knees felt weak whilst her heart pounded ferociously. She allowed herself to be led to a settee and sank upon it, her eyes never leaving Lady Semple's face. Nothing had as yet sunk in. Half in a daze, she asked, "Did I hear correctly? You gave birth to me?"

"Lydia, will you leave us please?" asked Lady Semple.

With a scornful toss of her head, Lydia left the chamber. Lady Semple sat beside Meg and gently took her hand. "I know this will be difficult, and that you will doubtless never forgive me, but I must tell you a story. It happened eighteen years ago, here at Pentworth Park, on a warm summer's day . . ."

"Bear down, your ladyship! Bear down and push!"

The pain hit hard. Charlotte felt a desire to scream but fought it back. She reached above her head to grip the back slats of her four-poster bed, clenched her teeth, and bore down, allowing herself one long, low groan.

"Very good, m'lady. I can see the baby's 'ead just now."

"What is taking so long, Mrs. Chester?" she cried. "You would think the fifth would simply drop out." Wearily she wiped the back of her hand across her forehead. " 'Tis so hot!"

" 'Twon't be long now." Plump, gray-haired Mrs. Chester smoothed back the damp, tangled strands of her ladyship's golden hair, wiping away beads of perspiration. Then she busied herself at the foot of the bed. "Ooo, look there. Its little 'ead's comin' down just now, m'lady. But 'tis not dark like the others. 'Tis a little blond head this time. A girl, no doubt, m'lady! After four boys, I wager 'is Lordship would be pleased with a girl."

Lady Lydia entered the room. "His lordship is partial to boys," she quickly corrected Mrs. Chester. "Normal boys, that is," she added in a venomous way. "I trust no surprises are in store. Do you not agree, Charlotte?" she inquired after a nasty little laugh.

Lydia's words caused a clench of consternation and anguish in Charlotte's heart. Ever since the birth of her firstborn son, each subsequent birth had brought with it a chilling fear.

Ah, William! Such a dear little boy. Even now, she could see his bright blue eyes and sweet smile. And so smart! William had talked early—walked early, too—and could read by the age of three. A perfect child, except . . .

Charlotte's heart still wrenched remembering that awful moment when Mrs. Chester held her firstborn high and a little twisted foot was exposed. First came shock, then, when she thought of her proud, perfectionist husband, fear. From the very first moment, she had known Cyril would reject this crippled child. How right she had been! Cyril, his male pride wounded, could hardly bear to have William in his sight. Never once had he kissed the child, held him on his lap, or tossed him playfully in the air as he eagerly did his next three sons who, mercifully, were born normal.

"William is but a little boy," she had pleaded countless times. "Can you not show him some affection like you do the others?" Sometimes she could not keep tears from her eyes. "Granted, he's crippled, but he is still your *son*! He loves you. He's so hurt when time after time you give him that blank, cold stare and turn away."

"I cannot countenance a crippled heir" would come

Cyril's unyielding response. "Keep the child out of my sight." Then he would glare at her with flat eyes. "This is entirely your fault, Charlotte. Had you but warned me about your uncle. . . . Ah, well, at least my other sons have not been affected with your uncle's abnormality."

What could she say? The bitter truth was, Cyril was right. Though she had never given it a thought, she had known her uncle was born with a clubfoot. *Her* family—and therefore *she*—was responsible for the tragedy of William's twisted foot.

Poor lonely little boy, no wonder he had died when he was twelve. They said it was consumption, but Charlotte knew better. Being the smart, sensitive child he was, William had sensed early in his short life that no matter how hard he tried, his father did not want him. Only to herself had Charlotte admitted the bitter truth of it: Her little William, his spirit crushed time and time again, had died of a broken heart.

Please, Lord, don't let it happen again. Throughout the next three births, and now this one, she had prayed this fervent prayer. If she bore another crippled child, its fate would be to be shunned and belittled. And how could she herself bear more knife-edged remarks from Cyril that made it clear he held *her* responsible?

It will all go well, Charlotte reassured herself. No sense going off corkle-brained; she was too worried by half. She deserved for things to go well—had, after all, presented Cyril with three fine, normal sons.

Lydia flipped open her fan and began fanning herself. "You are worried about having another clubfoot, are you not, Charlotte? I can see it in your eyes."

A pity Lydia had just returned from a few months' stay on the Continent! There was no doubt her hateful sister-in-law was hoping for the worst. If only Lydia had children of her own—at least then she may have shown some sympathy, may have known what it was like to live through nine months of ever-mounting dread.

Charlotte glared at her, for once making no attempt to

hide her distaste. "Will you kindly leave, Lydia? I do not need you here." Never before had she been so blunt with Cyril's sister, but today she didn't care.

Lydia's nostrils quivered with resentment. "Very well, I shall be outside. Cyril should be home from hunting soon. Let us hope you have good news."

Was that a threat? With the utmost disquiet, Charlotte watched her sister-in-law leave the bedchamber. No time to ponder on it, though. Here came another wave of pain—so wrenching it made her grasp the back rails.

"Push, m'lady!"

"Goodness, how can I *not*?" she cried. She was almost there, groaning, shoving through that intense final agony she had experienced many times before. It continued for what seemed like forever until suddenly there was a long, sliding woosh! and out slipped the baby. Charlotte heard a slap, followed by a lusty wail. With her remaining strength, she raised her head off the pillow. "What is it, Mrs. Chester? Pray, tell me! Hold the baby up so I can see."

"A girl, your ladyship!" Mrs. Chester sang out glee-fully. Charlotte could just see the top of the midwife's white muslin cap bobbing up and down. "Cutting the cord, your ladyship. You have a fine little girl . . . so fair . . . just wait 'til 'is lordship . . . *oh, 'pon my word, oh, dearie me.*"

Through a haze of dread Charlotte heard herself asking, "What is it, Mrs. Chester, is something amiss?"

Shaking her head, clucking in sympathy, Mrs. Chester held up a blond, fair-skinned, lustily wailing baby girl. " 'Tis a sweet babe, m'lady, but look, 'er little foot's misshapen—twisted around. What a pity, though 'tis not as bad as poor little William's."

"Clubfooted," Charlotte repeated in a horrified whisper. "A girl and clubfooted." Tiny black dots started swarming before her eyes. They grew steadily larger until they all meshed together and, mercifully, she fainted dead away.

* * *

When Charlotte opened her eyes, she found the baby washed, wrapped in a soft blanket, and tucked into the crook of her arm. Lydia stood over her. Mrs. Chester was gone.

"So you have done it again," Lydia said in a harsh, ringing voice. "Another cripple. How could you do this to Cyril?"

Charlotte tried to arise to a sitting position, but fell back exhausted, half whispering, "Perhaps he will love this one—"

"Do not count on it!" Lydia raged. "Was it too much to ask that you produce fine, strong sons? How can you possibly think Cyril could accept this child—crippled, and a girl? This time he will never forgive you."

A shiver of fear ran through her at the very thought of Cyril's endless anger. From the child came a mewing sound. Charlotte let out a tormented moan and reached a finger to stroke gently the baby's tiny nose. "My first little daughter," she whispered, "oh, what have I done?" She cast pleading eyes at her sister-in-law. "Help me, Lydia. She is but a helpless, innocent baby. Perhaps when he sees her—"

"Help you?" Lydia cut in, laughing bitterly. "Why should I help you? I, who have been not much more than a servant to your high-and-mighty ladyship all these years!" Then Lydia seemed to calm herself, though her eyes still held a hateful glimmer. "But there is a way out, Charlotte, if only you do as I say."

"Tell me!" Charlotte begged, her mind still dazed and unbelieving.

"Listen carefully," Lydia began, "I've been talking with Mrs. Chester. She informs me that this very morning she attended one of the scullery maids at Hartwick House who had got herself with child. The girl died of a bloody flux, but the baby lived." Lydia's eyes bored into Charlotte's. "The baby is a girl. Brown-haired, brown-eyed, straight of limb."

The unthinkable slowly dawned in Charlotte's mind. "Lydia, do I hear you correctly? Are you suggesting—?"

"I am *telling* you we shall exchange babies. It is the only way. Mrs. Chester can make the switch and be back within the hour. I have cautioned her to be discreet, but there's no cause to worry. The doxy had hidden her condition, so it was unbeknownst to anyone until today."

Charlotte regarded Lydia with suspicion. "Why are you doing this?"

"Don't deceive yourself that it's for you," Lydia answered harshly. "I would rather die than see my dear brother humiliated again."

Of course, Charlotte should have known. Lydia possessed a fanatical attachment to her brother. He could do no wrong, as far as she was concerned, and she had so far spent her life attempting to please him. Charlotte squeezed her eyes shut, as if to block out her growing despair. The solution Lydia suggested was dreadful. Frantically, she searched her mind for an alternative solution but could find none.

As if reading her thoughts, Lydia spoke again, softer now, as if she actually possessed a modicum of understanding. "Face the truth, Charlotte. Do you really want this baby to grow up shunned and unloved like William? Any other sort of life would be better for the child."

"Where will you take her?" Charlotte asked, choking over the sob that rose in her throat.

"Don't ask," Lydia replied impatiently. "All you need know is that the child will be safe on a large estate. We will explain that the child is a scullery maid's by-blow, and when she grows older, she can be trained for some sort of servant's work."

Lydia was right. Charlotte asked herself how could she possibly relive the agony of those twelve years William was alive. How could she allow her precious baby to face a parent who didn't love her—nay, despised her? Cyril would be cold and cruel—even more so this time, because this newborn was a girl, and Cyril had no use for girls.

But that wasn't all. Charlotte cringed at the memory of all those years spent vainly trying to appease Cyril. How obsequious she had been! Ignoring his harsh attitude—always begging for a smile, a kind word—trying to avoid misery and arguments at all costs. Too much! She could never go through all that again.

Sick at heart, Charlotte responded in a quaking voice, "All right, but no one must ever know."

Lydia smiled faintly. "Leave it all to me." She left the room and within the hour returned with Mrs. Chester, who was carrying a tiny bundle. "We have brought your little daughter," Lydia said, and reached to take the crippled newborn out of Charlotte's arms.

Grief and despair suddenly struck Charlotte's heart. How could she bear to let her daughter be spirited away? In one last desperate gambit, she decided she would throw herself on Cyril's mercy—or tell some lie—anything but let her baby go. She clutched the warm little bundle tighter. Over a sob, she cried, "No, no!"

"Don't be a dunce, Charlotte." Moving swiftly, Lydia snatched the fair-skinned baby from Charlotte's grasp before she could move. Lydia quickly switched tiny bundles with Mrs. Chester and proceeded to press a crying, dark-haired newborn into Charlotte's unwilling arms. "Here is your new daughter. Looks much like Cyril, don't you agree? So like him with that dark hair and olive skin. Not to mention the straightness of her little limbs."

Charlotte knew that Lydia spoke the truth. It would be best for all—Cyril, her daughter, and yes, herself—if she let her imperfect child go. Otherwise, only a path of misery for all lay ahead. Still, she reached out a shaking arm toward her child. "Wait! She must have a name."

"Hmm . . ." For a moment Lydia seemed to ponder, then turned to the midwife. "What is your given name, Mrs. Chester?"

"Me, m'lady? 'Tis Meg."

"The scullery maid's name was Eliza Quincy," Lydia continued, "So, Meg Quincy. Is that good enough for you?"

"Meg Quincy," Charlotte whispered, looking toward her child. "I shall always love you, Meg. I shall always—"

"Don't be maudlin, Charlotte," Lydia interrupted. "Mrs. Chester, take the baby home with you. I then shall make arrangements to remove her from Pentworth Park." She turned back to her sister-in-law. "I shall leave you now. You can get acquainted with your daughter—why not call her Allegra? It's a name I've always fancied."

Alone again, Charlotte looked down at the dark-haired baby that was not her own. It was crying. Charlotte turned her head away. She had no desire to comfort this stranger.

Lady Lydia wasted no time in ordering that the deformed child be swiftly and secretly removed to Auberry Hall near Cambridge, beside the River Cam, where, living in regal splendor, dwelled her cousins, the Earl and Countess of Wallingford.

Chapter 15

". . . So now you know, Meg, why I nearly fainted in London last month when I heard your name. You and Cousin Caroline helped me to a chair, remember? When I opened my eyes and said I was fine, you smiled. Oh, how my heart leaped! 'Twas William's smile. Not only that, you had the exact look of Edward about your eyes! At that moment, I knew that before me stood my own true child."

Throughout the revelation, Meg had sat unmoving, increasingly shocked by the unfolding tale of incredible deception. Words wedged in her throat, but she managed, "So that's why you insisted I become Allegra's lady's maid?"

"Of course! I was beside myself with joy. After all those tortured years, at last I had found you. I had never imagined you were so bright—caring—pretty." Charlotte fondly trailed her fingers along Meg's cheek. "Nay, not pretty, beautiful. Spirited, too, and independent, despite your humble status, despite the limp. I had no intention of losing you again."

Tenderly Lady Semple covered Meg's hands with her own bejeweled ones. "There's been a weight upon my heart since the day you were born. Not a day has passed I haven't remembered my beloved, lost child. A day? Never an hour—never a minute—hardly a second—has gone by without my regretting my despicable moment of weakness that allowed Lydia to spirit you away."

"Did you ever look for me?" asked Meg, somewhat forlornly.

Lady Semple shook her head. "Time and again I wondered what had become of you, but it was fruitless to ask. Lydia would never tell me. Besides, even had I found you, what could I do? The dye was cast, Allegra was my daughter now."

"How cruel of Lydia to keep my whereabouts a secret!" Meg burst out in a fury.

"Lydia is not known for her spirit of benevolence." Charlotte sighed. "I consider my sister-in-law the cross I must bear. No husband, no children—the poor woman is embittered by jealousy and an unfulfilled life."

"My lady, you are too kind to her by far!" Meg protested.

"Oh, I have not always been this kind! I cannot tell you how many times I blamed, and hated, Lydia. But every time I did, I reminded myself the ultimate guilt lay with me. If only I had possessed the courage to stand up to her! If I had, I would not have lost my daughter."

"But what of Allegra?"

Charlotte squeezed her eyes shut, as if the very thought was painful. "I did my best by Allegra—gave her everything my own true daughter would have had, except for one thing: love. The sad truth is, I never loved Allegra, not from that very first day. Oh, I tried countless times, tried even harder when I realized she sensed my lack of attachment. But from the beginning, Allegra was a loud, selfish, willful, mean-spirited brat whom I could barely tolerate. Everyone admires my earnest endeavors to marry off Allegra, but little do they know!" Lady Semple gulped hard to keep her tears in check. "It was far from motherly love that motivated me. I could hardly wait for the day when Allegra would become a husband's responsibility, not mine, and she would be gone from Pentworth Park forever."

The door opened. Lydia walked in with an inquisitive frown. "Well, Charlotte?"

"Yes, she knows!" Lady Semple cried, "I am overcome with remorse over my actions!"

"Try feeling gratitude instead," Lydia replied with a haughty sniff, "gratitude to me, as well as to that scullery maid who by chance birthed a girl the very same day." She peered down her nose at Meg. "I trust you realize Lady Semple took the only sensible course. You should be grateful. My brother eschews cripples—cannot *bear* to have them in his sight! Had I not intervened, you would have had a miserable life."

Sudden anger surged within Meg at the abrasive woman who stood glowering at her from across the room. *Aunt Lydia.* What irony! Here was a woman of her own flesh and blood who could hardly wait to get rid of her. Meg stood to confront her. "I have had a *good* life? Is that what you presume to tell me?"

Lydia bristled. "You had a roof over your head, did you not? Plenty to eat? I saw to that by sending you to my Cousin Elinore's estate. Was not Lady Wallingford good to you? Did she not allow you to learn to read and write? Be grateful I did not dispatch you to the workhouse!"

Speechless, Meg shook her head with disbelief. " 'Tis beyond me what to say." She turned toward Lady Semple—her mother?—still not quite believing. "So now that I know, what do you intend to do?"

Charlotte nervously twisted her handkerchief. "I . . . I had not thought . . ."

"Nothing can be done at this late date," Lydia broke in, her voice smoldering. "Nothing is changed, nothing is about to change." She turned to glare at Charlotte. "You have now indulged yourself; what good have you accomplished? You cannot plan to confess to Cyril! What, pray tell, would *that* do?! In your wildest fantasies, can you imagine he would immediately proclaim to the world that Meg is his daughter? And what would he do with Allegra? Give her a mop and bucket, and pack her off to the servants' quarters? *Lady Meg,*" Lydia spat the name out, her lip curling in a sneer, "one day a servant, the next the daughter of a marquess? Ha! I think not. You must be practical. As far as the world is concerned, Allegra is still your daughter, and though you might fervently wish otherwise, Meg is still a maid."

Charlotte dabbed at her eyes. "What makes you think I cannot go to Cyril?"

"You get in a twitter if he so much as frowns at you," Lydia scoffed. "Imagine how furious Cyril would be over such a deception! Such wickedness, it strikes me, would be grounds for divorce."

"*Divorce?*" Stark fear glittered in Charlotte's eyes. "Oh, no, I could never bear the disgrace! Lydia," she protested weakly, "have you forgotten this all was your idea?"

"Was it?" Lydia returned a mocking smile. "As far as Cyril is concerned, I knew absolutely nothing of your wicked deception, and furthermore, would have been shocked had I known. And Eliza Quincy passed away years ago. No, you won't get anybody else to take the blame. And that, dear sister-in-law, is why you shall remain silent." She turned to Meg, confident in her ability to quell a servant's rebellion. "And why you, too, shall remain silent. Don't even think for one moment this changes your circumstances. After that disgusting spectacle I witnessed at the river today, I want you gone from Pentworth Park. Tomorrow will be none too soon."

Meg stared silently into Lydia's angry face, knowing that from now on she must live with the knowledge of who she really was and how she had been cheated. Not only that, she must survive the hurt of knowing *her own mother had rejected her*! She turned to Charlotte. "Do *you* want me to leave?" she asked, fearful of the response.

"It is of no import what she wants," Lydia interjected. "There's only one sensible course to follow."

Meg's gaze did not waver from her mother. "What *she*

says doesn't matter, m'lady; I want to hear it from you. Do you want me to go?"

"Oh, dear." Lady Semple's handkerchief was by now thoroughly damp and twisted. For a long moment she sat staring at the floor, unwilling to meet Meg's gaze. Finally she sighed and said softly, "I would like to tell Cyril, but I cannot. I could never stand up to him—I cannot now. And Allegra—I can only imagine her fury." Her face brightened. "But I shan't desert you. You shall *not* leave!" She flashed a quick glare at Lady Lydia. "I shall insist Meg *not* go with Allegra to Hartwick House. She shall have a home here at Pentworth Park as long as she likes."

If I stay, Meg thought, *I would not have to go through the anxiety of finding another position. If I stay, I would catch a glimpse of Richard from time to time.* Crumbs from the table, but was that not her fate in life? She could never expect more, but perhaps what little it was would sustain her for the years she must remain in service. "Are you sure this time I would stay here at Pentworth Park?" she asked her mother. "Not be compelled thereafter to follow Allegra?"

Lady Lydia glowered. "The whole idea is idiotic, Charlotte. Meg must go."

Distraught, Lady Semple arose from the settee to face Lydia. "But I cannot bear to lose her now. All these years . . . you cannot know how happy I was to find her. And now, to let her go again? I cannot!"

"You can, and you will!" decreed Lydia.

Meg took a step toward Lady Semple. "Stand up to her, ma'am!" she urged. "We discussed this once before, remember? How 'tis better to face your fears? If you don't, then . . . I wish you hadn't told me! Of what use is it to have a mother who is . . . who is a"—she yearned to utter *coward*, but the word was so harsh—"who is unable to stand up for herself?"

Her mother's face twisted in anguish. "Oh, my

daughter, I cannot face Cyril. What he would think—what he would *do*! My knees turn weak at the thought."

"To be frank, m'lady," Meg retorted stoutly, "I would rather be dead than live in such fear of another human being."

Lydia stiffened immediately. "Leave us, Charlotte. I must talk to Meg privately."

"But—"

"Leave!"

Without another word, Charlotte crept away, dabbing her eyes, closing the door softly behind her.

Eyes blazing, Lydia turned to Meg. "You will *not* stay, despite Lady Semple's unfortunate importuning."

"That is a decision I shall make, not you"—Meg paused, finding a perverse pleasure in the thought of what she was about to say next—*"my dear Aunt Lydia."*

"Why you impertinent . . . !" Eyes flashing, Lydia drew back her arm. Meg did not flinch from the impending slap, but instead stared Lydia down with a cold, steady gaze. Finally Lydia dropped her arm to her side. In a stony voice she continued, "You're to disregard Lady Semple's foolishness. You will leave tomorrow."

Meg lifted her chin, meeting Lydia's icy demeanor straight on. "Why should I leave?"

Lydia smirked triumphantly. "Because *I* run Pentworth Park, not your mother. With Allegra gone, we shall have no need of another lady's maid. Therefore, if you stay you will toil belowstairs. Rest assured, I shall have you scrubbing hearths, emptying chamber pots, turning mattresses twice a day. I vow I shall make your life unbearable!"

A sly look then crossed Lydia's face. "Since your mother has no money of her own, I'm prepared to offer you a stipend of forty pounds per annum out of my own pocket. Not a princely sum, but 'tis more than enough to set you up."

Meg did a quick calculation. What with the additional expense of food and lodging, she could barely get by on that amount! Whatever had she done to make this woman hate her so? Meg returned a puzzled frown. "Why are you so anxious to get rid of me?"

"I am not obliged to explain myself to a servant," Lydia replied icily. "Suffice to say, because of my largesse, you'll live comfortably for the rest of your life—so long as it is away from Pentworth Park. Frankly, with your low status, and your"—her eyes flicked downward—"affliction, you are most fortunate indeed. Rest assured, you will never receive a better offer."

Meg could feel the thin chill that hung on the edge of Lydia's words and knew she meant them.

"You would be a fool to turn my offer down."

With terrible regrets assailing her, Meg realized this was the course she should follow. "All right, I accept."

"You must cut yourself off from Pentworth Park, never to return, never to enter into any correspondence with its inhabitants, or the inhabitants of Hartwick House—*all* the inhabitants, you understand my meaning?"

"Yes." *Richard—my love—my Richard, I shall never see you again. But perhaps 'tis best this way.* "I shall leave tomorrow, never to return."

Meg left the room with a heavy heart. Down the hallway, not far from the door, Polly was waiting, her face strained with anxiety.

"Polly!" Meg halted. "Have you been eavesdropping?"

"Me?" Polly pointed at herself, eyes wide with innocence. " 'Pon me word, no! But I know 'ose ear was pressed against the door bold as brass—Lady Allegra's!"

"Oh, no." Meg felt her heart skip. "How long was she there?"

"Long enough to 'ear you was kissin' and carryin' on with Lord Beaumont down by the river."

"Blast!" How humiliated she felt that Allegra had overheard Lady Lydia's distorted description of the scene at the river!

"But not long enough," Polly hastened to add, "to 'ear

the part about you bein' Lady Semple's real daughter. Oops!" Polly slapped her hand over her mouth. "I 'ad not meant to eavesdrop. I was just passin' by and—"

"No matter," Meg cut in sharply. "Where is Allegra now?"

"Dashed up the stairway lookin' like a thundercloud."

"I shall speak to her."

"Why? If you don' mind my sayin' so, she ain't deservin' of your sympathy. Best look after yoursel'." Polly regarded her with awe. "I jes' can't believe it! You, the daughter of a marquess? Lady Meg! Lor', I always knew you were somethin' special."

Ignoring Polly's chatter, Meg thought a moment. "You're right, why should I speak to her? Lord knows, I have problems enough of my own. Besides, with her kind, today's heartbreak is forgotten by tomorrow." *Not so the case with me.*

Trailed by Polly, Meg climbed the stairs to her room, pulled her box from beneath the bed, and began to collect her meager belongings. A flare of anger overcame her, and she sat hard upon the bed and thrust her twisted foot in front of her. "Cursed foot! If not for this twisted, ugly *thing*, I would be the daughter of the house, not Allegra."

Polly plunked down next to Meg. "Indade, 'tis not fair. *You* should be Allegra."

"And Allegra should be Meg. Ah, well . . . what is done is done, and nothing will change my fate at this late date."

Polly bristled. "That wicked girl has your rightful place! You shud take it back. If Lady Semple won' help, then, go to Lord Semple yoursel' and tell 'im the truth."

"No," Meg answered flatly. "If her ladyship sees fit to keep her secret, sees fit to reject me still as her daughter, then so be it. I don't need her—or any of them!"

Polly frowned with concern. "But what are you going to do, Meg? Where will you go?"

"I shall make arrangements to leave on tomorrow's mail coach for . . . Brighton, I suppose. Then, once there . . ."

For a moment Meg couldn't speak. She'd been offered a chance at a new life, but so sick at heart was she still, it brought her no pleasure. "I've not decided yet," she finished lamely.

"You may not like it out there in the world all by yurself." Polly worried. "Here, at least, you 'ave friends and a roof over your head. Lady Semple said you could stay, did she not? Why not change your mind?"

"Never. I intend to put miles and miles between myself and both Pentworth Park and Hartwick House—the more miles, the better."

"But 'tis so unfair! Just think, Meg, you're the daughter of the Marquess of Semple. An' the legitimate daughter, no less. Ain't life strange? All yur life you 'ave despised the nobles, an' now, come to find out you *are* one."

Meg managed a faint smile. "Do you believe I would have been another Allegra?"

"Lor', no!"

"I like to think you're right on that score, Polly—I would have been considerate, and done good works, and been kind to my servants. Now all I want is to get so far away from here, I shall never be confronted by reminders of who I really am." So far away that she would never again witness the pitiful weakness in her mother. So far away that . . . *Richard*. Her heart twisted.

"You don' fool me, Meg. I know from the look in yur eye. You're thinkin' about Lord Beaumont."

Meg nodded. At this point, she was beyond pretense.

Polly paused, then asked, "Was wut Lady Lydia said about you two true?"

"No . . . and yes. I was not after him, not the way she described it. But still . . ." Meg sank disconsolately to the bed. "There was some truth to her story. Ah, Polly, I thought I loved him, but you're right. In the end, he grossly insulted me." Meg bit her lip to hold back tears. "He asked me to be his mistress. That tells you something, does it not?"

"Wut it tells me is the man must be desprit!" Polly returned stoutly. "I've no doubt 'e cares for you, even if 'e thinks yur not noble born. Why, you're so pretty and bright! And since 'e cannot have you as 'is wife, 'e wants you on any terms." Polly eagerly continued, "So what did *you* say?"

"I told him no, of course."

"So what did 'e say?"

"Nothing." Meg paused, remembering. "Although I do recall he had a somewhat devastated look in his eye."

"There you are," Polly replied in triumph. "Lord Beaumont is good at wearing a mask most of the time, but this time it must have dropped away. Oh, Meg"—Polly grasped Meg's hand—"'tis clear Lord Beaumont is smitten with you. Why not tell 'im the truth? If 'e knew you was Lord Semple's real daughter, wouldn't 'e be wild with delight? Wouldn't 'e marry you in an instant?"

Meg recoiled. "Go against Lady Semple's wishes? I could not do that! Already—unexpectedly!—I have developed an affection for my mother. I have no desire to go against her wishes and shall keep her secret to my grave."

"Then, why not accept 'is offer?" Polly asked, unabashed. "Wut's wrong with bein' a mistress? Lor', if 'twas me, I would live in sinful luxury rather than go off to Brighton to fend for myself."

"'Tis a matter of honor, Polly," Meg said firmly. "Now, that's the end of it."

Somewhat sadly Polly headed out of Meg's room, saying, "Well, then, I 'ad best get to 'aulin water for Lady Allegra's bath."

Moments later she returned. "Lady Allegra wants ter see you. She claims 'tis urgent." Polly frowned. "That girl is up to somethin'. She has that sly look in her eye."

"But what?"

"I dunno. But I 'ave a feelin' you ought ter find out, if fer no other reason than yur own protection."

Chapter 16

In the main salon at Hartwick House, Richard sat slumped in a chair. Moodily he stared out the arched Venetian window, not hearing the nightingale that sat atop an oak tree singing its good night, but rather hearing Meg's appalled *Do you think I can be bought?* when he had asked her . . .

Perdition! He didn't want to think about it.

Vickers appeared and announced, "Lord Edward to see you."

Before Richard could reply, Edward stepped past the butler, his expression a mixture of inquisitiveness and agitation. "Pray tell me what on God's green earth is going on!" he demanded as Vickers withdrew. "I cannot get a word from anyone except the servants, who, I can assure you, are all agog. All I know for certain is that Meg has done something terrible, Mama is in tears, Allegra's sulking in her bedchamber, and Aunt Lydia appears taken with a frenzy."

"Is not 'frenzy' her usual condition?" Richard questioned dryly. He slumped further into his chair.

"Aunt is outdoing herself today," Edward replied. "Something happened. I have no idea what, except, from what I gather, it involves you and Meg, and was witnessed by Aunt Lydia."

Richard felt a heaviness in his chest. He had no desire to talk, and wished Edward would go away. But of course Edward would not. He glanced up wearily. "Yes, 'something' happened today. Meg and I were at the river . . ." He proceeded to recount the exact truth of the matter. ". . . but when I offered to make her my mistress, you cannot imagine her reaction. Suffice to say, she said no."

"What a surprise," Edward sarcastically replied.

Richard let out an anguished groan and began pacing the room. "That aunt of yours made her appearance at exactly the wrong time. True, we were kissing, but Lydia always suspects the worst. To her, a simple kiss would look like—"

"A kiss is a kiss, Richard. Face the truth. It isn't Auntie who has upset you. You're undone because your little lady's maid rejected you."

With an oath Richard flung himself into the chair again. "Meg is so unpredictable. I . . . I hardly know what to think of her."

"The trouble with you, Richard, is that far too many young chits have thrown themselves at your feet."

"Of what significance is that?"

"The significance is, you've become a pompous ass, spoiled rotten in the bargain." Edward pointed an accusing finger. "In your colossal conceit, you expected Meg to be thrilled at your odious invitation. To your astonishment, she declined, leaving you enveloped in this brown study, which is, I might add, entirely of your own making. Gather your wits, man! Meg may be a servant, but far smarter than most, and strong-headed besides, with a mind of her own." Edward grinned. "My dear Lord Beaumont, you have met your match. Meg would as lief pick oakum in the workhouse as be kept by you."

To Edward's surprise, Richard squeezed his eyes shut, as if attempting to shield himself from the truth. "Obviously," he replied through gritted teeth.

After a long moment of studying his friend, Edward's countenance lit as if a light were dawning. "My prophecy! Do you recall that night you announced you would never marry?"

"I remember," Richard answered tightly. "You accused me of being more of a romantic than I might think."

"I predicted that someday you were going to fall madly, agonizingly, totally in love, and—"

"And when I did, I would look back upon that conversation and realize I sounded like a jackass."

"Well?"

"You were right." Reluctantly, as if he could hardly bear to utter the words, Richard declared, "I have fallen in love, Edward, madly, agonizingly in love—with a maidservant!" He gave a choked laugh. "Oh, God, Edward, I love her. I don't know what to do."

Edward took a moment to wipe the smile of triumph from his face, then said gently, "She is leaving, according to the servants' rumors."

Richard jerked his head up. "What!"

"You already knew that Aunt wants her gone from Pentworth Park forever."

"But it was not Meg's fault—none of it!"

"Apparently Aunt was most insistent. Mother cried, seemed quite distraught for reasons I cannot fathom, but to no avail. Auntie would have Meg gone on tomorrow's mail coach."

Richard vaulted from his chair, sped to the door, and flung it wide. "My horse, Vickers!"

"Whatever are you planning?" asked Edward. "Bear in mind, nothing has changed. Your . . . er, romance, is still quite hopeless."

"Stop reminding me," Richard replied brusquely. "I shall return with you to Pentworth Park. You are to tell Meg I wish to see her."

"But why?"

"Oh, have no fear, Edward, I have not forgotten my obligations." Richard's voice was cold, exact. " 'Tis merely that I wish to apologize for my ungallant behavior and, if possible, dissuade her from leaving."

"Shall you meet at the river?"

"Your drawing room."

Edward recoiled. "Entertain a mere servant in the drawing room? Have you taken leave of your senses? Aunt Lydia would throw a fit."

"Call her a mere servant again, and I shall—" Richard muttered an oath, and stopped abruptly.

Not the least intimidated, Edward smiled in sympathy. "Ah, Richard, have you entirely lost your sense of humor? You really do love the little chit, don't you?"

"Are you going to help me, or are you going to stand here with that stupid grin on your face?"

"Of course I shall help you, but, please, not the drawing room. Wait in the garden—at that secluded spot by the fountain. I shall sneak into the servants' quarters and fetch her down. But you had better say a prayer she will even condescend to meet you, after the shabby way you insulted her. In fact—"

"Just do it, Edward!" Richard interrupted, his voice hoarse with frustration.

What could Allegra want? Meg wondered. Revenge, most likely, and an opportunity to vent her wrath. At the door of Allegra's bedchamber, she took a deep breath in order to compose herself. *I am walking into the lion's den,* she thought as she entered. Allegra would be furious.

Allegra's portmanteau was spread upon the bed. Beside it, a large trunk and a jumbled heap of clothes. "What is this?" Meg inquired.

"So there you are!" Hair in disarray, cheeks flushed red with excitement, Allegra scurried here and there about the bedchamber. "Where have you been?"

"I—"

"I am aware of your perfidy." Allegra paused long enough to glare daggers, then hurled an armload of clothing upon the bed. "I assume my mother has dismissed you?"

"Yes, but—"

"Before you go, I need you. Get over here and make

some order of all this." She began hurling garments from the messy pile into the portmanteau. "Fold these neatly."

Meg stood unmoving. Calmly she inquired, "Allegra, what are you doing?" She surprised herself. She had addressed her mistress without the title. How easily a simple "Allegra" had rolled off her tongue! Not that her omission had been intentional . . .

She wondered if she should correct herself and decided no. What a heady, gratifying feeling to address Allegra directly instead of through a servant's humble pose! Aware she had just passed a milestone in her life, she silently vowed never again to be subservient to Allegra, or, for that matter, to allow anyone to treat her with disrespect.

But if Allegra noticed her lapse in protocol, she failed to say so. She appeared in a high state of excitement. "Get my jewels," she snapped, "and my ribbon box. Be quick!"

Meg stood fast. "You will address me in a civil manner. I am not your servant anymore."

Allegra heard her that time and was so taken aback she stopped and stared. "How dare you! No one has ever talked to me like that before."

"Then, 'tis time someone did."

"Well . . . I . . ." Allegra sputtered, then stopped, at a loss for words. Finally she managed in a more conciliatory tone, "I've no time for this now. You must come help me."

As Meg watched her former mistress's discomfit, it occurred to her that Allegra was like many a bully who, when confronted, showed their true cowardice and backed down. *I should have done this sooner.* But at least this was a lesson learned for the future, when the stipend would save her from having to work as a servant. "I ask again, what are you doing?"

"If you must know"—Allegra continued to fumble through her clothes—"I am eloping. Naturally, Mama and Papa are not to know."

A soft gasp escaped Meg's lips. "Elope? I cannot believe Lord Beaumont would consent to such a scheme."

"*Not* Lord Beaumont." Allegra gazed at Meg in triumph, savoring her astonishment. "I plan to marry his younger brother, Henry. We leave at dusk for Gretna Green." She hurled herself upon the overfilled portmanteau. "Blast! I cannot get this closed." She paused long enough to cast Meg a warning glance, her eyebrows pinched together in a scowl. "Tell, and I shall have you dismissed immediately."

Meg laughed. "I *am* dismissed, remember?"

Nonplussed, Allegra mumbled, "Well, then, without a character."

Meg shook her head in disbelief. "Allegra, have you lost your senses? Surely you put no credence in your Aunt Lydia's tale. What happened at the river today was not as she described. We hardly—"

"I don't care!" Allegra interrupted harshly. "Part of it is true, is it not? 'Tis enough to know that Richard lowers himself to dally with mere servants. 'Tis enough to know he thinks so little of me." She shook her fist in the air. "Richard shall rue the day he toyed with my affections!"

"Lord Beaumont intends to marry you. Surely one incident, grossly misinterpreted, should not cause you to ruin your reputation over a scoundrel. There must be more to this. What has Richard done that you should treat him in this manner?"

"The blackguard refused to love me!" Allegra wailed. "I offered him my heart. In exchange, he acted as if he could not stand to touch me. When he looks at me I see deep in his eyes he despises me."

Meg groped for answers. "But even if he did despise you, which I am sure he does not, is that a reason to run off with a man whose reputation is in ruins? Whose own father has practically disowned him?"

"Henry adores me, whereas Richard doesn't love me and never will. Well, then, will he ever be sorry!"

" 'Tis utter folly to marry Henry. He's a gambler, a drunk, and a disgrace to the family."

Allegra set her jaw. "Nothing you can say will stop me."

Meg racked her brain to find more reasons to dissuade Allegra. "If you go through with this elopement, I warrant you will make the biggest mistake of your life. Do you really wish to humiliate Lord Beaumont? Think of your mother, how devastated she'll be when—"

"My mother?" Allegra flashed a look of bitter rancor. "Mama doesn't care a fig about me. She wants to get rid of me. I doubt she really cares which brother I elope with, so long as I am away from here." Allegra's chin lifted in defiance. "Henry loves me. He's the only one who does. Not Richard, not my mother, certainly not my father . . . they'll all be sorry." Allegra halted abruptly, and slanted Meg an astonished gaze. "What am I doing? Confiding in a servant this way, especially *you*."

A portion of Meg's anger and disgust with Allegra melted away. The poor girl had grown up ignored by her father, merely tolerated by her mother, with no more love than . . . than . . . *I have had.*

"You must help me right now!" Allegra suddenly pleaded, changing the conversation to a concern more pressing to her. "I need you to carry my bags down the stairs and accompany me to the river to the spot where Henry is to meet me."

A curious thought jarred Meg. "Why are you telling me all this? If I inform his lordship, he is bound to chase after you."

"That is why you *must* keep quiet, at least until we reach the border. After that, I don't care what you say. By then, he could never catch up with me."

"I cannot change your mind?"

"No."

Resigned, Meg declared, "Then, I shall accompany you as far as the garden, but no farther."

Minutes later, as darkness fell, Allegra, dressed in a

hooded cape, stood at the end of the garden, attended not only by both Meg and Polly, but also by two footmen she had summoned to haul her considerable baggage.

Allegra gripped Meg's arm. "Before dinner, you must go to the drawing room and inform my parents I shan't be down. Explain that I am indisposed and shall be going to bed early. That should do it, don't you think?" she added smugly. "I'll wager they'll not suspect a thing."

Meg was beginning to have suspicions of her own. She regarded Allegra curiously. "You have a strange way of harboring a secret. At least four servants already know."

"All sworn to secrecy," Allegra answered hastily.

"Are you sure you *want* to elope?" Meg asked warily. "You've told so many of us, I get the impression you *want* your parents told, you *want* your father and Lord Beaumont to catch up with you before the knot is tied."

"Have you lost your mind?" Allegra screeched. "Why would I do that?"

"You would know better than I," Meg answered quietly. "If this is a scheme to get attention, you have gone much too far. Things could not turn out as you expect."

Allegra tried to scowl fiercely, but could not manage it. "You could not be more mistaken." Then, turning her back on Meg, Allegra grabbed her portmanteau and, followed by the two footmen hauling her trunk, disappeared into the night.

"I think you 'ave it right, Meg," said Polly. "If she's elopin', 'ow come she let you, me, and at least two footmen in on 'er little secret? Might as well shout it from the treetops."

Meg nodded in agreement. It seemed strange indeed.

"Why ever for?" Polly asked, then answered her own question. "Of course! Allegra's been ignored and slighted, which mus' just kill her, and so—"

"—what better way to draw attention to herself, at the same time wreak revenge, than to elope with an unsuitable scoundrel?" Meg finished. "Making sure, of course, her father gives chase and stops her before she crosses the border and actually marries the man."

"Tha's it! Oh, the foolish girl!" Polly had to pause and catch her breath. "Me 'ead's so full of all that's 'appened today 'tis about to burst. So will you tell her ladyship Allegra's elopin'?"

"I have no idea what I shall do," Meg answered. Her head was bursting, too.

"Well, I say let 'er go and good riddance. Let 'er marry that young fool. Allegra's gone, Meg! What a blessing! Just think, now you kin tell his lordship who you really are, so you kin take your rightful place. An' just imagine"—Polly's face beamed with anticipation—"then you kin marry Lord Beaumont an' live happily ever after."

Meg laughed wryly. "You're spinning fairy tales."

"But with Allegra gone—?"

"I would still be a servant no matter what course Allegra takes. Lady Semple doesn't possess the courage to confront his lordship with the truth. Even if she did, given his lordship's pride and stubborn nature, she would doubtless accomplish nothing more than have us both banned from Pentworth Park forever."

"Then, why not jus' stay?"

Meg tried to smile. "No, I must go tomorrow. I should be deliriously happy, Polly. I shall be given a stipend, enough that I need never be a servant again."

"You don' look all that happy about it."

"But I am, Polly, it's just that it hasn't sunk in yet, that's all. Of course, I shall be deliriously happy."

When she reached her chamber, Meg flung herself upon her narrow bed, relieved to be alone so she could at last release her tears. How strange life was. Only weeks ago she truly would have been deliriously happy to be on her own, but that was before she met Richard, and fell in love with him. Yes, she had fallen deeply in love with a man who was totally unobtainable.

For a long time Meg lay gazing miserably at the ceiling.

Her fate was sealed. If she lived to be a hundred, she would never forget him, nor find another like him. She would never marry. Instead, she would devote herself to the apartments she intended to keep, and to her art and poetry. Also, she would take in orphans, try to find a child or two, crippled like herself.

One thing she knew for certain: She was still plain Meg Quincy, daughter of nobility or not. Best to forget she had ever learned who she really was. As for Allegra . . . should she tell? The question hammered at her. Perhaps she should go to his lordship this instant, or her ladyship, or even Richard. On the other hand, she could simply not say a word . . .

A knock sounded at the door. When she opened it, she was so surprised she blurted, "Lord Edward! Whatever are you doing in the servants' quarters?" *My brother,* the thought struck her as she looked into a pair of blue eyes she realized now were exactly like her own. A pity he would never know.

Edward, wearing his mischievous grin, tapped his finger to his lips. "Shh, come with me."

"But—"

"Now! This instant! Somebody wishes to see you, out in the garden."

Meg froze. "I've said all I care to say to Lord Beaumont. You may go back down and tell him I never wish to lay eyes on him again."

"Very well, then." Edward turned to leave.

"Oh, wait!" Meg called suddenly. The answer she had sought had suddenly become crystal clear. She *would* tell on Allegra. Lord Beaumont would be the first to hear, in plenty of time to stop the silly girl.

Chapter 17

Deep in the shadows of Pentworth Park's formal garden, Richard waited. Crickets chirped, but he hardly heard them. The scent of jasmine hung heavy in the summer night air, but he paid no heed. Would she come? After the mindless insult he had perpetrated upon her, he could not be sure. Miserably he wondered what he would say if Lord Semple happened to come strolling along his moonlit flagstone pathway and discovered his future son-in-law lurking amid the shrubbery.

What a hobble he was in! To what depths had he sunk? Before he could devise an answer, two figures emerged from the shadows.

"Richard, I trust 'tis you," came Edward's loud whisper. "Here she is. Well, er . . . uh, I shall be getting on."

"Fine. Do get on, Edward." The moon went behind the clouds as his friend's dim form receded into the darkness. In what little remained of the moonlight, Richard turned his attention to the small figure standing before him. He could just make out her white cap and prim gray dress. It occurred to him he had never seen her dressed otherwise, but what difference? No matter what she wore, to him she was still beautiful.

"Good evening, m'lord," came Meg's voice politely.

He tried to speak, but discovered a catch in his throat and had to pause a moment to clear it. "I'm so happy you came, Meg." He took her small, soft hand in his, drew her into deep shadows cast by the fountain and a tall clipped hedge, and turned to face her. "It was imperative I see you." Despite himself, an urgent trembling edged his voice, betraying his customary lofty indifference.

"I shall only stay a minute," she replied, not coolly, but in a manner that held no warmth. "I'm leaving tomorrow, as I am sure Edward has apprised you. Actually, I'm grateful you sent for me. There's something I must tell you."

His heart clenched at the words *I'm leaving,* but he asked evenly, "Something to tell me?"

"I warn you, you will be shocked."

"I doubt it. I am well-nigh unshockable."

"Really?" she asked skeptically. "Then, you'll not turn a hair when you learn that Allegra has eloped with Henry."

Through the moonlight, he could see her well enough to gather she had tilted her head back, waiting expectantly, no doubt, for him to recoil in astonishment. True, her news had hit him like a thunderbolt, but not in the manner she expected. "When did they leave?" he inquired flatly.

"Within the hour. As we speak, they're traveling in all haste toward Gretna Green, but plan to stop later tonight at an inn. I have not informed his lordship and her ladyship as yet, but now that you know, I'm sure you'll want to do it. If you and Lord Semple leave immediately, you should have plenty of time to stop her and bring her back."

He would not have to marry Allegra! Richard felt such joy he could have soared to the clouds. *Thank you, Henry, a thousand thanks!* Then he remembered his reason for being here, and brought himself to earth posthaste. "You were right to tell me, but I shall not lift a finger to stop her. Allegra's made her bed."

"You won't?" she asked in surprise. "Perhaps you should reconsider. Allegra gave me the impression she *wanted* to be stopped."

Richard decided the time for shallow parrying was

over. Tonight Meg would get nothing from him but blunt honesty. "I don't give a groat what Allegra wants. All I care is, I am *rid* of her!"

"Fine, then," she replied, appearing to accept his pronouncement with equanimity. "Now, as for why you asked me here, I'm not unmindful of your reasons, but as far as you and I are concerned, we still live in different worlds." She started to turn away. "I must go inform Lady Semple of Allegra's elopement immediately."

He clasped her arm. "Meg, I have to talk to you."

She pulled against him. "Why? Haven't we said all there is to say?"

"I must apologize—"

"Please, no! We could talk 'til doomsday, and our circumstances would still be the same." To emphasize her words, she placed her palm on his chest to push him away. It was only for a moment, but her mere touch was enough to set his pulse racing so madly, he had to breathe deeply for a moment to keep himself from trembling. My God, Clarice at her most lustful moment had never set him off this way! "We had no time to talk at the river," he barely managed smoothly. "I would prefer you not think ill of me."

"Rest assured I shall not," she answered civilly, "even though you grossly insulted me."

Oh, why was she not like all the other women in his life—meek, adoring? But, then, if she were, she would not be Meg, and he would not be making a grand fool of himself here in the middle of Lord Semple's garden.

With an effort, he pulled himself together and continued, "Hear me out, Meg. It was wrong of me to make that odious proposal. I should have known that you, being the honorable person you are, would reject me. My only excuse is—" He stopped abruptly, shocked at himself. The words he had been about to speak, he had never uttered in his life before, except to his mother, which was a different thing entirely. But even if he were to say the words, what good would they accomplish? Stiffly he continued, "Suffice to say, I most humbly beg your forgiveness. I—" Sensing the futility of it all, he stopped again. "This is madness," he softly declared, and was compelled to press his arms against his sides so he would not reach for her.

"Oh, Richard . . ." The gentle softness in her voice was almost more than he could bear. ". . . 'tis all so hopeless. But you'll soon forget about me. Tomorrow I shall be out of your life forever."

"You should *not* have to leave over one stupid incident. I shall talk to Lord Semple. I shall make it clear—"

"No, Richard, I must leave." Her reply was sad, accepting. "There are reasons having nothing to do with you that compel me to go."

"What reasons?" he demanded. "You must tell me."

"You will never know."

The evident resignation in her voice forced him to face harsh reality: She meant it. She would be gone tomorrow and never come back. There was nothing he could do to stop her, and yet . . . *how can I let her go?*

Forgetting his resolve, he circled his hand around her waist and drew her closer. He longed to crush her to him and fought for control, but the tender softness of her body caused a feeling of abandon to overcome him. Urgently he tugged off her cap, and like a madman thrust his fingers through the silkiness of her tumbling hair. She offered no resistance, but instead lifted her face to him. "You are so beautiful," he whispered, knowing, but not caring, that in this current passionate, abandoned state, he was about to offer up the forbidden words.

"I love you, Meg," he whispered, his breath hot against her ear. She gasped and tried to pull away, but he held her fast. "No, don't . . . I ask only that you listen."

"Richard, we cannot—"

"Hush!" He lifted her gently, swung her to the foot-high rim of the fountain, and drew her so close every curve of her body fit snug against his own. Rocking her gently, he declared, "I fell in love with you that first moment I saw you—sitting on the floor behind the Earl of Wallingford's settee. Your cap was off. You have no idea how dazzled I was by the glow of candlelight shimmering in your hair."

She seemed to shiver in his arms. He reached his fingers to brush her cheek and discovered it was damp. "Tears? Oh, God, I didn't mean to make you cry."

"It's just ... I cannot bear to see you hurt," she replied. "You're such a kind man, though you go to great lengths to hide it."

"Only kind?" He thrust her at arm's length, and squinted at her through the darkness. "Have I no other qualities that impress you?" he inquired with mock severity, amazed that he could retain his sense of humor.

Meg felt her heart melt. Up to that moment she had made a valiant try to resist him, but his humor brought her close to both tears and laughter. "You're not only kind," she answered, softly laughing. "I have seen beyond that arrogant facade of yours. You're a thoughtful, brave, humorous, honorable man."

"Does this mean we have dispensed with Master of Idleness?" he inquired lightly.

"Oh, indeed we have!" She paused, grew serious, and touched her hand to his cheek. "Those are only partly the reasons I love you. Mostly I love you because the mere touch of your hand sends little shivers through me, and I feel feelings I never felt in my life before. Ever since that kiss yesterday, I have felt a burning desire for another—"

"Ah, Meg!" he cried, smothering her last words as his mouth hungrily covered her own. She returned his kiss with reckless abandon. Blood pounded in her brain, made her knees tremble. What a divine ecstasy this was! When he lifted his mouth, he whispered, "I am so happy you love me, Meg," then showered kisses around her lips, her ear, and along her jaw, ending with a tantalizing kiss in the hollow of her neck.

"I want you so badly, I could take you right here, this moment," he whispered hoarsely.

What am I doing? His words brought her to the realization that if they didn't stop, they would soon end up on the ground beneath the yew trees. "Richard, no," she murmured, and forced herself to wrench away. "We cannot possibly . . ." She could hear his ragged breath, feel his quivering. "God knows, I want you, too, but 'twill get us nowhere."

With a tortured groan, he answered, "I cannot let you go, Meg. With Allegra gone, there must be something—"

"Nothing!" She stepped back determinedly. "I cannot be your wife; I shall not be your mistress. There's nothing left for us but to say good-bye."

Without another word, he wrenched away and turned his back on her. She could hear his struggle to bring his breathing back to normal, and in the gathering silence, Meg thought of Polly's fairy tale and allowed a foolish fantasy to dance through her head:

Richard will throw caution to the winds. He will seize me in his arms, declare he will marry me, servant or no; Society be damned!

If only he knew her true identity!

But he would never know, she reminded herself sorrowfully. She could never, ever claim her rightful place and should be content that at least she would not be a servant anymore.

Finally Richard turned and spoke again. "I would give anything if we could be together, although I know 'tis impossible."

"Sensible words, m'lord." How stuffy she sounded, trying to cover up her wretchedness! And how silly she was! If, in the remote event he should ask her to be his wife, she must say no. And yet, how she longed to hear him at least ask her anyway! She waited, sensing he was struggling with himself, but he remained silent, and only the chirping of the crickets filled the night. "I must go," she said at last, her throat tight. "Her ladyship must be informed about Allegra."

Before he answered, he took a moment to look about

and breathed deeply, as if savoring the ambience of this warm summer night. "Good-bye, Meg. I shall carry you in my thoughts forever. I shall think of you every time I hear a cricket chirp, every time I sniff the scent of jasmine in the air."

The moon came out from behind the clouds, and she could see his expression. He looked as if someone had struck him in the face.

"We never had a chance," she whispered, her voice close to breaking.

"There is nothing more to say, then, is there? Well, you had best go tell your news about Allegra." There was such sorrow in his voice, it was all she could do to keep from reaching for him. She managed not to, though, and he turned and walked away.

Chapter 18

The poignant strains of a Beethoven sonata led Meg to the music room, where she found Lady Semple alone at the pianoforte, playing with her eyes closed, an expression of sorrow covering her face.

"M'lady?"

Her mother stopped abruptly and opened her eyes. When she saw it was Meg, she gave her such a look of remorse, it made Meg's heart wrench. "You wish to see me?"

Meg smiled. "You play beautifully."

Tears sprang to Lady Semple's eyes. "Oh, if only . . ." She bit her lip and flung out her hands in simple despair.

Meg stepped purposefully into the music room. "You don't look well." *So much left unsaid!*

"Neither do you, Meg, I can see the strain on your face. But after all I put you through today . . ." She let the sentence fade, and for a moment bowed her head in her hand. In her small voice, she inquired, "What did you wish to see me about, my dear?"

"About Allegra . . ."

Meg related the details of the elopement. When she finished, Lady Semple, who had listened with increasing horror, cried, "I cannot believe this! That poor, misguided girl! How could she have allowed herself to be taken in by such a rake?" After a moment's pause, she exclaimed, "This is all my fault. I have made such a muddle of things. If I had only loved Allegra—if I had only—"

"Stop blaming yourself," Meg interrupted gently. "Guilt is but another useless emotion. You did your best. Besides, there's still time to go after them, if you inform his lordship immediately."

"Yes, yes, of course," said Lady Semple. "And perhaps, if we catch them in time, there will be no need to inform Lord Beaumont."

"He already knows."

"Oh, my heavens! He must be mortified."

"Not entirely, madam."

"Why do you say that?"

"I told him I was almost positive Allegra *wants* to be caught before she ties the knot with Henry. But even so, he claimed he would not lift a finger to get her back."

To Meg's surprise, Lady Semple, despite her chagrin, had to stifle a smile. "I must confess . . . but no! Such a thought is wicked of me! Of course I shall inform his lordship immediately, but first, I must know . . . you have seen Lord Beaumont? Spoken with him?"

Meg yearned to reveal her tempestuous scene in the garden, but all her life she had been taught that as a servant she must be discreet, keep her emotions to herself. Then she remembered she would be gone tomorrow, forever; what was the harm? How refreshing, to confide in someone besides another servant! And what better confidante than her very own mother? "I should not burden you, m'lady, but Richard and I . . ."

Lady Semple listened to Meg's explanation in stunned bewilderment. When Meg finished, she asked, "You truly love Lord Beaumont?" Meg nodded. "And Lord Beaumont"—her amazement was such she could barely get the words out—"loves you?"

"He held me in his arms and kissed me, less than an hour ago."

"But you know how men are, my dear. Could you not have mistaken a stolen kiss for love?"

"He declared his love for me, m'lady."

"Dear Lord!" Lady Semple gasped. Then, as if a new

thought had struck her, she clasped her hands together over her heart. "Did you tell him about . . . you know, about—"

"Your secret is safe," Meg reassured her. "Lord Semple will never know I am his daughter." She swallowed the despair in her throat. "Nor will anyone else, including Richard. It would have done me no good to tell him, especially knowing we must part." Her voice choked. She had always been the mistress of her emotions, but this time she could not control her sorrow. A sob rose in her throat. "Oh, madam," she cried, "I shall never love another!"

"My darling little girl!" Lady Semple sprang from the bench, circled Meg in her arms.

Meg let the tears come, resting her head on her mother's warm, comforting shoulder. *At last! I am in the arms of my mother.* What a joy this would have been, if not for the sad circumstances.

Charlotte patted her lovingly on the arm. "You are still so young. Surely you will find someone you will love as much as Lord Beaumont, perhaps more."

"Never!" responded Meg, allowing herself the rare luxury of crying even harder. But after a short time she took herself in hand and broke from her mother's embrace. "Forgive me," she said, wiping away tears with the palm of her hand, "I've never been in love before. I never knew 'twould be like this."

"I understand." Lady Semple's mouth curved into a wistful half smile. "I loved Cyril once, back before little William was born. But that was long ago, and now . . . this is my fault!" Her voice anguished, she repeated, "All my fault. I cannot bear to see you crying, after all the horrible things I have already done to you." She breathed deeply, lifted her chin. "I shall talk to his lordship, tell him the truth. Just think, if he were to accept you as his daughter, you could marry Lord Beaumont!"

"No!" Meg cried in alarm. "That's simply wishful

thinking on your part. Think of the scandal! 'Twill never work. 'Tis unthinkable you tell him."

"The time for lies is ended," Lady Semple stoutly declared.

"You will ruin yourself." Meg clasped her mother by the shoulders, fairly shaking her. "Listen to me! You see me crying now, but I assure you, you've seen the last of my tears."

"But you have been so mistreated!"

"True, but I've had a lifetime of coping with hardships of one sort or another. I shall cope with this."

"You will not have to, child." A glint of purpose appeared in Lady Semple's eyes, the first Meg had ever seen. "Since you advised me, I have twice made an attempt to stand up for myself—not with very good results, I must admit, but at least I made the attempt, and, thanks to you, have gathered the courage to try again."

"You need to think upon this, m'lady."

"No! I shall discuss this matter with his lordship this instant. You shall accompany me."

"Oh, no!" Meg pulled back in dismay. "What with his lordship's temper, this could cause a hellish scene. You said yourself, you could be exiled. You must think of the consequences."

"Think?" echoed Lady Semple, cheeks flushed in agitation. "All I have done my whole life is think! I've avoided every scene, measured each action. 'Tis time I acted." She bobbed her head with determination. "Come, Meg. Let us pay a visit to your father."

Meg noted the obstinate angle of her mother's chin and knew there was no sense arguing further. All she could do was hope there would be no dire consequences.

"I believe his lordship is in his study."

At the study door, Meg caught her mother's arm. "I want you to know I love you, no matter what happens. If you change your mind, 'tis all right, I shall understand."

Lady Semple took in a deep breath, as if to draw up her courage. "I shan't change my mind. Let's go inside."

Until now, Meg had seen little of the lord of the manor, other than to pass him occasionally in the hallways. So she had only a vague impression of Cyril, Lord Semple: tall and thinnish, his pinched, acerbic face dominated by an aristocratic nose and cold dark eyes.

He was seated behind his carved mahogany desk, scribbling with his pen. He did not look up, but stated sternly, "Not now, Charlotte."

"Cyril, I must speak to you," Charlotte began, voice quavering.

He glanced up scowling. "You are well aware I don't wish to be disturbed at this hour."

Meg sensed her mother's whole body trembling and wondered if she would have the strength to stand up to this imperious, powerful man. *This is my father,* she reminded herself. Her mother had loved him once, but why? Meg tried to dredge up a modicum of filial affection, but found none. Rather, he appeared so formidable, she realized her own knees were shaking. *But I must be strong, for my mother's sake.*

"I ... I ..." Charlotte cleared her throat, licked her lips.

Realizing her mother could not continue, Meg took over, saying boldly, "Sir, Allegra has eloped with Lord Beaumont's brother. As we speak, they're on their way to Gretna Green. They could not have gotten far, however, and there is ample time to stop them."

Lord Semple dropped his pen. "*Allegra?* Eloping with *Henry*? Is this a hoax?"

"No indeed, sir, but if you hurry—"

"Allegra ... Henry?" He was shaking his head, as if to convince himself the news was true. Finally he burst out, "Priceless!" seeming exceedingly bemused. "If ever two people deserve each other, 'tis those two!" His lordship looked askance at his wife. "You actually want to stop her?"

"No . . . well, yes. The poor girl is making such a terrible mistake, I thought—"

"Let her go! If she wants a scapegrace like Henry, by God, let her have him!" Cyril slammed a heavy fist to the desk. "No dowry! That money-grubbing rascal will not get a farthing! I shall instruct our butler that Allegra is never to darken this door again."

Lady Semple stared at her husband in amazement. "Must you be so harsh?"

"That's the end of it!" he sternly proclaimed. When Charlotte made no move to leave, he inquired sarcastically, "Is that all, Charlotte, or have you brought me more good news?"

Charlotte opened her mouth to speak, but was trembling so much she could not utter a word.

"Out with it! Or must you stand there quaking in your boots"—his lip curled in contempt—"as usual." He peered pointedly at Meg. "I am curious as to why you brought a servant with you, particularly this one."

Still Charlotte said nothing. Meg would not have been surprised if she had burst into tears or even swooned. "We can do this another time, m'lady," she whispered.

"No, no, I shall speak!" Lady Semple suddenly cried. Meg saw her jaw tighten, and knew that from some secret source, her mother had gathered the strength to carry on. Standing stiffly, hands clenched at her side, Charlotte gulped a deep breath, and in a steadier voice continued, "What I came to tell you, Cyril, is that Meg is not a servant. Meg is your daughter."

During the ominous silence that followed, his lordship's countenance remained immobile as he gazed up at his wife with deliberate blankness in his eyes. Finally he slowly arose to his full height and gazed imperiously down at his wife, breaking the silence with a softly put, "Why, Charlotte, what a surprise."

"I know this comes as a shock."

He coolly answered, "You mistake me. I have known since the day she was born that Meg was my daughter and Allegra was not. I did not know where Meg was, of course; Lydia would not tell me." He cocked an eyebrow. "I am only surprised you told me. After all these years, however did you find the nerve?"

Lady Semple was so stunned, she reeled backward. "You . . . you *knew*?" she gasped.

"Answer my question, Charlotte," Lord Semple snapped. "Why now?"

" 'Tis time you answered *my* question!" declared Lady Semple, pulling herself tall. "You say you *knew* about Meg? I demand an explanation!"

"Demand?" asked Cyril. "Well, dish me if our meek little lamb has finally found some spunk!"

Charlotte narrowed her eyes. "I want the truth, Cyril."

Meg waited uneasily for his lordship's reply, ready to spring to her mother's defense should he disparage her newfound courage.

Lord Semple weighed his wife with a critical squint. Seeming to make up his mind, he appeared to relax, and in a more civil tone said, "I never intended to tell you, Charlotte, but since you have finally spoken up, I believe I do owe you an explanation. Sit, the both of you."

While Meg and Lady Semple seated themselves, Lord Semple appeared immersed in thought, drumming his fingers on the dark green leather of the desktop. "My word, this puts a new light on things," he said. "There remains no reason not to tell you, now Allegra is gone. Never cared for the girl, actually. Even had she been my own, I would have been hard put to feel any real affection for her. As for my sister, at long last her lies have brought her down. Only makes sense, as it *was* all Lydia's doing." He peered at his wife. "You've told Meg all of it?"

"That I know of," Charlotte replied. "But what is it you know, Cyril?"

"Yes, yes, in good time." Lord Semple reached for his

Sevres snuffbox. Meg waited, hardly controlling her impatience, as with infinite care, he sniffed a pinch of Violet Strasburg up his nose. "It all began with a visit from Lord Harley. You remember him, my dear?"

Lady Semple furrowed her brow. "I believe so. He was in the habit of coming down from London for our weekends, years ago. Dashing sort of fellow . . . had a way with women, as I recall. Yes, I remember now, I was obliged to keep a close eye on the maidservants."

"The very one. He was considered the rake of London for a time. Long since gone, poor fellow. Dead from debauchery."

"But what has he to do with us?"

"On one of your fine weekend gatherings, he bedded Lydia. Damme, if he didn't get her in the family way."

Charlotte was stunned. "What! Lydia? I cannot believe it!"

Lord Semple gazed at his wife with a bland half smile. "Well, I know 'tis hard to think that Lydia could ever . . . but, as you might recall, she was not so unattractive back then, although already doomed to spinsterhood. I cannot explain why she did it, except Lord Harley could be most charming and persuasive, and, too, I might speculate she could not face her old age without, having . . . well, er . . . a fling."

"But when did this happen?"

"You have not yet caught on? Think back to when Lydia took her grand tour of Europe, or so everyone was told. In reality, I was obliged to send her to stay with our distant cousins in Scotland, to hide until the baby was born."

An astounded look of discovery spread across Lady Semple's face. "That was at the very same time I was with child! Are you saying . . . ?"

"I am saying Lydia is Allegra's mother. There never was an Eliza Quincy."

After the shocked silence that followed, his lordship continued, "Lydia birthed a girl, you see. I had instructed her to leave the baby there, in Scotland, but, damme, she brought it with her when she returned! Stubborn woman, caused me no end of inconvenience. Mother love, I s'pose. Insisted upon leaving it with a farm family close to Pentworth Park."

"So then when I gave birth to Meg, and she was . . ."

"Clubfooted, m'lady," Meg interjected calmly, "you cannot hurt my feelings; I'm quite used to it."

". . . clubfooted, Lydia saw her chance to switch babies."

Lord Semple nodded. "Lydia seized the opportunity, imploring me to go along with her scheme. I was doubtful. Allegra was already more than a week old, although, as it turned out, she still could pass for newborn. But I had other misgivings." Lord Semple looked momentarily abashed. "Suffice to say, Lydia kept cajoling me—kept insisting it was for my own good, that I could save myself the embarrassment of rearing another crippled child. 'After all, 'tis only a girl,' she kept hammering at me, 'it's not as if it were a son.' The woman would not desist until she wore me down."

"So you allowed her to make the switch," said Lady Semple, her voice holding the beginnings of deep anger. "Allowed your own daughter to be banished!"

His lordship had the decency to rub a nervous hand across his forehead. "I've come to regret it, Charlotte."

Meg, who had listened in growing astonishment to her father's tale, thought her ears were deceiving her. The great Lord Semple admitting he was wrong? Unbelievable, yet there he sat, arrogance gone, suddenly looking older, frailer, shaking his head with regret.

"You think me a monster," he said, "and I was, back when William was born. Pride kept me from loving my crippled son, or so I thought, but after he died"—to Meg's astonishment, Lord Semple's voice broke and his eyes dampened—"I gradually began to realize I had loved him all the while! And had never showed it! Ah, how cruel I was! Now the day doesn't pass I don't regret my behavior."

Tears rolled down Lady Semple's cheeks. She stood up, reached both arms toward her husband. He came around the desk and clasped her in a tight embrace. "Why didn't you tell me?" she implored.

"You didn't ask, Charlotte, and I have my pride. Can you forgive me for not having loved our son?"

"Yes, yes, of course!" Charlotte cried. The two clung together, caught up in mutual sorrow. Meg got up to leave the room, but Charlotte spied her.

"Stay, Meg. Cyril, what shall we do? I cannot bear to part from Meg again. She is our daughter!"

"I know very well now who she is," replied Lord Semple, his voice near shaking. "You think I don't care? You think I feel no remorse when in my own home I see my daughter dressed in servants' garb, working like a slavey?" Resolutely he drew himself up. "Declare Meg as your daughter, my dear, if that is what you wish. I have long since ceased to care what people think. Lydia shall leave, of course. Both she and Allegra are henceforth banished. From this day on, their names will not be spoken in this household."

Charlotte frowned. "But can you not imagine how tongues will wag?"

"Let them wag," Lord Semple stoutly declared. "Meg is our daughter now. The ton will accept her or have me to deal with."

Charlotte, seemingly accepting his response, offered, "There's something else you should know, Cyril. 'Tis the most delightful news. Lord Beaumont is in love with Meg."

"Indeed?" Cyril's countenance lightened. "So much the better. To Meg shall go the wedding and the dowry."

This is wrong! thought Meg. She had been listening with increasing concern, and no longer could she remain silent.

"M'lord and lady, I cannot be your daughter, cannot

accept the wedding or the dowry. I shan't be staying, and shall leave tomorrow, as planned."

They both looked at her askance. "But I thought you would be ecstatic!" protested Lord Semple.

"From the bottom of my heart I thank you, but I wouldn't dream of staying. You must not claim me as your daughter! It will cause no end of scandal if you do. No, 'tis best for me to slip away to Brighton and live my own quiet life."

"The deuce! That is poppycock," Lord Semple exclaimed.

"Leave us, Cyril," said his wife.

"But—"

"I said, leave us!" Lady Semple's voice rang with newfound confidence. "I wish to speak to Meg alone."

Lord Semple took a step, then turned to Meg. "It is my heartfelt wish you stay. There is much I must make amends for. But if you decide otherwise, rest assured I have no desire to see you struggling for an existence. I shall provide you with an annual stipend with which you can live quite comfortably."

Without waiting for a reply, Lord Semple strode out of the room.

After his lordship left, Meg's mother made haste to remind her, "But what of Richard?"

"I shan't be marrying Lord Beaumont—not now, not ever."

"Only an hour ago you were crying on my shoulder, saying how much you loved him. Now you plan to leave? What kind of love is that?"

"I do love him, only . . ."

"Only *what*? You said he loves you, did you not?"

"He loves me enough to be his mistress, not his wife."

"But all that has changed now."

"Has it?" Inside, Meg shriveled a little. "Oh, I've no doubt he would gladly marry me if he learns of my true identity, but I would never forget he wanted me only after he discovered I *wasn't* a servant!"

"But, Meg, surely you could compromise!"

"That's not my nature," Meg said, with quiet, desperate firmness. "He should want me for *me*. No arguments, please! I've made up my mind. I go tomorrow, as planned, without his ever knowing who I really am." She gripped her mother's arm. "I trust you'll not tell him?"

Lady Semple shook her head in bewilderment. "Not if you prefer I don't . . . but I simply cannot understand."

"I hardly understand myself, but there's the end of it, and I go tomorrow. Now, may we talk of something else before I go upstairs?" Meg smiled and hugged her mother. "You did it, m'lady! You stood up to him! And see what happened?"

"I should have done it years ago." Lady Semple had a glow about her, Meg noticed, a confidence that had been missing before. "It was you, Meg, who gave me the strength, who had the wisdom to see my fears were all of my own making."

"It appears he, too, was tormented over this, in his own way," Meg observed.

Her mother smiled. "Yes. A weight is off both our shoulders. And I cannot believe I shall never be obliged to cope with Lydia again!"

Meg answered softly, "I often wondered why she seemed so partial to Allegra. Now I guess we both know."

Meg was in her room when Croft knocked at her door and announced, "Someone to see you." The lofty butler's eyebrows were twitching, a sure indication he was scandalized. " 'Tis Lord Beaumont," he added incredulously, "waiting for you in the drawing room."

Meg, unable to resist her opportunity, peered imperiously down her nose at him, and in her snobbiest manner replied, "Tell him I shall be down at once, Croft."

What could Richard possibly want? Meg wondered as, with a heavy heart and dragging feet, she headed for the drawing room. They had said their good-byes. What further pain must she endure?

He was standing by the windows when she entered, hands behind his back. Upon hearing her step, he turned. "Meg!" he exclaimed, and strode across the room to meet her, taking her hands in his, a gleam of purpose in his eye.

She replied wearily, "Oh, Richard, we *said* our good-byes."

"Never! I hardly got home and off Thunder before I realized, I must have you."

"But I already told you, I shall never be your mistress."

"I don't want you for my mistress, I want you for my wife."

"Wait!" she said with a gasp. "You have stolen my breath away."

" 'Tis I whose breath is stolen." His arms went around her. "Marry me, Meg. I cannot live without you."

She placed a firm hand on his chest to hold him at arm's length. "Lord Beaumont marry a servant? Think of the scandal!" she reproved.

"Scandal be damned," he answered. "I would give it all up in a minute . . . my title, my inheritance . . . my life is nothing without you."

Meg felt as if the clouds had parted and the world was suddenly bathed in sunshine. She looked deep into Richard's dark eyes and asked, "Truly, you would marry me, knowing I'm but a servant?" He nodded. "And you would give up your title and inheritance, if need be?"

"Henry can have it all. Oh, Meg, don't make me wait; say yes!"

"Yes, I shall marry you."

With a cry of gladness, he pulled her to him and gave her a kiss that was demanding, yet surprisingly gentle. Finally she turned her head away and for a time buried her face silently against his chest, profoundly grateful for so many things. She had found her mother . . . she had found security and love . . . and she no longer need deny herself the touch, the arms, the ecstasy of loving Richard, Lord Beaumont.

At last she pulled away, an impish smile on her face.

"You had better sit down. I have something to tell you."

LOVE LETTERS

Ballantine romances are on the Web!

Read about your favorite Ballantine authors and upcoming books in our monthly electronic newsletter, LOVE LETTERS, at **www.randomhouse.com/BB/loveletters**, including:

·What's new in the stores
·Previews of upcoming books
·In-depth interviews with romance authors and publishers
·Excerpts from new romances
·And more . . .

To subscribe to LOVE LETTERS, send an E-mail to
loveletters@randomhouse.com,
asking to be added to the subscription list. You will receive monthly announcements about the latest news and features.

So follow your heart and visit us at
www.randomhouse.com/BB/loveletters
for sample chapters from current and upcoming Ballantine romances.